**How was he supposed to keep her alive when he was her biggest threat?**

He tore the thick, wooden, iron-barred door off its hinges by the simple expedient of sinking his fingers into the metal crosspieces and setting his feet, then yanking back with every erg of strength he possessed. Metal squealed and snapped, wood exploded, and a wild-eyed Mari scrambled out of the stinking darkness inside the crypt. Her hair curled wildly, streaming back from her face; she was still screaming, her cheeks paper-pale except for splotches of hectic color high on each cheekbone.

Hanson's hands closed around her shoulders. He half-spun, bringing up the gun, pointing at whatever Dark lurked in the crypt's chill blackness.

She struggled frantically, kicking and clawing at him, probably mad with fear. "Easy, sweetheart," he said, the undertone of Power in his voice slicing through her screams. "Easy. I'm here. It's all right. I'm here."

Whatever was inside the crypt retreated. A foul stench of rotting flesh and swamp water boiled out of the stone cube. *She was in there alone for how long? I am going to torture that gargoyle to death. I swear it on my sword, I am going to clip his wings down to nubs and pull out his claws before I slit his throat an inch at a time.* "Easy, sweetheart. Shhh, Mari, Mariamne, I'm here. It's me. Relax." *Come out so I can kill you,* he thought, the gun never wavering. *Come on.* "Be easy, sweetheart. I've found you, it's all right. What were you thinking, hmmm?"

She stiffened, staring up at him, her blue eyes ringed with white. The perfume of her fear, Power trembling, ready to escape her control, folded around him. His nerves tingled, bathing in it, drinking in the smell of his witch. In that moment he understood far more about the Dark than he ever wanted to. He was hungry for her, hungry for her light. What would he do if she denied him?

For Tricia and Ali, with love.

Other books by Lilith Saintcrow

Dark Watcher
Storm Watcher

Coming in 2005
Fire Watcher
Cloud Watcher
The Society

# Storm Watcher

\*\*\*

# Lilith Saintcrow

Storm Watcher
Published by ImaJinn Books

ISBN: 1-933417-00-5

10 9 8 7 6 5 4 3 2 1

PUBLISHER'S NOTE:
This book is a work of fiction. Names, characters, places and incidents are products of the author's imagination or are used fictitiously. Any resemblance to actual events or locales or persons, living or dead, is entirely coincidental.

Books are available at quantity discounts when used to promote products or services. For information please write to: Marketing Division, ImaJinn Books, P.O. Box 545, Canon City, CO 81215-0545, or call toll free 1-877-625-3592.

Cover design by Patricia Lazarus

**ImaJinn Books**
P.O. Box 545, Canon City, CO 81215-0545
Toll Free: 1-877-625-3592
http://www.imajinnbooks.com

# One

*Her face, chalk-white, smear of blood on one pale cheek, dark hair falling back. She fell, her green dress fluttering, the silk making a small ripping sound as her fingers twisted, tearing the material.*

*She fell.*

*"Theo!" A long, despairing scream. Rain lashed, stung her eyes. "Theo! No!"*

*She fell, and Mari's throat swelled with the enormity of the scream. It tore out of her, rivaling the thunder, and the Power rose, striking like a snake.*

"Mari," he said, quietly. "Wake up. It's all right."

Mariamne Niege struggled upwards. *Darkness and rain, Theo's pale and blood-streaked face, the Darkness pressing close, full of teeth and claws. And his face, his familiar face, bloodless, eyes blazing red through a merciful haze.*

"Mari. Wake up." His hands were on her shoulders, fingers biting in, the entire room rattled under the lash of his voice. *He must be upset.* She opened her eyes. Blessed relief burst under her breastbone. *Awake. I'm awake. Just a dream. No, not just a dream. Gods.*

The covers lay rumpled at the foot of the bed. She must have kicked them off. Mari blinked, choking back a scream. He leaned on the edge of the bed, holding her shoulders, a darker shadow in the darkness of her bedroom. "Shhh, hush, it's all right. Just a dream, Mari. Breathe." He sounded calm, as usual. "In through the nose, out through the mouth. Just breathe."

"Theo," she gasped. "Theo—"

"It's all right," Hanson said, but his voice made the window rattle in its frame, made the bookshelves groan. "Just relax, Mari. Okay? There's nothing here. I promise."

"Not yet," she said, taking in a deep, jagged breath. "Not yet. But it kills Theo. And it'll kill *me,* too."

"Of course not." He slowly let go of her shoulders, finger by finger. "Theo has Dante. And I won't let anything happen to you. You know that."

Of course she knew. He was a Watcher. *Her* Watcher.

*I've got a half-human man with guns sleeping on my couch. How on earth did this happen?*

Mari shivered, a galvanic shudder racing under her skin.

The torn T-shirt she wore to bed did nothing to protect her from the chill in the air. "Why is it so cold?" she finally asked, when her ragged breathing had eased and she could think without the trembling candle flame of the future under her skin.

"I think your friend Brandon 'forgot' to pay the gas bill on time," he answered. He almost touched her shoulder, two fingertips hovering a bare half-inch from her skin. Heat flooded her. It was one of the Watcher tricks. She'd seen Dante do it for Theo more than once. "You should move from here, Mari."

"Where else could I go? I can't afford a house, like Theo. Not until after school." She pushed her hair back from her face, grimacing as she peeled a curl away from her lips. Now she was comfortably warm, and some small part of her was sneakingly grateful. If she'd been alone, sleep would have been impossible for the rest of the night.

"I'm sure we could find something," he said dryly, pulling the covers up. His long black coat moved oddly in the darkness, as if it were a living thing riding his back. There was no slim shadow poking up over his right shoulder, though, which meant he wasn't carrying his sword. Had he been sleeping in his coat?

Mari shivered. *Past and present stay with me, future I wish not to see.* It was a rhyme Suzanne had taught her to keep the visions away.

Too bad it worked less and less. And Suzanne...

*No. I don't want to think about that.*

But the vision of Suzanne rose, her arms lifted, the pale oval of silver light swallowing her whole. The spell had wrecked everything. No matter that it had been necessary. The Crusade couldn't enter the city to hunt down psychic women, not as long as Mari, Theo, and Elise were the Guardians.

And Suzanne, watching from the other side of the Veil. Suzanne, who had given her life so her three students could live safely.

*It should have been me,* Mari thought bleakly. *It should have been me.*

Hanson tucked her in efficiently and stood with his hands in his pockets, shoulders drawn in to hide how tall he was. The dimness shone off his pale hair, his eyes glowing briefly as he contemplated her. "There. Safe and sound." His tone was gentle. Mari shivered again, even though she wasn't cold.

It wouldn't have been so bad if the Watchers weren't so unfailingly gentle, despite being armed to the teeth. Mari had never heard Dante even raise his voice to Theo, and he meekly did whatever she told him to do. Hanson was the same way. Mari had the sneaking suspicion he would throw himself off a bridge if she asked. *That's the training,* he'd explained to her once. *Circle Lightfall trains us to protect and to obey, Mari.*

And of course the only time they ever disobeyed was when 'safety' was an issue.

"Thanks," she managed, around the lump in her throat. "Hanson?"

"I'll be on the couch," he said. "We'll find you another place to live tomorrow, Mari. If you'll let me."

"I can't. They need me." She closed her eyes. She could still see the Watcher's fuming, dark red aura printed inside her eyelids.

Her Watcher. *What am I going to do about this? We can't keep this up, him sleeping on the couch and me...What am I doing? Just waiting. What am I waiting for?*

Sometimes being a witch wasn't comforting at all. Mari suspected if she asked the question out loud, the answer would become depressingly obvious. It usually worked that way.

"I'll be on the couch, Mari," he repeated. "Call me if you need me."

She watched behind her eyelids as the dark red glow faded, little by little, from the room. He went slowly, probably reluctant to leave her. Mari took deep breaths—in through the nose, out through the mouth—smelling leather, and male, and the scent of dark magick. He was so careful not to push her, careful with her housemates, careful to stay out of sight while she was in class. So everlastingly, frustratingly, mind-numbingly careful.

*I wish he'd just ask me, so I could say no, and we could have it over with. But then again, I'm not sure I would say no.*

Mari kept breathing, her heartbeat slowing. The vivid images began to fade. That was one mercy; she didn't remember the visions in their gaudy Technicolor detail very often. But they were becoming far more frequent. And the last three had been all the same.

*It's a true vision, not just a dream. Theo's going to die. And so am I.*

She stared at the darkness behind her lids until she fell into a thin, troubled sleep. If she dreamed again, she did not remember it.

# Two

Hanson heard Mari's alarm go off, the loud sleep-shattering buzz prodding her out of bed. Heard her curse as she hit the snooze button.

He waited, his eyes closed and his attention split between the defenses on the small house, the sound of rain tapping on the roof and the subliminal sound of Mari breathing, cloth sliding against cloth as she moved in bed. He forced himself to stay absolutely still, breathing evenly, silently.

Ten minutes passed, clicking away on the clock hung on the wall over the couch. Then the alarm went off again.

"Oh, *gods.*" Mari groaned and hit the button again. Hanson found a smile tilting up the corners of his mouth, dispelled it. He sat up, folded the blanket, and laced up his boots, tying them quickly. Then he stood, stretching, hearing Mari slide out of bed and click the alarm fully off instead of to snooze. The sound of rain against the roof intensified, as well as the sound of water coursing through the gutters.

He played his usual morning game. *Let's guess her mood. Well, she's going to the bathroom first, usual enough. But she's touching the wall in the hall, and that means she's tired.* He yawned, tasted sleep in his mouth, and grimaced. A little tingle of Power to clean off his teeth, a little more to clean off his boots and coat. It reminded him of life on the streets. Only he hadn't had magick then. He'd had to live with being dirty.

Mari liked him clean, though. Though *like* might be too strong a word. She seemed to tolerate him better when he engaged in basic hygiene.

He made his way into the kitchen, listening for her.

*Brushing her teeth first? She must really be upset. There, there's the shower. Thank the gods the water heater's electric. If she had to take a cold shower, she'd turn blue all over.*

He had to take a deep breath, looking at the avocado Formica counter. The kitchen was ugly, but he barely noticed. His hands moved automatically, getting Mari's coffee jar from the freezer, measuring into the filter, adding filtered water to the coffeemaker, putting the whole mess together. He strained his ears. *She just dropped the shampoo. Bad night. She'll be worn thin today. Have to watch out for her. When she's tired those damn visions hit her hard.*

The coffeemaker gurgled into life. Hanson ran his hand back through his hair, feeling it cover his fingers. He grimaced again, tapping a knife hilt. *Got to get my hair trimmed. Wish you could do that with magick. Maybe Mari...*

He listened intently. Three other people lived in this house. College students all, renting rooms from the man who owned the house. Hanson didn't like any of them. The feeling was emphatically mutual. The house's owner, a greasy lounge lizard, had made some trouble over Hanson staying—something about leases and occupancy—until Mari had spoken with him.

Just thinking about standing in the landlord's orange shag-carpeted living room, while Mari smiled and pleaded very politely with the man in the skintight bell-bottomed jeans and polyester shirt unbuttoned almost to the waist, made Hanson's skin tighten with rage. Remembering the reek of cigarette smoke in the air and the man's greasy eyes lingering on Mari's earnest face and tumbled blond curls was enough to make a growl rise in his chest. He could have ended that problem with a single bullet, but the potential trouble for Mari had canceled that scenario.

It was a pity.

Mari's blue and green coffee cup rattled against the counter. The floor groaned.

A Watcher's rage could tear this whole flimsy house down.

*Careful,* he told himself. *Duty and honor, Watcher. Don't make things harder than they already are.*

A Watcher's first duty was protection. It was hard enough looking after a foolhardy water witch, but Mari seemed to have no regard for her own safety. The fact that Mari's precognitive visions were so strong they overrode her conscious mind added another dimension to the task.

He heard the shower shut off and imagined water slicking down her blond hair, dripping from her skin. Taking another deep breath, he rested his fingertips on the counter. *Don't, Hanson. Just do your job, okay?*

And that thought conjured up miserable images of Astrid, lying broken and bloody in the shattered wreckage of her smoking house, her white scarf tangled and bloody around her throat.

He'd failed that time. Circle Lightfall had sent him to protect her, and he'd failed. A stray Dark predator had broken open her house, witch-wards and all, torn her apart and drained the Light

from her while he'd been busy fighting off the Crusade. And
he'd been too miserably late to stop it, afraid of making further
contact and frightening her again, hiding in the shadows because
he'd been too clumsy.

The Dark rose inside Hanson's bones, spikes of broken glass
and barbed wire dragged along his nerves. He shoved it down.
"Dammit," he said softly, not caring that he was speaking out
loud. "Think about something else, Watcher."

He poured the coffee—milk and sugar for Mari, just black
for himself—and waited a few moments until he heard Mari
banging about in the bedroom, dresser drawers slamming shut.

*Let's see. I'll bet she'll wear the blue sweater. She'll be
feeling cold today. I'll also bet she'll wear that pair of jeans
with the plaid patch on the knee. Boots, too. Probably the
navy-blue coat, since it's raining. Two final exams today. No
wonder she's nervous.*

When Mari finally came yawning into the kitchen, Hanson
carefully handed her the cup of coffee. He watched her take a
sip and nod, blowing across the scalding liquid to cool it.
"Thanks," she said. "Did you get any sleep?"

He nodded, pushing his hair back from his forehead. "It's a
comfortable couch."

Mari's expressive blue eyes met his. She had pulled her
wet hair back into a ponytail, but as soon as it dried, blond curls
would tumble around her pretty face. She wore a threadbare
blue sweater over a white dress shirt, and a pair of jeans with a
green plaid patch over one worn knee. Her earrings were
mismatched—one was a collection of tiny, blue crystal drops,
and the other was a silver hoop. Four plain bands of silver circled
the fingers of her left hand.

Her head would barely reach his collarbone. Hanson found
his mouth had gone dry. Blue eyes, slightly cat-tilted, water-
clear skin, her balanced cheekbones, and a wistful mouth all
combined to make her pretty when she was, as usual, solemn. It
was when she truly smiled that the full measure of her beauty
came out, like the moon sliding out from behind clouds and
glittering in still water. And of course, there was the fact that
she was a Lightbringer, glowing in the dark landscape of Power.
The more Lightbringers in a city, the less violent crime, the less
unhappiness. They were gentle souls, the healers and teachers
of humanity, blessed with gifts normal people didn't understand.
Blessed, but persecuted by the Church and hunted by the Dark,

always in danger. If not for Circle Lightfall and the Watchers, there would be far fewer Lightbringers in the world.

The shifting cloak of Power over Mari smelled of ocean and cinnamon, tides and spice. Since the spell that made her and her friends Guardians of the city, the blue glow surrounding her had become ever more visible to Hanson's senses. And to the predators.

The Dark.

He pushed that thought away, too. *This is going to be a day of unpleasant thoughts,* he told himself, and his fingers tightened on the coffee mug.

Mari was still studying his face. "I'm really sorry," she said. "I can't afford an apartment." She glanced at the other end of the kitchen. On that side of the house were the other three bedrooms, and her three housemates who still slept. One of them, Brandon, was becoming more of a problem. The other two, slightly psychic women attracted to Mari's glow, were uneasy with Hanson and the unphysical smell of Watcher he carried.

He had to try twice to talk through the lump in his throat. "It's okay," he said, unable to look away from her face, from the fragile arc of her throat, the dark circles under her eyes. "I mean, Circle Lightfall could help, but you don't want that. Don't worry, Mari. I've slept in worse places."

"Maybe I could rent Elise's other half of the duplex." Mari looked down into her coffee cup. Then her blue eyes came back up, fastened on his face. "But I can't afford it, and she's got bills to pay, too."

"Mari." He knew where this conversation was going. She would ask him what she was supposed to do. He would make a suggestion, and she would back away, frightened, unless he dared to interrupt her. His hands threatened to shake. If she kept looking at him that way, he would want to touch her jaw line, skate his fingers over the softness of her skin, feel the narcotic jolt to his nerves. The temptation was enough to make him start to sweat.

She sighed. "I know. All right. Look, I have my last two finals today, and I've got to get going."

"Breakfast?" he offered.

The slight smile that touched her lips made his entire body tighten. "I'll grab a pastry or two on the way. I suppose you're coming?"

That was an easy question to answer. "I'm your Watcher.

Where you go, I go."

He meant to say it lightly, but her eyes widened and her smile faded. He could have kicked himself. *Did I have to remind her why she's so afraid of me?*

"Mari—"

"No," she said at the same time, holding up her slim hand. He saw the blue traceries of veins in her wrist, the delicate bones standing out under the skin. He stopped immediately, frozen in place. "Not another apology, Hanson. It's not your fault. I'm pretty certain of that."

He waited until he could be absolutely sure she wasn't going to speak again. Seconds ticked by, and he heard another alarm clock go off. Gretchen's, he guessed, by the annoying high-pitched buzz. "Mari?"

She finished her coffee in one scalding gulp, grimaced, and put the cup in the sink. "I've got to run. Come on."

He didn't trust himself to speak again. He nodded, carried his own cup to the sink, dumping the rest of the coffee out, and then set about rinsing the cups while she went back to her room to fetch her backpack and books. The kitchen was pristine again except for the lingering smell of coffee. Hanson looked down at his shaking hands.

*Control.* He watched as his fingers slowly went still again. His hands were scarred and callused, one small healing scrape across the back of his left wrist from the Slider he'd dispatched yesterday. His fingers were thicker, blunter, his palms ridged with the calluses of sword and knife. And the other calluses, from trigger and recoil. Not like Mari's slim fingers and beautiful, cupped palms. *Okay. Control. You got it.*

When she came back, shrugging into her heavy wool coat, he held her backpack for her. "I'll carry your books," he said, as he did every morning.

"Thanks," she said, as she had every morning since he'd been allowed into her house. "Just don't drop them this time, okay?"

"Given the choice between dropping a book and seeing you hurt, Mari, I'd drop a book every time." He tried to say it lightly, but failed.

"You're so serious," she told him, blond curls already beginning to spring free and tumble around her face. She was pale today, dark shadows under her blue eyes, a vertical line between her dark-blond eyebrows. "Lighten up a little, okay?"

He nodded. *If you wanted me to, I'd dance a jig right here. Just ask, Mari. Ask me for something, anything.* "Okay."

She examined him for a few more moments, and then took her backpack, her hand brushing his.

A spike of narcotic pleasure jolted all the way down to his bones. *Lightbringer,* he thought, staring at her bowed head while she slung her backpack over her shoulder and sorted through the stack of books, taking four of the heaviest. "Gods," she mumbled. "Just a little more work on that thesis, and I can get a real job and get up early to slave for a wage instead of paying to do it."

He took the books, both hoping and fearing the brush of her fingers again. It was better than being around other Lightbringers. They made the Dark melded to a Watcher's flesh *hurt*, as if rusted spikes were being driven through his nerves. It was every Watcher's dream to find a Lightbringer whose presence didn't hurt. One that could actually stop the agony.

Most Watchers never made it that far. They fell to the Dark or died of despair. To find the witch that could actually *ease* the pain of being a Watcher was like opening up a Cracker Jack box and finding a million-dollar lottery ticket inside. Especially since almost every Watcher had only one last chance to redeem himself.

Hanson's last chance was flipping through the leftover books, making sure she didn't need any. "Okay." She glanced up at him. "Hanson?"

He shook himself into full awareness, adjusting his long black leather coat so it hung correctly, hiding most of his weaponry. He would have to check with Dante. Things had been too quiet lately. *Never trust the quiet,* the Watchers said. "Yes?"

"Just checking. Come on, I'm almost late."

*Just checking? Like I'd be anywhere else.* He followed her down the hall and out the door, determined not to make any mistakes today.

# Three

Rain spattered the library windows, but inside mellow electric light lay quietly against bookshelves and bowed heads, students studying or catching a quick nap. Mari tucked a stray curl behind her ear and walked up to the checkout desk, hitching her backpack a little higher on her shoulder. She wasn't wet. The walkway between here and the Dolroyle building was covered. Two back to back, hour-and-a-half final exams and a bolted sandwich in the cafeteria, another quick gulp of coffee, and she had four and a half hours to work on her thesis before she had to get to the Rowangrove to help Theo put out some new stock.

"Hey, doll face." Crutcher pushed her steel-rimmed glasses up on her wrinkled forehead. "Back for another go at that thesis?"

"Got two pages to go and the rest of the bibliography to finish out," Mari said, smiling. The smile was genuine, relief and fresh worry. *Brewstonski and his essay questions. The man should be barred from teaching.* Mari accepted the stack of books and papers, letting out a slight groan at their weight. "Then I'm free for a few weeks' worth of biting my fingernails until the exam results come in."

"Well, you're bound to carry through. What's your G?" Crutcher's pink lacquered acrylic nails drummed on the counter. *I don't know why they call her the Dragon Lady.* Mari's smile widened. *She's perfectly nice.*

"Three nine seven," Mari confided. "Would have been a four point, but Brewstonski nailed me on an exam two quarters ago and that was half the course grade. He saw reason when I quoted one of his own books back to him to prove him wrong, but I only barely squeaked through. He almost cost me a scholarship."

"He's a bastard," Crutcher agreed. "He sends students away in tears. Man's a sadist. Did you want that copy of Cicero's *De Amicus?*"

Mari's heart leapt against her ribs. "You got it?" she whispered. "Really?" Then her face fell. "Oh, damn. If I get it now I'll never finish that bibliography. How about I work like a demon for the next four hours and take the Cicero at the end of that?"

"Stronger woman than me." Crutcher's thin lips tilted into a brief smile, her crimson lipstick feathering at the edges. "I'd have said to hell with the thesis. Probably why I'm a librarian. I'll keep it safe for you, never fear. Where is your young man today?"

The question was like a pinch in a sore spot. Mari shrugged, hoping she didn't look too guilty. Crutcher always asked about Hanson, seemingly fascinated by him. "Around, I guess. I don't know." The thought that he was probably watching her right now, maybe somewhere out in the rain, invisible to any of the nonpsychic people, didn't send a shiver up her spine. Instead, it was oddly comforting. "He might be along later. Why?"

"No reason. Just wondered." But Crutcher's sharp, watery eyes were a little bit too narrowed. "Well, go on and finish that thesis, girl, so you can take this Cicero off my hands."

Mari nodded, picking up the now towering pile of books and paper. "Gods above," she said, "whoever said being a scholar was *easy* work? Thanks, Mrs. Crutcher."

"You're very welcome," the librarian replied easily, and went back to checking in a pile of economics texts.

Mari found her usual table, setting the stack of books down. The papers were her notes, guarded with care by Crutcher. Less notes, now that she was almost done with the damn thing. *Only a ringing conclusion left to write.* She settled into her usual chair, a yawn catching her off guard. *And a damn bibliography to finish. I don't suppose anyone will ever read the bloody thing, but it's a relief to be almost done.*

A hand came over her shoulder, holding a latte in a paper cup. "Here," Hanson said in her ear. "If I know you, you just now had something to eat."

Mari sat back down, sheepishly. He'd avoided the chair's swift scraping back as she leapt halfway to her feet. "Thanks," she managed, watching him drop into the chair to her left. *He sits there because his back is to the wall*, she realized, feeling foolish. How long had he been sitting there and she hadn't ever thought of that?

He settled down and seemed to go completely still, only his eyes moving in careful arcs over the entire library. Sharp-faced, handsome man, icy blue eyes, his pale hair dusted with glitters of water. *He only ducked outside for a moment, or he used some Power to shake the water off.* Her heart started to calm its wild pounding. "You're welcome," he replied. "How did it go?"

"I think I might have passed." She found herself watching his hands, resting easily on his knees. He never seemed to completely relax, not even when injured or obviously exhausted. Instead, he seemed to send off a kind of radar in all directions, invisible waves of his attention constantly scanning the environment. "Hanson?"

"Hm?" As soon as she said his name, his attention shifted, his pale-blue eyes now fixed on her face.

Funny how that didn't seem to detract from the attention he was paying to the rest of the library. And not quite so funny was the way his attention made her cheeks feel hot and her pulse speed up.

"Where do you go when I'm in class? I never see you, but I get the feeling you're around." The question popped out before she could stop herself, and she watched his face for signs of disappointment or anger. If there was one thing Mari had learned about men, it was that they didn't like to be questioned.

He didn't look angry. He only looked faintly surprised, and then one half of his mouth curled up. The resulting lopsided smile—sardonic and amused, eyes almost sparkling—was actually kind of charming, even though it was delivered by a man wearing a long black coat and a sword on his back. He also wore so many other weapons, she was surprised he could move without clanking like the Tin Man. Mari was so used to the slight shimmer of magick hiding his weapons from ordinary people that she barely noticed it now. "I just hang around where I'm not likely to be seen," he said. "Make sure there's nothing hiding in the corners. Most normals are fairly unobservant. They just assume I'm part of the furniture."

The thought of anyone *overlooking* him was so ludicrous it made Mari laugh softly, her hand cupping her mouth as she set the latte down. Drinks were forbidden in the library, but Mari was careful and Crutcher usually turned a blind eye as long as nothing spilled.

His lopsided smile became a grin as he watched her laugh. Then his eyes drifted past her, and the smile fell from his face so quickly she was surprised it didn't shatter on the carpeted floor.

Mari looked up and sighed. "Hello, Brandon," she said quietly.

Brandon Cochran, in a red rugby shirt and crisp new jeans, a gold chain around his beefy neck, grinned down at her. "Yo, Mari." He affected a too-cool gangsta street drawl. "Wuzzup?" He pulled out the chair next to her and plopped into it, nearly knocking over a stack of history books. Mari rescued her latte just in time. *If I spill on the table here, Crutcher will never forgive me. Why does he have to be so pushy?*

"I'm kind of busy here, Brandon," she said, searching for the right tone.

"No problem, baby. I'll be quiet as a mouse. You won't even know I'm here." The wide grin hadn't left his tanned face. He had dark eyes thickly fringed with dark eyelashes, a fashionable jock haircut sat uneasily on his round head. The football scholarship meant he didn't have to work at much besides keggers and touchdowns. Mari had long ago made peace with the fact that not everybody went to college to actually better themselves.

Mari squashed down a sudden flare of unease. Brandon's pupils were dilated and he was moving a little strangely. They were extremely still one second, then jerking into motion the next, as if he was nervous. He wasn't sweating, and he wasn't wet either. So he hadn't been outside. Where had he been? In class? That was vanishingly unlikely.

"I'm *really* busy, Brandon," Mari repeated patiently, taking a sip of her latte. His aftershave rolled around her. *Probably the same kind his daddy wears.* She tried not to wrinkle her nose. The Library was quiet, the murmur of soft conversations, the hum of computer monitors and copy machines, and the sound of rain on the windows turning into a low background hum. "Is there something you wanted to talk about?"

"Kind of," he said. "Ya know, your pet goon, Mari. We don't like him." He leaned back, giving her the eye. *The gunfighter riding into town,* she thought sardonically, and had to choke back a laugh.

"What on earth are you talking about?" *Can you just go away and let me finish my thesis?* Then she chided herself. Brandon couldn't help it. He had been raised by a distant millionaire father and a domineering alcoholic mother, and he was searching frantically for any way to fit in. Right now it was baggy pants and gangsta talk. He was so *young.* At his age, Mari had been studying hard for her associate's degree and working nights to support herself. *Sometimes looking young for your age is a curse,* she reflected, and took a shallow breath, trying not to inhale too much of the aftershave. *Maybe I'm unsettled because of the visions.* She tried another shallow breath. He was *drenched* in perfume.

And something else. Mari's nostrils flared as she tried to isolate the scent and failed. It was like something burning; a wet, heavy, vaguely familiar smell.

"Ya know," he repeated, nasally, "that guy you let sleep on

the couch. We don't like him."

"Really." Mari tried not to lift her eyebrow. *Theo would know how to handle this, why do I feel so nervous? Why can't I be more like her, or even Elise?* "Look, Brandon, I pay twice my share of the rent because of that. Aren't you happy?"

He spread his hands, leaning back so the chair tipped up on its back legs. "Yo, relax, cuz!" he sneered. It sat uneasily on his broad face, and Mari tried not to look at the steroid-assisted muscle rippling under the rugby shirt. She'd once dated boys like Brandon: too big, too clumsy, and too quick with their fists. "I'm just *sayin'*, that's all. You… uh… you wanta go to a party with me tonight?"

*Gods above and below grant me strength.* Mari sighed. "No, thank you. I have to work. Look, Brandon, did you pay the gas bill last week? It was awfully cold in the house this morning."

"I did it," he said, sticking out his lower lip just like a three-year-old would. Mari suppressed another sigh. It wasn't fair. She wanted to *push* him, just to get him to go away and give her some peace and quiet. "I swear I did. Hey, you're always workin'. Come on, blow off a little steam tonight. It'll be a primo party, I swear."

"No thanks," she said, gently enough. *Amazing. I can't even feel Hanson. Is he still sitting there?* She wanted to look but didn't dare. If Brandon hadn't seen Hanson, they might avoid unpleasantness. "Can you call the gas company and make sure there's not some sort of problem, Brandon? It would mean a lot to me."

"I paid it," he said, his lower lip pooching out even further.

*Oh, for the sake of every god that ever was, I'm only ten years older than you. I'm not old enough to be your mother!* Mari suppressed the flare of irritation. Rain spattered the windows, a comforting sound. Mari's shields thinned, taking in Brandon's emotional state. It was a risk. She was tired, and other people's emotions had always threatened to drown her before she'd painfully learned to control her gifts. Suzanne had gone a long way towards teaching her complete control. Yet now, since the Guardian spell, those gifts had grown, and Mari sometimes wondered if she would sink into the sea of confused emotion other people seemed to live in.

The thought of being trapped in that sea of screaming bedlam was enough to make her entire body go cold.

Brandon was a chaotic swirl of dirty yellow and green, an

acrid taste laid against her tongue. *Oh, no.* Mari sighed again. *He's been taking some kind of drug.*

"Look," she said again, pitching her voice low and reasonable, just a little Power to calm him, "I have a lot of work to do, Brandon. Why don't you go and I'll see you later?"

"Oh, I'll just watch ya work, cuz," he interrupted blithely, stretching his arms out as if he was going to try the old yawn-and-put-the-arm-around-the-girl trick.

Mari's lips thinned. She flinched away from his arm. If his skin touched hers and she got a jolt of whatever drug he was on she might scream or convulse.

Hanson's hand dropped onto Brandon's shoulder. *Oh, no,* Mari thought.

"She's busy, friend," Hanson said, his voice neutral, soft. "I think you have business elsewhere."

Mari braced herself. But Brandon's dark eyes went flat and empty, and his aura flushed with dark, metallic Power.

"Catch ya later," Brandon mumbled, and slowly hitched up to his feet. Hanson's fingers unloosed.

"Now go and pay the gas bill, Brandon," Hanson said, low and distinct. Mari's jaw dropped. "While you're at it, pay the next couple of months' rent for *everyone*. Just because you want to."

Brandon nodded. He looked very young with his pupils dilated and his mouth slackly open. "Yeah," he said.

"Go on, now." Hanson gave him a slight push, his callused fingers against the other man's shoulder.

Mari watched the younger man bumble away, his huge shoulders sloping, his aura twisting with the peculiar dark fuming bruise of Watcher power. "That's dangerous," she said quietly, "giving him a *push* like that. He's on something, and it could make him dangerous."

"He's not dangerous," Hanson said. "Stupid and annoying, but not dangerous."

"Hanson." It was no use. It was done. She looked down at the table, her notes spread out, now jumbled in a mess.

Hanson's eyes were on her, a weight she could feel against the side of her face. "Mari, if he'd touched you... He was intent on disturbing you, and he did *not* look peaceful. I could follow him outside and beat some sense into him, but that would make you angry."

"He's just a spoiled little boy," she said, staring at the cover of a book on early Christianity in the Roman Empire. "I can handle him. I did it for two years before *you* showed up. I'm kind of busy right now, Hanson. Maybe you should go find someone to menace or something."

As soon as she said it, she was ashamed of herself. It was something Elise might have said, sharp and rude. He'd stopped Brandon from touching her. He deserved a "thank you," at least.

For a long, heart-stopping moment, all of his attention was on her. She felt it, as if the air had gone hot and still. Mari fiddled with a pencil, staring at a sheet of notes about the French Revolution from a course two years ago. She had doodled a Celtic cross on the paper, thick black strokes of ink and pencil shadings.

Then the sense of his attention faded. When she finally looked up, he was gone. She looked around the library, twisting in her chair, her annoying hair falling in her face so she had to blow the blond curls back.

Nothing but quiet students and bookcases and mellow electric light. And the sound of the rain.

Mari sighed and put her head down on the table, her elbow bumping a huge text on socioeconomic conditions in first-century agrarian communities. *Gods. How did this get so tangled? I should be happy. I'm about to finish my thesis, and get my degree, and get a job... but I feel so empty inside. And why did I take it out on him? He was* protecting *me.*

The vision rose up, trembling, in front of her. Theo's bloodstained face, Mari's own scream, the face of the Darkness mercifully obscured except for its glowing eyes and sharp glittering teeth. Mari counted to twenty, taking deep slow breaths. *Past and present stay with me, future I wish not to see. Past and present stay with me, future I wish not to see.*

It took many repetitions until she was able to sit up again, and a few more deep breaths before she could pick up her latte and look at the work she had yet to do. *This is going to take some time. I can't concentrate.*

A whiff of lemon drifted across her face. Mari smiled. Lemon was Suzanne's favorite scent, and it reminded Mari of her teacher.

*Stop your ninnying and get to work,* Suzanne would have said, kindly. *Enough time for dithering after the work is done.*

Mari took another drink of her latte. *I'll worry about Brandon and Hanson later,* she decided, and settled down to work.

# Four

Hanson watched as Mari left the University as dark fell, walking down the Avenue with quick strides. Her backpack was hitched on one shoulder, her books wrapped in a plastic shopping bag and held to her chest. She walked with her head down, the rain flashing on her hair under the streetlights. She didn't glance around, but the tide of Power surrounding her—shifting shades of blue, like a light shining through blue silk—slid small fingers out, waving anemones searching out danger. The Teacher had at least left all three of the Guardians with excellent shielding.

It was no substitute for a Watcher, though. Even a Gray could crack witch shields and kill a Lightbringer. They were so vulnerable, too vulnerable. It was the price of the gifts they carried.

Hanson drifted behind her, checking the street. Rain slid off his hair in rivulets and slicked his coat down. The tide of pain through his bones was normal and ignored.

*I should have been more careful.*

Yet it had been so close.

The boy had made Mari visibly uncomfortable, but she had tried to be kind. She had actually gone pale, and her mouth had turned down slightly. The stink of some kind of stimulant was on the boy, and he had tried to touch her.

Rage rose, the Dark twisting inside his bones. The thought of anyone threatening Mari made a tide of black fury roar through him. The thing the Watchers had melded to his flesh fed on the rage and pain, an endless feedback loop of violence and Power. It was good fuel. Dangerous, but good.

He trailed her, automatically expending the thin trickle of Power that would keep the normals from noticing him. They rarely looked anyway. Most of them were in a kind of deathly daze, robots going from work to home to watch TV to buy more goods and then back to work to pay for what they'd spent. Hanson, in contrast, had a very simple life, few if any needs beyond his weapons and maybe some caloric intake for the day if he hadn't fought anything Dark and fed off killing it.

His only *real* need was waiting on the street corner, clutching her books to her chest, her shields suddenly thinning so that bright blue flared up, a beacon in the rainy gloom.

*Oh, no.* He sprinted forward, slipping past two old women huddled under a red and white umbrella, clucking to each other as they hobbled through the rain.

Hanson arrived just as a red Toyota bulleted by, doing at least fifteen over the posted limit, throwing up a sheet of water. His hand closed around Mari's arm and he hauled her back from the curb. He had to be careful. Denser muscle and bone gave him greater strength and endurance, and he didn't want to hurt her.

Mari's eyes were wide and blank, her face papery-white. *At least she didn't get a face full of water,* he thought as he neatly guided her off the street corner and into the shelter of a bank entrance. "Mari?" *Gods, don't let her be hurt. This is going to kill me, because if the Dark doesn't get me my heart will explode.*

Her teeth chattered, and her arms were rigid around the books. Little jeweled raindrops glittered against her blond curls. She must have been using a turn-aside to keep the water away. She didn't resist when he stopped her. He could have touched her while she was locked in the vision, her pupils dilated. Could have touched her hair, or her jaw line, or even found out if her lips were as soft as they looked.

*Dammit, focus on your work, Watcher!*

He risked a little more Power, to keep them hidden. She didn't need prying normals poking at her. The temptation was almost too much, even for a Watcher. Just one brief touch. Just a single moment.

He froze. Habit kept him scanning the street, his awareness sliding over familiar buildings. He had watched her from almost every roof on this street before he'd made contact, learning her schedule, watching over her before Dante had been sent to make contact with Theo. After that, everything had moved quickly. Almost too quickly.

It took only five minutes. Then she blinked, life coming back into her eyes. Her lower lip quivered. Hanson glanced over the street. Clear, even though the light was failing. Night was the best time for the Dark to come out. Mari would glow all the more brightly without the static of normals out and about on the street.

"It's all right," he said, as soon as consciousness flooded her eyes again. "You're on the corner of the Ave and Seventeenth, the BankTrans building. You're safe."

She nodded, shivering. He held his hand an inch from her coat sleeve and sent a tingle of Power flushing through her. Her shields thickened, and her cheeks flushed. Heat steamed off her coat. "A-a-accident," she stammered. "F-f-four cars... the f-ffreeway… off the Dextrose exit."

He made a soothing affirmative noise, letting her know he was listening. She flared through the spectrum of Sight, sending out waves of Power so concentrated he was surprised, as always, that the normals couldn't see it. "I want to get you off the street, Mari. Please?"

She nodded. "The Rowangrove," she whispered. "Elise… and Theo."

"If they're there, they'll help. If not, we'll call them, I promise." He pitched his voice low and soothing, shoving down the urge to touch her cheek and reassure himself she was all right. His heart was beginning to slow down a little. This was the worst time. Right after one of her visions, she was disoriented and physically drained. There had been times he'd had to keep her from stopping in the middle of a busy street, carry her home and put her to bed,. She couldn't help it. The visions literally took her over. He just thanked the gods he was around now to keep her safe.

"Hanson?" She blinked and looked up at him. "*There* you are. I looked for you in the library."

The thought that she had actually looked for him made his chest go unexpectedly tight. "I made sure Brandon got a cab," he admitted. "The library's fairly safe, and it was daylight."

"Oh." Now her eyes were fully awake. "You're all wet," she finally said, the shopping bag rustling as she shifted the books.

"I'll carry those." He subtracted them deftly from her arms and was rewarded with a thin, tremulous smile. *Please forgive me, Mari. I almost touched you.*

"You really made sure Brandon got a cab?" She looked alert now, and started off down the street. "It's pouring."

He didn't answer. Instead, he trailed behind her, slightly to her right. The rain had intensified while they stood under the overhang, and the streets were awash with the overflow. The Rowangrove was four blocks away, and Mari's hair was dark and slicked down by the time they had gone a block. She tilted her face up to the rain once, and Hanson kept a close watch on the pavement in case she tripped.

The Rowangrove, warm mellow light shining out through its windows, finally folded them in its familiar incense-scented calm. The 'Metaphysical and Occult Supplies' printed in gold foil under the graceful arched letters on the front window always made Hanson wince. *A witch running an occult supply store. No discretion at all. Then again, they're Lightbringers. They don't* understand *the Dark.* He held the front door for Mari, shifting the stack of books to one arm, and followed her through the sheet of energy that was the protections applied to this place. The Lightbringers were well shielded, but Dante and Hanson had each added layers, Watcher shields and traps, to keep the Dark away. Only the fire witch had objected, but the other two had patiently waited, and finally she had given in, throwing up her hands and stomping away.

Theo's other shop, the Magick Cauldron, had been gutted during the Crusade's all-out attack last year. Instead of rebuilding on that site, the green witch had decided to move right onto the Avenue. The subsequent increase in customers meant that all three witches were busy helping out, and the Watchers did a fair bit of heavy lifting and small repairs.

The odds against three Lightbringers in one city—all three reaching adulthood intact, all three singly more powerful than most of Circle Lightfall—were astronomical enough. The fact that both Dante and Hanson had bonded with two of them was even more fantastical. Sometimes Hanson had the uncomfortable feeling there was more than simple chance at work here.

He usually tried to forget that thought as soon as it rose to the surface. Another Watcher proverb: *Don't attract the attention of the gods, for those the gods heed die young.*

The green witch was sitting on the floor, and she looked up from an open box of books. "Mari!" She sounded delighted. The air turned suddenly heavy with the smell of growing things.

Theodora Morgan, Guardian of the City, tucked a strand of dark hair behind her ear. Her eyes, the color of sunlight through leaves, widened. She moved, almost overturning the box of books. "And Hanson. Hello. You two look wet clear through. Come in, have some tea. Dante?"

Hanson's fellow Watcher appeared from the door marked "Employees Only," carrying what appeared to be another heavy box. "Here's the last of the overstock books, Theo," he said, his black eyes flicking once over both Hanson and Mari, gauging potential threats, and then dismissing them. He rarely noticed anything other than Theo nowadays. Hanson understood. "Mari, hello. Duty, brother."

"Honor, brother," Hanson replied automatically. "A word with you, Dante?"

"Of course." Dante was taller than Hanson, built like a football player. He was oddly graceful for all his bulk, and his long black coat pooled on the floor as he bent, depositing the box next to Theo, who smiled at him. Oddly enough, that made Hanson cough slightly and look at his own witch stamping water free of her boots.

Mari shook her head, drops flying from her long curls. "It's like the sky is trying to drown us," she said, sliding her backpack off her shoulder. "I nearly walked out in front of a car again," she added, squishing over to the glassed-in counter that held the ancient cash register. "Hanson had to pull me back."

This made Theo's dark-green eyes turn even darker, and her eyes met Dante's for a long moment. "Well, it's a good thing he was there, then. We'll make some tea. Elise should be along any moment."

"That's good." Mari put down her sodden backpack and shoved her wet hair back. "I need a spell. There's an accident."

"Of course." Theo's voice was husky, soothing. Hanson's bones began to ache. Even Mari's nearness couldn't protect him from the pain of being near other Lightbringers. The clean, pure light spreading from Theo's aura dragged broken glass over his nerves, taunting the Dark that lived in him. He stood motionless, holding the books, while Theo accepted Dante's steadying hand, brushing off her green silk dress with her other hand. "How did the exams go?"

Mari peered out the front window, a deep line between her eyebrows. "Theo, I need to talk to you." She slid her coat off her shoulders instead of letting Hanson help, and that vaguely disturbed him. Her aura, now that she was inside the shop's shields, began to burn more brightly, her shields slipping. She felt safe here.

"Dante, would you get Hanson dried off and get some tea?" Theo moved gracefully, skirting Dante. Her bare feet padded softly against the hardwood floor, almost-dancing. Hanson controlled the urge to step back, flinching from the light she carried. Instead, he followed Mari to the counter, scanning the front of the store out of habit.

"Absolutely," Dante replied. "Come on, brother. You look half drowned."

Hanson set the books down on the counter. "Mari?"

She gave him a startled look, hanging her dripping coat on the wrought-iron stand. Precious first editions and research texts, as well as some of the more expensive items, peered out from behind glass doors on the shelves behind her. "It's okay," she said, with a bright smile. "Thanks."

There it was again, that distance. She was frightened of him.

*Terrified.*

Hanson took a deep breath. "Call me if you need me," he said, and took two steps back, unable to tear his eyes away from her face. Bedraggled, wet, and completely beautiful, she pushed her hair back and grimaced again, digging in her pocket for a ponytail holder.

Then he turned on his heel and stalked away, following Dante into the small walled-off space in the back of the store that held a sink and a counter, a few boxes of stock, odds and ends, and the door to the bathroom. A rippling blue and green curtain covered the doorway. "What's up?" Dante said, ducking slightly to fit through the doorway. His voice was pitched deliberately low, the harsh hurtfulness of Watcher magick reined and controlled.

Hanson shrugged as he came into the room. "Does it strike you that it's too quiet?" He raked his hair back with stiff fingers. "And I had to use a bit of Power on a civilian today. He was bothering Mari. One of her housemates. Drugged."

Dante whistled out through his teeth. His harsh, severe face settled back into its usual watchful lines. He reached up and plucked two coffee mugs from a rack, then took two more. "Dry yourself off, will you? You're making a mess."

"He was on some kind of stimulant, Dante, probably meth. I can't convince her to move out of that damn house." Hanson closed his eyes briefly and concentrated. The Dark rose in him, harsh and hurtful, then a *phsshht* of steam puffed out from his clothes. His coat creaked, settling. The leather was spelled not to shrink and to repel water, but the downpour outside was too much for a simple turn-aside charm.

"Just means you have to keep your eyes and ears open, hmm? Do you need to make the problem disappear?" Dante poured hot water from the coffeemaker into the cups. Hanson sniffed. Peppermint tea and chamomile.

"That's the problem," he answered. "She's so fucking frightened of me that it makes my teeth ache. If I get rid of the boy she'll suspect it, and I can't lie. What am I supposed to do?"

Dante shrugged, contemplating the gentle steam rising from the teacups. "Better to apologize than to ask for permission, right?"

"Yeah. Sure. How well would that fly with *your* witch, Watcher?" Hanson accepted a cup of peppermint tea. "Wish I had some vodka for this."

"Against regs." Dante appeared lost in thought, but Hanson

knew better. Dante was at his most dangerous when he looked sleepy. "What else is pulling your chain, blue-eyes?"

Hanson's shoulders dropped a fraction of an inch, as if in relief. "It's that obvious?"

"I've been under fire with you for eight months. I'd be pretty shoddy if I couldn't read trouble on the horizon. Come on, give, this won't stay hot forever."

"She's having those visions again. In her sleep. She hasn't slept through the night for two weeks. Not only that, but she wakes up screaming about the green witch. And about dying." Hanson wrapped his hands around the tea mug, enjoying the heat. He didn't need it. The Dark parasite changed his metabolism to adjust to external conditions, but it was... pleasant.

So many things were pleasant now that he'd found Mari. Now that he could see her... and occasionally touch her.

*That should be enough for you,* he told himself severely. *Don't get arrogant, Watcher. That's your sin, isn't it? Arrogance? Just do your job, and count yourself lucky she doesn't run away screaming every time you appear.*

"That's serious," Dante said, suddenly looking wide awake. His black eyes met Hanson's. "Since that spell, it's gotten worse. Theo can't stop herself. She wants to heal every goddamn stray dog and wasted junkie that wanders past. She'd drain herself right down to death if I wasn't around. And that fire witch."

"Yeah, she's a problem," Hanson admitted. The redhead was more than a problem. She was a foolhardy nuisance, with far too much Power and a temper to match her hair. "We need someone to cover her."

"There's nobody to spare."

"I know. So what do we do?"

Dante sighed. "Something's coming, Hanson. I wish we could consolidate defensive positions and start a regular patrol. If there was a Lightfall safe house around here that would solve the problem. But they're just as scared of the Circle as they are of us. What a goddamn mess."

"You've got that right." Hanson shook himself and checked the shields. They were vibrating with Power.

"All we can do is watch, and wait."

Hanson's shoulders sagged another fraction of an inch. "I was afraid you'd say that."

# Five

By the time Elise banged in the door, shaking her long hair out, her green eyes sizzling with light, Mari had almost finished her story.

"He was higher than a kite, Theo. I swear, I don't know what I'm going to do."

Theo shook her head slowly, thinking. Her liquid eyes shifted past Mari, who sat cross-legged on the floor, shivering, her hands curled gratefully around a cup of chamomile tea. "Here comes Elise. We'll get this figured out. If all else fails, you can stay with me. I'd like that. And I'm a better landlord than that—"

"—freaky dude you're renting from, Mari," Elise finished, setting her guitar case and battered black messenger bag down. Her nose-ring twinkled, and her pale cheeks were flushed. She had the fair clear skin some redheads are blessed with, and between Theo's calm beauty and Elise's high-cheekboned, aristocratic face, Mari felt like even more of a drowned water rat. "Did I hear a crisis in the brewing?"

"One of my housemates 'forgot' to pay the gas bill on time. Again. It was Siberia in there this morning. Hard to believe it's technically summer," Mari replied. "And the same roommate showed up high in the library and invited me to party."

"Let me guess." Elise snapped her fingers, and sparks popped. She undid her clear plastic raincoat, scavenged from a thrift store, with a practiced flick. "The poor little no-neck rich boy with the football scholarship."

As always, Mari immediately envied Elise's casual confidence. "You must be psychic," she said, trying to keep the sharpness out of her voice. "It's been a long day, Lise. Can we take a number on the sarcasm and get back to it tomorrow?"

"*That* wasn't sarcasm," Elise answered with a broad smile. "That was *truth*. Big difference. If I was doing sarcasm, someone would be bleeding. Hey, you guys hungry?" She twisted her long, wet hair back and secured it with a scrunchie, and then stalked over to the counter to hang up her raincoat. "Where's Stoneface and Prince Charming?"

"Dante and Hanson went downstairs to clear up some of the shipment we got today," Theo said. "And, I suspect, to give us some privacy."

"Tactful of them," Elise snarled. "I'm *starving*. How about pizza?" She scooped up the phone, leaning on the counter, her torn *Pascaloosa* T-shirt sliding down and revealing generous cleavage.

"I can't afford—" Mari began as usual, pulling her knees up and resting her chin on them.

"Pish, posh." Elise waved one elegant hand, tipped with red lacquered fingernails. "My treat. You're a student, Mari, you're supposed to be broke. How did the exams go?"

"I think I might have passed," Mari said. "But my thesis—"

"No problem. You could do that standing on your head. Hey, Rocko, it's Elise Nicholson. Yeah... Nope, I'm at the Rowangrove. Can you have someone bring us a vegetarian, a pepperoni, and an extra large Supreme? Sure, you bet. Cash... Yeah, at the K-Bar. I guess so... Thanks, baby." She dropped the phone back in its cradle. "So what's going on? I'm hearing that Mari needs a place to live and that those jerks with the guns are making trouble again."

"Dante isn't a jerk, Elise. He's perfectly polite." Theo's voice held only a shadow of irritation, which was shocking enough. But she also looked at Elise with her dark eyebrows drawn together, a faint frown on her usually serene face. "Why are you so *angry?*"

"It's my nature, Theo m'love," Elise replied, hopping down from the counter and stamping across the hardwood floor. Steam rose from her clothes. "Comes with being able to light candles with a look. Now, what's the real problem? I know my personality isn't the issue here, for once. Mari's got to find a new place to live and something else is going on. So what gives?" She dropped down beside them, and immediately Mari felt better. As rash and prickly as Elise was, she was also absolutely trustworthy and fiercely loyal once she'd given her devotion. *She'd give you the shirt off her back,* Suzanne had often remarked, *while she scolds your ears off for losing yours.*

"I've been having those dreams again," Mari admitted. "And they're so much worse now."

"Well, what are they?" Elise asked. As usual, the three of them together made the air crackle with electricity. Mari sighed, her shoulders easing slightly.

"Something Dark." she whispered. "Rain. A storm. I'm stumbling, I can't find my way. Then Theo's there, and her face is all bloody...and the Dark is laughing. It's got sharp teeth and red eyes...and then I know I'm going to die. Then...I do."

"And you're sure it's a vision and not a dream?" lise asked.

Mari sighed, closing her eyes. "Of *course* I'm sure," she

said. "Even *I* can tell the difference."

"I didn't mean it that way," Elise said. "Okay, so what do we do? Theo?"

Theo, a vertical line between her dark eyebrows, sketched a rune on the hardwood floor. "Well," she said, "there are a few things that give me hope in this vision of yours, Mari. You say that you just see me bleeding, not dead."

"But I know you die—" Mari began, and Theo held up her hand.

"Just a moment, Mari. You know what Suzanne always used to say about seeing the future. 'Be careful of *seeing,* and even more careful of *knowing.'* You don't actually see me die, do you?"

"I see you fall." Mari stared at the rune Theo was tracing into the floor. *Ken*, the torch, for clarity. "And the Dark."

"Well, the Dark is worrisome," Theo admitted. "But we have Dante, and Hanson. They've both proved to be very… ah, useful."

"I don't know if I'd put them in the plus column, Theo," Elise immediately objected, of course.

"Stop it, Elise," Mari snapped. "Leave it *alone!*"

Both Elise and Theo stared at her, Elise's eyes wide with surprise, and Theo's soft and thoughtful. Mari clapped her hand over her mouth. It wasn't like her to burst out like that.

Elise's mouth twitched upward at the corners. "I never thought I'd live to see *you* lose your temper," she said. For Elise, that passed as tact.

Mari peeled her fingers away from her mouth. "I'm so sorry, I—"

Theo waved it away. "The question right now is, where are you going to live? I'd like you to come stay with me for a while. We can put some of your furniture in the garage."

"I've got that whole side of the duplex," Elise said.

"But you need the rent money from that," Theo pointed out. "It's much easier if Mari stays with me. And if your housemates aren't paying the bills, it's bad for all of you. How about that?"

Mari thought it over, running her fingers over the smooth slick metal of the rings on her left hand. "But they need me," she said tentatively.

"Not as much as we do," Elise snorted. "I'm free Saturday. How about we start packing you up and moving you out then?"

"I think that's a grand idea," Theo said. "Mari?"

Mari rested her chin on her knees. "I guess so," she said, trying to ignore the guilt that immediately crashed down on her.

Gretchen and Amy were nice girls, and they needed her. So did Brandon.

"Here come Dante and Hanson," Theo said, just before there was a rap on the front door. "And the pizza's here."

Mari glanced over and saw a young man with stack of pizza boxes.

"Good deal." Elise bounced to her feet. She was across the store in a moment, snapping her fingers to some private beat, and met the delivery boy just as Dante and Hanson appeared from the door leading to the stairs.

Hanson immediately looked at Mari, who was just hauling herself up from the wooden floor. Theo had risen to her bare feet and was looking up at the ceiling, a thoughtful expression on her face and her dark hair falling down in an unbroken wave. "You know," she said, "this just might be the best thing for your housemates."

"How?" Mari looked down, trying to avoid Hanson's eyes. She could still feel him staring at her.

"Well, they won't have to deal with Hanson anymore," Theo said, and the amusement in her voice made Mari grin. Something about Theo always made her feel better. *Theo could have made van Gogh cheerful*, Mari thought, and her grin widened. "There," Theo said, with evident satisfaction. "*There's* our Mari. Don't worry so much, sweetie. We'll be all right."

"Okay, everyone," Elise called from the door. "Food. Yes, even you two. Gods. I'm feeding my best friends' boyfriends. Stoneface, you want to get us some plates? And you, Blue Eyes, you want to get the girls something to drink? I left a bottle of rum here, that'll do for me. Mari, Theo, you guys want to tell me where we're eating? These aren't going to stay hot forever."

Mari looked at Theo, who smiled softly, amusement evident in the tilt of her chin. "Yes, ma'am." Theo snapped Elise a salute. The Watchers were already obeying, Dante making a low comment to Hanson, who gave another one of those bitter laughs and glanced back at Mari.

It was all usual, and Mari should have felt relieved. Instead, fresh worry began to bite at her. What if her vision was true and Theo was about to die? What would change the vision? And the accident, there had to be something that would avert the wrecked metal and shattered glass and the screams she'd seen.

"Mari?" Theo took her arm. "You're still worrying. Come on, have something to eat, and then we'll do some magick. Don't worry so much. We'll be all right. *All* of us."

"I hope you're right, Theo." Mari bit her lip.

# Six

Mari walked with her head down, leaning into the wind. The rain had slacked to a fine drizzling mist, and jeweled her hair with sparkles whenever she walked under a streetlight. Hanson matched her step for step, occasionally glancing down at her bowed head. She'd been unusually silent all the way through dinner, and when the Lightbringers retreated to the basement to work some magick she hadn't even glanced at him. The Dark twisted uneasily in Hanson's bones. Had he made her angry? Displeased her?

He'd discussed with Dante the feasibility of doing a citywide recon, just to figure out why it was so quiet. Unfortunately, none of the witches were likely to stay under cover while the Watchers patrolled. Dante had promised to bring it up to Theo.

Mari walked slower and slower, and then she finally stopped under a streetlight, looking at the wet pavement. Hanson waited, scanning the street out of habit, and she finally looked up at him, blinking.

"Hanson?" As if reminding herself who he was.

Oddly enough, her ignoring him didn't hurt as much as it might have. As long as she took his presence for granted, she would allow him to stay near and protect her. "You all right?" he asked.

She nodded. "I want to ask you something."

He steeled himself, nodded. Her aura shifted, turned a deeper blue, light shining out into the wasteland of the city. The street was clear, but he wasn't sanguine about waiting out in the open with a Lightbringer. *Stop it,* he told himself. *If anything attacks, you'll get her under cover and deal with it. Like usual.*

"Do you know how to anchor somebody?" she asked.

Of all the questions in the world, he hadn't expected that one. "Anchor?"

"Like Theo and Elise do for me, when I do my Madam Zelda trick. Do you know how to do that?"

He considered carefully. "Maybe not with another Lightbringer," he said. "But I could anchor you." *What are you planning, Mari?* He couldn't ask that. *Obedience, Watcher. Obedience.*

"Would you?" she asked. "I need your help. I couldn't ask Theo and Elise. They're tired, and Theo wouldn't think it's necessary. She doesn't believe I saw her die." Mari shivered, her blue eyes turning dark and haunted. He had to force himself to stay still, overriding the urge to touch her, comfort her.

"Anything you ask, Mari. Of course." He stuffed his hands in his pockets, because now she was looking at him, her eyes shining and her face open, suddenly eased.

"Are you sure you can anchor me? I mean, if I slip too far—"

"I wouldn't let you slip too far, Mari," he said, then cursed himself for interrupting her. "I promise."

She nodded, biting her upper lip. It was a habitual gesture that only made her mouth look softer. "All right. Let's go home, and you can anchor me. My room's probably best."

That made his heart lodge in his throat. "Your room?" he asked. "Are you... I mean, will you be comfortable?"

"Well, if you haven't tried anything by now, you're probably not going to," she said tartly.

That wasn't what he was asking, but he shut up anyway, simply staring at her. Her cheeks were blushed from the chill in the air, and the damp mist was beginning to weigh her hair down, turn it dark. He played the game, memorizing the curve of her cheek, the line of her jaw, the exact arch of her eyelashes, the shape of her mouth. Memorized it again, storing it in that secret place inside his head. And again.

"Hanson?" she asked, now looking puzzled.

"I can anchor you, Mari," he said. "Just tell me what you want done, and I'll do it."

He meant it to come out lightly. Instead, he heard the seriousness in his own voice and cursed himself for it. His body wound tighter and tighter, like a guitar string before breaking. *If she keeps looking at me like that I'm going to... What?*

Mari watched his face, thoughts moving behind her blue, blue eyes. It would be so easy to reach out, to *feel* around the edges of her mind, find a corner to slink into, to watch. He had some psionic ability, most Watchers had a little, and she was the only witch who didn't make his entire body feel dragged through broken glass and rusty nails.

Yet he couldn't. If he violated her trust, she might send him back to Circle Lightfall. And he would have to go, knowing he'd screwed up his very last chance.

"You sound so serious." She impulsively tucked her arm through his. "Come on, let's get out of the rain. I feel the need for some hot chocolate."

"I have a serious job," Hanson said, trying not to mumble. *She's touching my arm. She's touching me. Damn coat, if I felt her skin... Stop it. She's touching me. That's what's important. She's walking with me as if she...*

"You could loosen up once in a while," she suggested. "Have some fun. You know, you're too grim all the time. It's like the world is this constant battle for you. I wish I could teach you how to relax."

He scanned the vicinity again, making sure. Nothing Dark inside the radius of his awareness. "If I relaxed, something might slip through and hurt you," he said. "That's what the training is for. I don't think I even remember what relaxed feels like."

She grimaced. He slowed his pace to match hers. "That's really sad. They did awful things to you. And to Dante."

He shrugged. "You don't understand," he said. "I wasn't a nice person, Mari. This is my last chance to make something of myself. To *be* something. That's serious, isn't it?"

"You never talk about... before."

*Don't ask me about that, Mari.* "It's not necessary."

"What happened to you? Who were you before they did that to you?"

"Mari..." For a moment he imagined telling her, played with the idea of letting her see. "That person's dead," he said finally. "He died a long time ago. Before I was even a Watcher."

She looked down at the pavement, and then slowly slipped her hand out of his arm. Hanson set his jaw and his shoulders. "Would it be so bad to tell me even a little bit about yourself?" she said finally, her steps slowing even more.

"Can we go somewhere safe?" he suggested. "It's too exposed out here."

"Please?" She was persisting, of course. Mari might be gentle and fluid, but her stubbornness was also fluid; water over rock, wearing away even the strongest resistance. She was doggedly persistent, usually at the worst possible time. "Hanson?"

"Please, Mari. Don't ask me that." *I can't tell her no.* His fingers itched—whether for a weapon or the touch of her skin, he couldn't tell.

The quiet of the rain-misted night grew close and dense. Mari slowed still further and glanced up at the sky. "What's that?" she asked. "Something's out there."

Hanson cast his senses out one more time. Nothing. Quiet. Too quiet. But he knew better than to doubt her sensitivity. "Come on, Mari," he said, daring to slip his arm over her shoulders and hurry her along. "Let's get you home, and I'll tell you anything you want to know."

"Promise?" She deliberately dragged her feet, looking up at him. Even here, out in a potential battlefield with the Dark perhaps drawing near, he still wanted to touch her. How was that for crazy?

"I promise," he said. *Astrid also used to tell me I was too grim,* he thought, and then cursed himself. That was the worst possible thought to have right now. "It's too quiet, I don't trust this. Can we speed it up a little, please? You know you don't like to see me fight."

That worked. At least, she sped up, her boots clicking against the pavement. "You really think something's out there?"

"It's too quiet," he replied, leaving his arm over her shoulder. Her light sank into his skin, painful pleasure spreading into his nerves. "And I trust your instincts."

"You do?" Oddly enough, that seemed to please her. She walked a little faster, their steps in unison now, Hanson's red-black aura spreading out at the edges of her clear light. It wouldn't deter a truly hungry predator, but it might make some of the weaker ones think twice about attacking her. Street lamps paraded down the street, their circles of light showing mist drifting in the air.

"Of course I do. You're my witch." He said this almost absently, scanning the street, even more uneasy when no visible threat appeared.

"I *am* nervous," she admitted. "What do you think it is?"

"If I knew, I wouldn't be on edge like this. Let's get you home." He immediately regretted the harshness in his tone, but she didn't pull away from him. Instead, she shivered and drew closer, and that thorny pleasure was worth any uneasiness.

"Hanson?"

*Maybe she's going to ask me again. I can't lie to her, I can't.* "Hm?" He settled for an affirmative sound, his free hand curling around a knife hilt.

"Thank you. For making sure Brandon got a cab. I know you don't like him. And thank you for keeping me out of the street." She watched the pavement unroll under their feet, either not daring or not wanting to look up at him, and he let out a soft breath of relief that turned into tension as soon as the street lamp two blocks ahead guttered out. Thick darkness congealed in the space the light fled. The hair on his nape rose, and the Dark inside him stretched, rusty metal grinding against his bones.

"Mari," he said quietly, "stay close to me, all right?"

She looked up at his face, and then her eyes flashed to the sliding pulsing blot of darkness drifting towards them. "Oh, no," she breathed. "What?"

"Maybe a *s'lin,*" he said, wishing she'd chosen another route home. *On the other hand, a good fight is just what I need right now. I wish she didn't have to see.* "Just stay close. If it's a *s'lin,* it might be a tiny one and relatively easy to kill. If it's a full-grown *kalak,* it'll be a little more difficult."

She stopped dead, staring at the shifting darkness, her pupils suddenly dilating so widely her eyes looked as black as Dante's.

*Oh, no.* Hanson tracked the blot of Darkness as it leapt from one street lamp to the next with nimble, mechanical grace. *A vision. Of course. Three in twenty-four hours. This just keeps getting better.*

Then training took over. He pushed Mari back—gently, gently—and to the side, into a doorway where the rain wouldn't catch her. A quick *command* and the layers of a keepsafe blurred over her, a protection to avert a blade or an attack of Power until he could reach her.

Then he stepped out into the rain. The Dark inside his bones growled, waking up. Something threatening *her*—threatening the only good thing that had ever happened to him—made every other rage he had felt in his long angry life pale in comparison. The knife hilt socked into his palm. He drew, spinning the hilt in his hand so the large black-bladed knife ended up reversed along his left forearm, a shield and a weapon all at once.

*Come on,* he thought, watching the Dark when it paused, as if uncertain whether it should attack or retreat. Mari shone with light that would feed the predator, but Hanson stood between them. His aura glowed red-black with Watcher power, ready to kill. *I'm just aching for a fight. Come on.*

The Darkness moved slightly, and Hanson's entire body went chill for a moment. The Dark symbiote melded to his bones countered, snapping him out of shock with a splash of adrenaline, hiking his body temperature.

It wasn't a *s'lin* or a *kalak.* The Darkness poured down a lamp post and resolved into a low, almost-humanoid shape—if the human in question had massive shoulders hunched with muscle and a habit of slinking on all fours. The head lifted, sniffing, and Hanson saw the flat silvery sheen of eyes.

There was only one Dark creature that fit *that* description.

*Belrakan.* Nasty, almost unstoppable, very good at camouflage, and very hard to kill, even for a Watcher. Called *Watcher's Bane.* He had to get it away from Mari. Even its presence would make her sick after a short while.

*Oh, fuck,* he thought, and reached for his sword with his right hand.

# Seven

Mari came back to herself, shivering, staring out from the sheltered doorway of an apartment building. The smoky smell of Watcher magick clung to her, and she cupped her elbows in her hands, chill working into her very bones. Nausea twisted her stomach.

Hanson was nowhere to be seen.

The vision had descended on her all at once, familiar and terrible. Theo's face, the blood, the screaming. Mari shivered again. "Hanson?" she whispered, not caring if she sounded like a ninny. He wouldn't leave her while she was having a vision, would he?

*Of course not. But something was there. Something hanging on the streetlight... and he said it was probably a s'lin.* She shuddered again. Not too long ago, she'd huddled in her bed while something like a giant manta ray glided over the city. Hanson had been just outside her bedroom door, but Mari had been too afraid to call him. It had *hurt*, that thing, scraping against her shields, but it had retreated once it sensed Hanson.

Or so Mari hoped. She didn't know why the thing had left. Dante and Hanson had fought it off the next day, while Mari and Theo and Elise huddled in Theo's house, reinforcing the shields. The thing had been after all three of them, and it had nearly killed Dante. At least, Mari privately thought, it was well nigh impossible to lose that much blood and have half your bones broken and still live. Hanson had been battered too, but neither of the Watchers had seemed to consider it any big deal. It was normal for them, nothing extraordinary.

Mari thought that was probably the point that Elise had decided she didn't want anything more to do with Circle Lightfall *or* the Watchers. Mari didn't blame her. If it hadn't been for Hanson's careful gentleness and the way he stared at her, Mari might have decided the same thing.

*Where is he?* She stretched her mind out cautiously, "looking" for him.

Other than the reverberation of bitter and Dark in the air making Mari's stomach flip uneasily, nothing. The entire city seemed hushed and expectant under the fine mist of rain. The night was utterly silent except for the faint drone of traffic.

And the sound of footsteps on the empty pavement.

Mari let out a long, sharp breath of relief and stepped out of the doorway, folding her arms over her rebellious stomach. Her greeting died on her lips. The man coming down the block wasn't Hanson. He was too thin, for one thing, and he had dark hair.

The cocoon of Watcher magick made it difficult to think. What had Hanson done? Where *was* he? It wasn't like him to just leave her. Not once in the entire time since she'd known him had he left her alone without telling her and cautioning her to stay somewhere safe. Was he watching from somewhere?

Mari struggled free from the sticky blanket of Watcher magick. It didn't want to let go of her, clinging to her shields, wrapping around her, slowing her steps as if she was wading in concrete. She managed to take a whole four steps up the sidewalk before the man stepped under a streetlight, the harsh orange glow streaking his dark hair. The two streetlights behind him were dark, and Mari saw a glitter of broken glass. *What happened?* she wondered, the world suddenly speeding up to its accustomed pace once she shook the last lingering traces of whatever it was away. She shivered again, put her head down, and hoped the man hadn't noticed her walking as if she was encased in mud. Her stomach felt like it was stuffed with something poisonous.

The man's footsteps slowed. *I'm only a few blocks from home.* Mari's heart hammered thinly. *Where is Hanson? This isn't like him.*

The footsteps slowed even more. Mari took a quick glance and saw a slice of pale cheek, a mop of dark hair. Flash of eyes. They looked oddly slate-gray in the street lamp glow.

"Excuse me," the man said. "Guardian."

Mari froze.

She had almost passed him, this thin, dark man wearing jeans and a hip-length leather coat. He wore a pair of boots, too, and stopped, his toes resting neatly together. Mari blinked and looked up at his face. "I beg your pardon?" It was weak, but it was the best she could come up with. Bile rose in her throat.

"You are one of the Guardians," he said quietly. Nice voice, deep and calm, far deeper than his slim chest would suggest. He was pale, his cheekbones standing out as if he was hungry, stone-colored eyes under a shelf of dark hair. Mari's nose wanted to twitch. She smelled cloves, and salt, and some pervasive, harsh perfume. *That's some aftershave.* Her heart took another skittering jump against her rib cage, almost making her gasp. Her stomach roiled.

"Um." It was all she could manage without throwing up.

"Here," he said, and held something out to her. "Your Teacher, Zsuszanna, left this. At the Library."

*Zhu-shanna? Does he mean Suzanne?* Mari stared at him, uncomprehending. "What are you?"

"I am Rossini," he said, dipping his head slightly. It managed to convey the impression of a respectful bow. "She left this, and I undertook to see it returned. There are more. Her notes, and other things—waiting at the Library. Underground."

"Notes?" Mari took the papers he offered her. It felt like six or seven thick paper sheets, folded in half. His fingers didn't touch hers, but he flinched back anyway, leaving the papers in her shaking, sweating hand. "What are you *talking* about?"

"The yellow witch," he said. "Your Teacher. She left those. I can only guess the spell was successful." he nervously glanced back over his shoulder. Mari blinked. He seemed somehow familiar, and she racked her brain, trying to think of where she might have seen him before.

"Why are you—" She had no clue what she was about to ask him, and she had to bite off the end of the sentence because she felt as if she had the flu, aching settling into her joints, the pizza she'd eaten boiling against the back of her throat.

"Look," he said, "time is short, and you're surrounded by enemies. Beware the Watchers, Guardian. They mean you no good."

That was like being goosed. Mari flinched. "You—"

"I will contact you again," he said, and turned sharply on his heel, his coat flaring briefly and settling oddly, as if something had moved against his back, under the leather. Two steps brought him to the mouth of an alley between two apartment buildings, and he disappeared into it, neat as you please. The darkness swallowed him without a murmur.

Mari shivered, swallowed bile, and wished she was home. *Okay, kids, everyone out of the pool. That was weirder than even I'm used to, and my standards for weird have gone up a lot lately, you know.* She looked down at the sheaf of paper in her hand. The misty rain was beginning to soften the thick paper.

She hurriedly stuffed it inside her patchwork purse, safe from the rain. Glancing around, she saw there was nobody else on the street. She might as well have been on the moon.

*Nobody would see if anything happened to me here.* She immediately chided herself for being silly and stupid, sweat breaking out on her skin. *I'm in the hands of the Goddess. And I've walked down dark streets before. It's not a big deal. Come on, Mari. Get home and curl up under some blankets. I didn't feel sick this morning. What's wrong with me?*

But as she approached the two busted street lamps, gooseflesh rose on her chilled skin. She slowed down a little, nervous, smelling sandpaper skin and wet fur, a distinctly animal reek that wasn't quite *physical* for all its eye-watering power. She stopped at the edge of the last circle of street lamp light before the dark of the two broken lamps, taking a deep burning breath. The smell made her wish she hadn't eaten.

*It's a good thing I left my books at the shop.* The thought had an undertone of dark, giggly panic she didn't quite care for. *If I had to run carrying them...*

She took a deep breath, closed her eyes, and forced her stomach to retreat by sheer willpower. *Come on, Mari. Come on. Just get home, where you're nice and safe. You can have a big cup of hot cocoa and listen to some music, what do you say? Come on, Mari. Come on.*

It wasn't working. She stood still, trembling, nailed in place. *Am I going to throw up on the pavement? Oh, gods, no. Please no.*

"Come on," she said out loud, startling herself. "Hanson would do it. *Elise* would walk right through this, you ninny."

*But I can't,* she thought miserably. *They're brave, and I'm just a coward.*

She opened her eyes and glanced both ways at the street again. Nothing and nobody. If Hanson was watching, she couldn't feel him.

*Beware the Watchers,* the strange man had said. *They mean you no good.*

*I want to throw up at home, if I'm gonna throw up.* That thought got her moving. It took all her waning courage to take a single step. Then another. Nausea rose hard under her breastbone, she swallowed hot sourness and then, all of a sudden, sprinted forward. Stumbling, gasping, fighting for air, she ran through the blot of darkness and didn't stop until she pounded up the front walk of her own house and fumbled for her key in her purse. It seemed to take an eternity. She finally found the key, jammed it into the lock, and twisted it.

Her door yawned open, and Mari almost fell inside, tearing the key free of the lock. She swung the door shut, locked it, and leaned against the wood, her ribs heaving and sweat standing out on her forehead. The house was dark and silent. Gretchen was almost certainly at work cocktail-waitressing. Amy was at her boyfriend's. And Brandon? Who knew where he was?

*That's the only good thing about this.* Mari tried to force her breathing to calm down. It didn't work. The nausea retreated. She gasped for breath, her pulse pounding in her ears. *Where's Hanson? Is he hurt, or dead, or... What happened to me? I had a vision. Oh, gods. Gods above. Anything could have happened to me. I just checked out and had a vision on the street. I'm lucky I didn't walk out in front of another car. What is* happening *to me?*

Trembling, sick, and disgusted with herself, Mari burst into tears.

The crying fit lasted only a few minutes, and Mari managed to back away from the door and peel her heavy, sodden coat off. She went down the hall and into the kitchen, turning the heat on as she passed the thermostat. Wonder of wonders, the furnace soughed into life. The gas must have been turned back on.

*Miracles do happen,* she thought, and picked up the phone in the kitchen, turning on the light. She dialed, wondering why her fingers felt so cold. *I'm numb. I'm in shock.* Her stomach gave two last dry heaves and subsided.

"What's wrong?" Theo, sounding breathless.

"It's Mari," she replied. "Something happened. Hanson's gone."

# Eight

The worst moment of his life was not coming back to the doorway and finding her gone, the shreds of the keepsafe fading in the rainy air. It wasn't even tracking her through the oozing pile of psychic sludge the *belrakan* had left behind. It certainly wasn't the pain. He'd had worse, even with the Dark symbiote crackling in his ribs, straightening shattered bone, repairing his lung, and fusing the ends of the break in his right upper arm. It wasn't the irregular flares of agony from his fractured femur. The Dark symbiote would take care of that too, once he had an hour or so to settle down and let it work.

The worst part was seeing the house, every window lit, and shadows moving behind the drawn curtains.

He thought perhaps something had broken into the house, but the shields were intact, and he saw a familiar green Subaru sitting in the driveway. Every other car was gone—well, at least he had that to be grateful for. None of Mari's housemates would be hanging around. If the pavement had been dry he would have left bloody bootprints.

He touched the front door with blood-slick fingers, let the shields register his presence, and felt a familiar swirl of dark-red fire. Dante.

The other Watcher opened the door, and his black eyes widened a fraction. "Honor, brother. You look awful." Dante stood aside so Hanson could slide into the front hall.

"Duty. Mari?" he croaked, his throat raw. *Tell me she's unharmed. Tell me she's safe.*

"She's fine. A bit shaken, but fine. Theo's with her." Dante didn't try to stop or touch him, just closed the door behind him and stood aside. Hanson made it down the hall and into the living room, where the familiar brown couch crouched in front of the television. The clock on the wall above mindlessly ticked off the seconds.

Mari bolted to her feet, her hair lifting in bouncing curls. Her eyes were wide and dark. "Hanson." The relief in her voice was enough to make fresh pain tear at his chest.

He crossed the room in two strides and had her by the shoulders, shook her slightly. She wore dry clothes, a pair of sweatpants and a green sweater, too big for her. Probably the green witch's. The other witch stood off to one side, by the television, her arms crossed. Hanson marked her and forgot her just as promptly, though her presence made his wounds start to burn as if salted ash was being forced into shredded skin.

"Are you hurt?" he demanded, his voice shivering the air and making the temperature in the room rise a good five degrees. He was bleeding heat into the air, the Dark symbiote using the pain to fuel the healing. "Are you *hurt?* Why didn't you stay there?" He checked her. She looked unhurt. Thank every god that ever was, she looked unharmed. "I left you under a *protection*, Mari, and you broke it. I came back for you. You *know* I'll come back for you. Why didn't you wait for me?"

Two crystal tears welled up in her eyes and tracked down her pale cheeks. "I... I had a vision," she whispered, "and when I came back... I thought something had happened to you, and I felt sick."

The Dark rose inside his bones, dragging spikes through his entire body. Yet more pain turned into more Power. His ribs cracked, the messy incomplete breaks smoothing out, mended by the symbiote. Heat drenched his skin. He would be ready to fight again soon. He could fight now, if he had to.

The trouble was, there was no enemy here to kill.

Hanson realized he was probably hurting her, his fingers sinking into her sweater. "Gods," he said, and had to try twice before his hands would unlock. The vision of Astrid's broken body receded slightly. Alive. Mari was alive. He hadn't failed.

"What was it?" Dante asked from across the room.

"*Belrakan,*" Hanson said, shortly.

Dante let out a short, sharp breath.

Mari blinked up at him and then looked down. "You're all bloody." She sounded pale and shocked. "And your face—" Her blue aura was jagged at the edges. Of course. The *belrakan* had probably made her ill. They were concentrated evil, pure Dark.

Hanson looked down at himself. His clothes were wet, shredded and soaked with drying, stiffening blood; his leather coat hung loosely, rent and torn. He dripped blood and water onto the cheap carpet, and his boots were caked with mud and yet more blood. "*Gods,*" he rasped. The thing had almost strangled him. His throat was bruised and tender. His face would be a mess of bruising and small scratches, both from the thing's hide and the concrete.

There were no words to express his thankfulness. She was

alive.

The green witch leaned forward, but Dante was already next to her, his arm over her shoulders. "No. Leave him be. He's dangerous right now, Theo."

"Mari?" Theo's voice, soft, dragged against his wounds.

"He won't hurt *her*," the taller Watcher replied. "Maybe now is a good time for that tea."

"What *happened* to him?" Theo asked, as Hanson checked Mari one more time, making absolutely sure she was uninjured. He smelled her hair. Cinnamon, the smell of ocean, and the clean summer smell of *her*. His witch.

"One of the bigger predators," Dante said calmly. "*Belrakan.* Called 'Watcher's Bane'. He's lucky to be alive." He drew her away. "Come on, Theo, a little bit of tea to warm everyone up and calm everyone down."

Hanson's hands dropped to his sides. He closed his eyes. The bloody darkness behind his eyelids pulsed once, and he took a deep breath, Power flushing him. He would mend. She was alive, safe, and unharmed. *I should never have left her.* It was his first absolutely coherent thought since the red rage of combat had taken him. *I had no choice. It could have made her even sicker. She's lucky, I'm lucky—everybody's lucky. Gods.*

Relief as jagged as the Dark reacting to a Lightbringer threatened to unlock his knees. He didn't allow himself to sway, but he felt as if he staggered.

"Hanson?" Mari's fingertips met his cheek. "What happened to you?"

Narcotic pleasure spiked, mixing with the pain. She was the only Lightbringer who could touch him, the only witch in the world who could ease his pain. His entire body shuddered. He was close, so close, to grabbing her shoulders again, pushing her back against the wall, and *proving* to his body that she was still alive and unhurt.

Hanson's scraped and bloody hands curled into fists. "Don't," he gritted out through clenched teeth. *Don't move, Mari. If you do, I might break.* "Do you have any *idea...*"

"What was that thing?" she asked. "It was *awful.* The place where it was. It was so dark, and I felt like I was going to throw up. And that man—"

"What man?" He pulled in a deep aching breath, rigid and motionless under her fingers, so close to breaking it wasn't even funny. "I should never have left you there alone. But I *had* to. It was a *belrakan*."

"It's all right," she said. Her voice hitched slightly. "I understand. I had a vision. I was out of it."

"I came back for you," he answered. "I will *always* come back for you, Mari. I just had to kill that thing and keep it away from you."

Her touch burned through his nerves, blurring, soothing, replacing the agony with a different sort of tension. *They always told us the Lightbringer would ease the pain,* he thought, taking another deep shuddering breath. *They didn't tell us it would feel this good.*

"Dante says you're lucky to be alive," she whispered. "You look awful."

Oddly enough, hearing her say it actually made his chest ease a little. If she felt sorry for him, would she let him stay with her? "Thanks," he replied, taking a deep breath and opening his eyes. "You must understand this, Mari. What you did was dangerous. I *will* come back for you. I need you to stay where I leave you next time."

"I didn't *know*," she replied with maddening illogic, but she still didn't move, resting her fingertips against his cheek, her thumb against his jaw. *I could turn my head and kiss her hand.* A shiver went through him. "How badly are you hurt?" she asked in a pale whisper.

That shook him out of the haze of sensation. *She's frightened,* the cold, clinical voice of control said inside his head. *Go carefully, Watcher. What you do now, she'll remember.*

"It's not bad," he lied as his leg wanted to buckle, the symbiote turning its attention to the incompletely-healed break. He wanted to move, ease the leg into a better position, but he didn't dare to as long as she touched him, afraid to lose the feel of her skin. "Looks worse than it is."

"Your coat." She stepped back, her hand dropping to her side. He almost twitched. The urge to grab her hand, clamp it against his cheek, and drown in the spiked pleasure was overwhelming. "Here. Take it off and let me see if I can mend it." Suddenly she was all business, though her voice shook. Her eyes cleared, and she ran her fingers nervously back through her hair. The resultant halo of stubborn golden curls made his mouth want to twitch into a smile. "Don't just stand there and gawk at me. Let me see it. And you'll need to clean up, too. Go take a shower. Your clothes—"

"I've got extra," he said, and slipped his coat off, wincing slightly as torn muscles reminded him how close he'd come to actually dying this time. When the symbiote finished repairing his bones it would move on to muscles, and he would be as good as new. *Useful little bugger,* he thought, and the ground-glass dragging of pain inside his bones sent a wave of nausea through him. It was the other Lightbringer. The more powerful they became, the more it hurt. And the more it hurt, the more the sudden balm of Mari's touch mattered.

He handed the heavy leather obediently over to Mari and then looked down at himself. "One moment."

There wasn't much Power. The symbiote was diverting most of it to the healing, bringing him back to fighting capacity as quickly as possible. The trickle he could use tingled down his body, fresh pain grating against his nerves. When he opened his eyes, the worst of the mud and blood was gone. "There," he said. "I won't foul the floor now. I'll be back in a few minutes."

"You almost died," she said, her tone dangerously quiet. Her hands shook visibly. So she wasn't quite as cool as she wanted him to believe. "And you're worried about the *floor?*"

He shrugged, helplessly. "I don't want to make things worse for you," he said. "It's hard enough for you here as it is."

She stared at him, her arms full of bloody, tattered leather. She appeared to be, for the first time since he'd met her, struck speechless.

*It doesn't mean she cares,* he reminded himself. *She could never care about a thing like me.*

"Tea," Theo said from the door. "Chamomile for you, Mari, to calm you down; peppermint and honey with a healing in it for you, Hanson, and I want you to drink every last drop." She carried a mug in each hand, her dark hair tucked behind her ears. The Power pouring out from her in a shifting tide of green made Hanson beat a retreat for the other hallway.

"I have to clean up," he managed, around the lump suddenly lodged in his throat. *I just said something wrong, I can tell from Mari's face. Damn my stupid mouth. I should never have left her there.*

He made it to the bathroom, closed the door, glanced briefly at himself in the mirror, and winced. No wonder she was so afraid of him

*What man?* he suddenly thought. It took him by surprise. He'd barely been listening to Mari, intent on making sure she was unhurt. *What man was she talking about?*

Later. Right now he needed to clean himself up. And not so incidentally, give the symbiote a little time to work so he didn't look so much like he'd been put through a Cuisinart.

The wave of shudders shook him, and he grabbed at the white porcelain lip of the sink. *I almost died. I could have died. It was a belrakan. I could have died.*

"Get a hold on yourself," he whispered, looking down at his hands. The worst of the blood was gone, but he would still leave dark handprints on the pristine sink unless he cleaned up after himself. "It's no different than any other day. You could die any day. You're cannon fodder so she can live, old son. She's more important. Now quit screwing around and *get a hold of yourself.*"

The porcelain creaked under the pressure of his fingers. He loosened his grip slowly, one finger at a time. "She needs you," he told himself. "Now stop it. It's not Astrid, she's not dead, and she *needs* you."

That managed to spur him, and he glanced up at himself in the mirror again. Pale blue eyes, gone dark and distant now, closed off. That was good.

*First things first. How about we get the blood off the face?*

# Nine

Theo and Dante left an hour later, Theo offering to open the store tomorrow so Mari could sleep in. But Mari needed the hours so she insisted that she could handle it. Theo finally gave in, biting at her lower lip as if worried and let herself be gracefully moved out the door. Dante closed her in the green Subaru with one last, measuring look at the tired old wooden house. Mari felt his awareness slide briefly over the protections. He was checking, she realized, and that made her jaw set so tightly she was afraid her teeth might splinter.

The papers still lay in her canvas purse. For the first time, she hadn't brought something to Theo. She hadn't told Theo about the strange man, either. *Rossini.* What kind of a name was that?

*On the other hand,* she thought wryly, closing the front door and locking it securely, *I've been hanging out with Hanson, no last name, no first name even. I'm hardly one to judge.*

He leaned against the wall. His hands were stuffed in his pockets, and his pale hair was now clean and shoved ruthlessly back from his face. His eyes were back to normal too—pale, icy blue, and fixed on her. "Feeling better?" he asked.

How could a man wearing guns and several knives, not to mention the sword poking up over his shoulder, sound so uncertain?

"A little," she lied, shifting her weight from one foot to the other. "Look, Hanson, I'm sorry. I was dazed. I felt sick. Three visions a day is too much."

He nodded. "It must be," he said softly, and he was looking at her that way again, his pale eyes absolutely level and absolutely focused on her. "You look a little tired. Going to bed?"

Mari shifted again, uncomfortably. *I'm an idiot.* She crossed her arms over her chest. *What am I so afraid of? He'd never hit me. I know he'd never hit me. He doesn't even raise his voice, ever. But... oh, gods, he scares me. He looks at me like I'm a five course meal—and he's starving.*

The air crackled with tension. Her arms tightened, defensively. "I was really worried about you," she said, finally. "And you looked... What *happened* to you? Dante told me those things kill Watchers."

"It was just a fight, Mari," he answered. "Just another predator. You're brighter now, more powerful. It brings bigger lions to the water hole."

She winced. The awful mottling bruises and scrapes on his face were fading. They healed quickly, at least.

*But how many times am I going to see him like that, bloody and limping and half dead?*

"You're brooding again," he said quietly.

"Come with me," she said. "Bring your things."

She brushed past him, stamped into the living room, and scooped his coat up off the couch. The leather was mostly mended, but she had another hour's worth of work on it before it was whole again. It was good practice. Some of the tears were nasty, as if razors had shredded the tough material. And it was so heavy. How did he move with all that weight?

"I can carry—" he started, but she gave him a look that silenced him and immediately felt guilty. He'd almost gotten killed tonight.

Because of her. Because of what she was.

She carried his coat down the hall and swept open the door to her room. Her purse lay on her bed, a forlorn little patchwork number she'd bought four years ago. It was tattered and rumpled and patched, its long strap repaired, like everything else she owned. Sometimes Mari thought she carried a field of fraying and patching around with her like the cloud around Pigpen in the old Charlie Brown comics. Not like Theo, so calm and impeccable. Or Elise, with her air of fierce glamour. No, just plain, boring Mari with her patches and holes and ragged edges.

*I've got to stop this, or I won't sleep tonight.* She took a deep breath and dropped down on her bed.

Hanson tented his fingers, pushed the door slightly wider. He carried nothing. "Mari?" He sounded so unsure she almost laughed.

"Come on in," she said. "Step into my parlor."

"Are you sure?" He looked puzzled now, a faint line between his pale eyebrows.

*Does he think I'm going to hit him?* Mari sighed. "You don't have to if you don't want to," she said. "I just thought… you know, that couch is a little lumpy, and the others… well, you can sleep in here. But no funny stuff. Okay?"

He took a single step over her threshold, and looked around

as if seeing the room for the first time.

Mari had warded the house, of course, but she'd laid another layer of warding over her bedroom. This was her sanctuary, the place she retreated to. The shielding shimmered as Hanson entered. Bookshelves leaned against the walls, and her desk sat under the window, the computer crouching mute and screen-dark upon it. A CD player and a messy pile of discs took up a shelf, and books jumbled everywhere, even atop her antique cherry wood dresser. The closet door was half open, revealing several different shades of blue, milk crates of papers and miscellanea stacked on the shelf above her clothes. She'd draped a sheer, blue beaded scarf over the lampshade, so the light was soft, aqueous, just the way she liked it. Her altar, a small table draped with white, was tucked almost behind the desk, with a small meditation rug in front of it. On the altar were two white candles, a cheap hand mirror laid facedown, a small glass jar of dried wormwood, and a string of pearls glowing mellow in the lamplight. And Mari's prize, a huge conch shell, crouched amid the other treasures.

She suddenly wished it wasn't so drab and crammed with dusty books. The bed was a queen-size, at least. She'd gotten the biggest bedroom in the house because she'd signed the lease. It was the one battle she'd been willing to fight with her housemates. "I'd offer you a chair," she said finally, "but I don't have one."

He took another step in, and then looked at the door. "Do you want me to close this?" he asked.

Mari's throat was suddenly dry. "I guess so," she said. "Unless you *want* to sleep on the couch."

He swung the door closed with a precise little click and then moved across the gray carpet, finally settling himself gingerly on the floor beside the bed, cross-legged, his back absolutely straight.

She studied him for a long moment, then pulled her legs up on the bed Indian-style, just like him. She started working on his coat. Power pooled in her palm. She teased it out in long threads, just like Suzanne had shown her, and started "stitching" together the long, vicious tears in the leather. "Does it hurt?" she asked, her head bent down and her hair falling and curtaining her face.

"Not much," he answered. "Thank you." What he was thanking her for, she had no idea. "Mari?"

"What?" Now she sounded irritated. She took a deep breath. It was the first time she'd *allowed* a man into her bedroom. He'd only come in to wake her up from nightmares before. It wasn't like actually inviting him in.

"You mentioned a man." His tone was flat, excessively neutral.

She glanced up, and then just as quickly looked down. "Yeah. He said…" The man's voice suddenly echoed in her ears: *Beware the Watchers, Guardian. They mean you no good.* "He said his name was Rossini."

*That's not quite a lie,* she thought. *He mentioned Suzanne. What did he call her? Some other name. But I'm sure he meant Suzanne.*

"Was he a witch?" Hanson asked.

She snuck a glance at his face. His eyes were closed, and he looked as if he was meditating. Did he meditate? She didn't know. She'd never asked what he *liked* to do. He always just followed her around. Her conscience pricked her, again. Hard.

*I haven't been very nice,* she realized. *He bled all over and then he cleaned it up without saying a word. He must have been really worried about me. How long has he been sleeping on that couch? Months. End of October to June… Six months? Eight. Gods. Eight months.* "I don't know," she said. "Hanson, I've never asked you what you like to do."

"Do?" He sounded startled.

"Yeah, like do you have any hobbies?"

"Hobbies?"

*Gods above and below, you twit,* she thought savagely, *quit repeating what I say. I hated that game in grade school and I hate it now, too.* "Never mind," she muttered, as a long rip in the leather closed seamlessly under her fingers. It wasn't precisely like sewing. It was like healing the material from the inside out. Suzanne had spent hours teaching her how to do it, how to concentrate.

She could feel him looking at her. "I used to like cars," he said finally. "Could have become an auto mechanic, I guess."

That startled her, a little. "What happened?" she asked, turning over another panel of the coat. There was a series of long, jagged claw marks there. *So that's where the blood on his back came from.* A chill ratcheted up her spine.

"I decided I liked money more."

Mari decided she'd had enough of cryptic men for the night.

Her eyes were hot and grainy, and her back ached from lugging her books around. And the fine trembling in her arms and legs reminded her she'd had three visions, none of them small ones. They were getting closer together and more powerful. To top it all off, her stomach felt bruised and tender, and her joints ached as if she had the flu.

Her concentration wavered for a moment, and some of the careful mending began to come apart under her fingers. "Dammit," she muttered, and forced herself to focus.

"Mari? It's not necessary, really. Don't exhaust yourself."

"That thing almost killed you," she replied more tartly than she meant to. "And I was absolutely no help at all. The *least* I can do is mend your coat."

He had no clipped answer for that.

"Want some music?" she asked, after a long silence. Outside, a car went by on the street, wet tires kissing wet pavement. The profound quiet of an empty house closed around them both.

"Sure," he said. "If you want."

"Put in the Joy Division," she suggested. "You said you liked that."

"You don't forget anything, do you?"

Mari's temper almost snapped. She took a deep breath, counted to ten, and counted to ten again.

It wasn't working. *Why am I so upset? Maybe I'm just tired. But... oh, gods, can't anyone do what I ask them to do, just once? Just once can we not have a committee decision where Mariamne Niege is involved? You know what's best, Theo knows what's best, Gretchen knows what's best, everyone knows what's best except me. And you do what I tell you, unless you can wiggle out of it by saying my "safety" is involved. Go to hell.*

"Fine," she gritted out between clenched teeth. "Forget the music."

He settled back down on the floor. He'd been getting up, slowly. Perhaps realizing discretion was the better part of valor, he shut up.

Mari took deep breaths, the tingle of Power in her palm never waning. She worked in grim silence until the coat was whole and heavy across her lap. It didn't make her feel any better, but at least she wasn't a complete dismal failure at it like she was at everything else nowadays.

# Ten

He heard her housemates come home—one of the women stamping in the front door, not caring if anyone was asleep, and the other's quiet, diffident passage a half-hour later. There were stealthy creaks and sounds as the nightly ablutions were performed, then the sleeping silence reigned again, broken only by the city sound of far-off traffic.

Hanson lay on his back, absolutely still. Beside him, under the covers, Mari breathed softly, deeply asleep, her hair tangled over her pillow. She had lain very still for a long time, obviously awake but silent, finally dropping off into unconsciousness. He hadn't taken his shirt off, or his jeans, but his weapons were piled next to the bed. He had a knife under his pillow, and his witch beside him. What could be wrong?

Something was bothering him.

He considered it, lying still, palms cupped up as his hands lay at his sides.

*She mentioned a man named Rossini. Have I heard that name before? And then she said he wasn't a witch, and changed the subject. Why? And why did she ask me to come into her room? She's never done that before.*

The front door banged open, and Mari stirred slightly, making a soft, protesting noise. Hanson's entire body turned to stone. He closed his eyes. *If you wake her up, I'll...* He stopped the thought. What could he do? Nothing except try to keep Brandon away from her, at least until the man made a move even Mari couldn't ignore.

Brandon bumbled in, muttering to himself. The front door banged shut, shaking the entire clapboard house.

Mari made another soft sound, then turned on her side. She flung her arm over Hanson's chest.

If he was stone before, he was frozen stone now. The darkness behind his eyelids turned into brilliant sparks and wheels of color. Her fingers brushed his arm, just below the sleeve of his T-shirt. She wore a tank top and a pair of sweats to sleep in, which meant her arm was bare, only the thin cotton of his shirt between her naked skin and his, except for her fingers. That slight touch poured fire up Hanson's arm, made his breath catch and damn near made him start to sweat.

It wasn't conscious. She was sleeping soundly. He could

tell from her breathing. But still…

Brandon's footsteps crunched down the hall, paused in the living room, then turned and stumbled towards Mari's door.

Hanson's eyes slid open a few millimeters. He saw the shielding over Mari's room resonating uneasily, both with Brandon's nearness and Hanson's own red-black, disciplined aura. The air in the room turned heavy, hot, and still.

He heard Brandon's heavy feet pause outside Mari's door. A long moment of perfect silence followed, Hanson's sensitive nose catching the heavy stink of alcohol. *He's mixed booze with the drugs,* Hanson thought, his lip curling despite himself. *Playing Russian roulette with chemicals.* He'd met plenty of Brandon's type, back in the old days, the ones that thought the right cocktail of substances made them invincible. *Come on, kid. Give me a reason. Just one little reason.*

Some other smell distracted Hanson for a moment, and his nerves tightened even further. *Dark? Can't be.* He dismissed it. Brandon was only human.

The sound of Brandon's heavy breathing filled the hall outside. Hanson's upturned hands tensed slowly. He could be up off the bed and across the room in less than a second. But if he moved, Mari would wake up, and he would lose the feel of her fingers against his skin.

And she was so exhausted, deep circles under her blue eyes, her cheeks pale as snow, and her hands shaking just a little. The *belrakan* had probably affected her more than she'd realized. This was the deepest she'd slept in weeks.

Hanson's hands curled into fists. Mari had agreed to move into Theo's house in four days. That meant he wouldn't have to worry quite so much.

Her doorknob rattled slightly. Hanson's breath hissed out, a low dangerous sound. *If he opens her door, I will kill him, damn the consequences.*

Mari sighed in her sleep. The shields over her room vibrated, a resonating note of Power.

Brandon's footsteps clumped heavily down the hall. Hanson heard him curse in the living room, then stamp into the other side of the house. Hanson inhaled smoothly, his aura slowing its spiking hurtful glare a little.

*That was close,* he realized. *I would have killed a normal. She just doesn't realize he's dangerous.*

It wasn't so hard to believe. You had to have a little bit of the Dark in you to really recognize evil. Lightbringers had no darkness to them. And Mari was a pushover. A hard-luck story, or a pair of bleary eyes brimming with tears, a sincere-sounding, "I'm sorry," and she would cave. She had no protective hardness in her. He would have called her an easy mark, back in the old days.

Mari murmured in her sleep.

Hanson stopped breathing.

The murmur stopped, continued, as if she was speaking to someone. Hanson slowly turned his head and found that by tucking his chin slightly he could look down and see her face.

While she slept, the worried line between her eyebrows was erased, and the pensive serious look was also gone. She looked content, a slight smile touching her pretty lips, a stray golden curl falling over her cheek and dropping past her nose. She pursed her lips, blew out between them, and his heart threatened to stop.

Moving slowly, he lifted his free hand and reached across his body, ready to freeze if she woke up. But she didn't. His fingers gently trapped the errant curl and pushed it back from her face.

Then his fingertips drifted down, touched her temple.

Between the touch of her hand on his arm and the feel of her skin under his fingers, his heart hammered. The pleasure swamped him in waves, an undertow of exquisite sensation drawing his nerves tight as guitar strings just before snapping.

He tore his fingers away. *Not like that. Not while she's sleeping.*

It was so goddamn *tempting.* He could slide into a corner of her mind, use the gift that had made him such a successful grifter, convince her she needed him, liked him.

His breath caught. He squeezed his eyes shut again, his pulse thundering at his throat and wrists and temples—and below the belt too.

*Don't think about that. Keep your mind on your work, Watcher. Don't get distracted.*

The trouble was, she was so eminently distracting. He would have never believed that a woman could raise his body temperature just by breathing. By tomorrow his shoulder would smell like her and the rest of him would smell like her room, her private sanctum. He would carry a reminder of being allowed into her room all day.

She sighed. Her eyelids fluttered. REM sleep, dreaming sleep. She was dreaming.

*I wonder what she's dreaming about. Is it a nightmare? Should I wake her up? Gods, no. Don't let her wake up. Let her sleep. Please let her sl-*

She moved slightly, and now her cheek was against his shoulder. Only the thin cotton of his sleeve kept her soft face from touching his skin.

*I. Am. Not. Made. Of. Steel. Dammit,* he thought, every word bitten off as savagely as if he'd been speaking. He'd been glad she had allowed him into her sanctum, closer in case of a nightmare, closer in case of an attack—but he hadn't realized what kind of pleasant unremitting torture it was going to be.

*Maybe I should sleep on the floor.*

Every fiber of his body rose in protest. He didn't *want* to sleep on the floor. He wanted to sleep next to her, hearing her soft breathing, feeling the touch of her satin skin on his.

Hanson invoked control. The memory of Watcher training rose under his skin, and the memory of the Trial, where the *tanak*—the symbiote—had been melded to his body. It had been sheer agony. Compared to that, even being around the Lightbringers and feeling broken glass grind into his bones was a picnic.

Mari stirred uneasily, her cheek pressing his shoulder. Hanson, his control reestablished by only the thinnest of margins, took a deep, soft breath in through parted lips. *Duty. Honor. Obedience.* He repeated it to himself, the Watcher's watchwords.

Maybe someday, in the distant future, she might allow him a little closer. But he had no right to even be this close to a Lightbringer, let alone the most absolutely perfect Lightbringer ever created.

"Thank you," he whispered, to the silence of her room, to the sound of her even and relaxed breathing. Her eyelids stopped fluttering. The dream was done. No nightmare. Her fingers still rested against his arm, and Hanson stared at the ceiling, willing himself to stay awake, to not miss a moment of her touching him.

# Eleven

*"I can See more now,"* Suzanne said. *"And so can you."*
Mari raised her head.

*The ocean muttered along the sand. It was a perfect tropical beach, the kind she had always dreamed of, white sugar sand and perfect blue water mouthing the soft shore. Warm air caressed her skin.*

*Suzanne stood tall and straight on the sand, barefoot, her yellow cotton sarong lifting slightly in the breeze. She wore a loose yellow peasant top, and she looked younger. The lines of worry on her face had been erased, but her hair was still steel gray, and still braided into a coronet atop her graceful head.*

*"I'm dreaming,"* Mari whispered. *"I'm dreaming."*

*"Not dreaming. Seeing. There is,"* Suzanne said quite dryly, *"a difference."*

*"Suzanne—"*

*"Listen. Time is short."* But Suzanne cocked her head, elegantly, and the sound of the ocean grew louder, reaching into Mari's bones.

I have to visit the sea again, *Mari thought.* It's been too long.

*"You must find the Library and complete the spell, Mari,"* Suzanne said urgently. *Her form rippled, shivered with an unearthly silvery light. Mari remembered that light from the spell that had made them Guardians. Had it come for her too? She threw up her arms, shielding her face, as the thundercrack of light spread out.*

*"Find... Library, Mari. Ask... your Watcher... He'll help..."*

*Mari fell, but the sand didn't catch her. Instead, darkness closed over her, darkness and an awful smell. She recognized that smell.*

*"Give it to me,"* the lipless sibilant voice said, as if speaking through mud. *"GIVE it to me!"*

*Mari struggled, desperation granting her hysterical strength. She tore her arm free of the iron grasp of darkness and ran, hearing the howling cheated scream behind her. A long twisting street laying under a blanket of fog, the wet oily glow from street lamps at even intervals, the stitch in her side gripping and something warm and wet dripping into her eyes.*

*Shutter click. Thunder rippled, tore at her ears. He was coming; there was no way she could escape. He was chasing her. Mari cowered behind the inadequate shelter of the air-conditioning vent.*

*"Make it stop!" Suzanne's voice over the sound of the storm.*

*"I can't!" Mari yelled back, miserably.*

*Suzanne's voice turned stern. "Make it stop, Mari! You can! I know you can."*

*A deep grinding roar. The ground shifted under her feet. Mari screamed, miserably, and then—wonder of wonders—there was Theo.*

*Theo materialized from thickly-gathered shadows, her heavy blue skirt weighed down with water from the lashing rain. She ran for Mari, her arms outstretched, and Mari gave a sob of relief and fresh pain. She knew what was about to happen, was helpless, helpless...*

*Then, the awful crunching sound. Theo looked down, a bubble of blood bursting on her lips. Water streamed down her chalk-white face, smear of blood on one pale cheek, dark hair falling back. She fell, her blue dress fluttering, the silk making a small ripping sound as her fingers twisted, tearing the material.*

*She fell.*

*"Theo!" A long, despairing scream. Rain lashed, stung her eyes. "Theo! No!"*

*She fell, and Mari's throat swelled with the enormity of the scream. It tore out of her, rivaling the thunder, and the Power rose too, striking like a snake.*

Mari woke all at once. No terrified lunge; the vision simply burst like a soap bubble. Her cheek rested on something warm and hard. There was a comforting, steady sound—someone's heartbeat.

She blinked. A yawn rose to her lips.

*I don't feel tired,* she thought, and curled closer into the warmth.

Then she realized her head was pillowed on Hanson's shoulder. She'd kicked off her covers and thrown her leg over his. He lay on his back, his arm under her head. Her arm was bent awkwardly underneath her, pressed against his ribs, and she had her other arm across him, her fingertips resting against his bicep right below the sleeve of his shirt. He lay completely still, breathing silently. The room was warm. Either someone had turned the furnace up or he put out a surprising amount of heat.

Mari froze.

*Oh, gods. How am I going to get out of this one?*

She could see the darker blond on his stubbled chin and the small scar just at the corner of his lips. The straight line of his nose, one dark eyebrow arching over his closed eye. With his eyes closed he looked strangely vulnerable. His heartbeat thudded under her ear, strong and steady.

Mari found that her breath had caught in her throat. He smelled familiar, maybe because he'd been close to her for so long, maybe because she'd just spent a whole night sleeping next to him. She could smell the faint, unmistakable tang of leather. Of course, he wore that coat all the time. The cold smell of steel and a warm male smell, something she'd never really thought about before. He smelled *safe*.

He'd slept in his black T-shirt and jeans, on top of the covers, and hadn't made a move once she'd turned out the light. Just laid there. Had he lain in the same position all night? Mari couldn't even imagine. She'd always been a rough sleeper.

Was he pretending to be asleep?

Mari, curious, moved her fingers slightly on his arm.

His breathing didn't even hitch.

Being around what the Watchers called *Lightbringers*—psychic women, though there were some psychic men who qualified—hurt the Watchers. Something about the Dark being allergic to Light. But Theo had told them Dante didn't actually hurt when she touched him, that the pain turned into something different. And Theo, cool impenetrable Theo, had actually blushed and mumbled when Elise, her coppery eyebrows arching, had asked just exactly *what* the Watchers felt when the right witch touched them.

His skin was smooth and hard under her fingertips. The bruising and scrapes had vanished. You wouldn't be able to tell that just last night he'd been limping and dripping blood and water all over the carpet, beaten almost to death.

Mari slid her fingers free of his arm. Her hair was tangled. She must have been tossing and turning last night until she settled against him. Her tank top was pushed up around her ribs, and her sweatpants were awkwardly twisted at the waist.

*I am in so much trouble*, she thought, and touched his face.

Rough stubble under her fingertips. She ran her fingers over the arc of his cheekbone, tracing the high curve. He had a nice face, she decided, when he wasn't so grim. She touched the small scar at the corner of his mouth. Where had he gotten that from? It looked wicked and painful, for all its small size.

Her alarm clock chose that exact moment to shriek. Mari snatched her fingers away from his face.

*Oh, no.* He'd slept between her and the door, which meant that she had to crawl over him to shut the alarm off, or get up and walk around the bed.

Hanson's eyes opened—pale, icy-blue snapping. He reached over with the arm Mari wasn't laying on and tapped the snooze button down. Morning silence descended on the room again.

He didn't look at her, just stared straight up at the ceiling.

*Maybe he's as embarrassed as I am.* Mari had to suppress a mad giggle. *Though that would be pretty damn hard to fathom.* She took a deep breath and pushed herself upright, pressing down briefly on his chest, flinching and pulling her tank top down so it covered her stomach. "Sorry," she said, pulling her knees up, unable to look away from his face.

"No worries," he said quietly.

"I'm sorry. That woke you up. I—"

"I was meditating," he said, interrupting her floundering. "It's all right."

"You must think—"

"Are you warm enough?" He moved for the first time, shifting his weight a little then curling up into a sitting position and swinging his legs off the bed. "Did you sleep all right?"

"F-fine," she said, and then could have kicked herself. She sounded like a stammering fool. "I barely even dreamed," she continued, taking a firm hold on herself. *Gods above, don't act like a ninny,* she thought. "It's the first real night's sleep I've had in a while."

"Good." He sounded pleased, even though his back was to her. "Mari?"

*If he asks me why I was touching him I'll die of embarrassment.* "I'm sorry. I—"

"Brandon came home late last night," he interrupted.

"What?"

"He stood outside your door, jiggled your doorknob." It

was that excessively neutral tone again. The tone he used when he wasn't sure if she would take offense. Hanson slid a knife out from under Mari's spare pillow and made it disappear. He stood up in one clean motion, scooping up the tangled harness that held most of his weaponry. His aura flared and then settled, the shields over Mari's room and the house reverberating as he checked them.

Mari looked at the covers she'd kicked off. Her pillow was on the floor on the other side of the bed. How the hell had it gotten *there?* "Maybe he wanted to talk to me," she suggested.

"At three-thirty in the morning?"

"He's just spoiled, Hanson. He's not dangerous."

"All right." He shrugged. Muscle flickered under the thin cotton of the T-shirt. *I was touching him*, Mari thought. *He's in good shape.* For some reason the thought made heat rise to her cheeks. "I'm going to visit the little boy's, unless you…"

"No," she said. "Go ahead."

He swung out through the door, and she felt him check the house shields again, his attention running over the layers of energy protecting her house from the outside world.

Mari bent over, scooped her pillow off the floor and clapped it over her face. She considered screaming, but she discarded the notion. He was likely to come back. So she kept her face buried in the pillow until her lungs cried for air, then she fell back on the bed, hugging the pillow to her chest and looking at her window.

Faint pearly morning sunlight filtered through the venetian blinds and the blue gauze curtains. The wandering Jew hung by the window glowed green, even in the faint light, a gift from Theo, of course. *Can't kill it, even if you try.* Theo had laughed. *Everyone needs a plant, Mari.*

She'd slept all night. Peacefully. And snuggled up against Hanson, too.

*I wonder if being near him stops the visions?*

It was something to consider. And what had she been dreaming about? She remembered a silvery light and Suzanne— or was it Theo? Sometimes the visions fled when she woke up, if she didn't pay attention to them. She couldn't quite remember. She'd been too busy looking at Hanson.

And not just looking, touching too.

Mari groaned. She was no good at boy-stuff. Elise went through men like they were Kleenex, dating for a couple of weeks and then dumping them unceremoniously. Theo hadn't dated as much, mostly because she was busy all the time with the store, but she also had no lack of male attention. The trouble with Theo was that she was oblivious to most men.

*I wonder if I should ask Theo's advice?* she thought, staring at the rainy sunlight coming through her window. *Elise would just snort and tell me he's a Watcher, and not to—*

*Beware the Watchers, Guardian. They mean you no good.* The man's voice echoed in Mari's memory, and she shivered. The thought of the awful sick weakness from last night made her skin crawl.

Her alarm went off again. Mari rolled over, bashed the snooze button, and then turned the alarm switch to off. *Quit mooning around,* she told herself sharply. *You've got work to do. Theo needs you to open the store, and you're going to be late unless you get showered and dressed. And you can finish the bibliography today. You can reward yourself with some Cicero tonight.*

She sat up, rubbing at her eyes, and was almost ready to get all the way to her feet when Hanson reappeared, carrying two of her blue coffee mugs. He wore his coat, too. It lay on him like liquid darkness, whole and looking new. Mari blinked. She'd done good work last night, apparently. She sniffed experimentally and found herself grinning, her hypothesis verified.

"Oh, gods," she said, "you brought coffee. You're wonderful."

She hadn't meant to sound so serious.

His mouth quirked up slightly. "Nice to see you happy," he said, and handed her the cup carefully, turning it so she could take the handle. If it burned his fingers, he made no sign. "I made myself some too. Mind if I drink in here?"

"Be my guest," she said. "I've got to get ready for work."

He nodded. "The shop."

"Yeah," she said, blowing across the top of the cup to cool the steaming liquid. "And then I need to go by the library and sweet-talk Crutcher into letting me use the laser printer there. I can't afford to get the thesis printed at a copy shop, but if I can get it printed then I can get a couple of copies and submit it to my advisor." She forced herself to stop babbling. "Boring stuff, huh?"

He shrugged. The movement was almost feline. "Not really.

I never had much time for school. If I'd known it was this interesting I'd've gone back."

"Interesting? Most people think it's deadly dull." She took a sip, almost scalding her mouth.

"Well, a whole lot of morons have no taste," he said, and Mari almost choked on her coffee, laughing.

*Gods above, did he just make a joke?* "No," she agreed, "they don't."

"It is interesting. That lecture last week about fifteenth-century sex mores was fascinating."

"You *heard* that? Where were you?" Mari found that she wasn't shivering in the morning, for once. The room was very warm, almost stifling, and Hanson seemed a lot easier than she'd ever seen him.

"Right outside the window." His blue eyes met hers. This time he didn't seem to be staring through her face like he always did. Instead, he seemed to be looking at *her*. Paying attention to her.

"But it was hailing," she remembered, scratching at her ribs through the tank top. *I hate sleeping in clothes. Guess I'd better get used to it.* For some reason, that thought made a flush rise to her cheeks.

Hanson shrugged again. "I've seen worse. It was an interesting lecture."

*It was in a third-story classroom, and there's almost no ledge under that window.* "I'm not even going to ask," she muttered darkly, dropping her eyes to stare into her coffee cup. "Well, thank the gods you don't have to do that again. Why didn't you tell me? We could have found some way to get you into the lecture halls."

He took a sip of coffee. "You might have found it distracting. And you were pretty jumpy whenever I was around, Mari. I didn't want to affect your schooling."

Mari found herself almost speechless. *So you hung outside a building during a hailstorm?* she wanted to ask, stopped herself just in time. "Look," she said diffidently, "maybe it's time we had a talk, you and me."

"You're going to be late," he said mildly, his eyes dropping.

*Great. Fine. Never mind.* The fact that he was right—she was going to be late if she dallied any longer—didn't help at all. She bounced to her feet, coffee sloshing against the sides of the cup. "Okay," she said. "Forget it. I've got to take a shower and get going."

She crossed to the closet, grabbed a random fistful of sweater, and managed to tear a pair of jeans out of a drawer, setting her coffee cup on top of the cherry wood dresser. Another random handful of underclothes and she turned around to find Hanson had stepped even further into her room so she couldn't possibly squeeze around him.

"Mari?"

Mari's heart leapt into her throat.

"I agree," he said, finally, his eyes on her. The smell of him—leather coat, clean male musk, steel and gun oil—boiled in the air between them, making Mari a little dizzy. "We need to talk."

Mari swallowed the lump in her throat. For a moment she'd almost been afraid, but that was ridiculous. He wasn't like any other man she'd ever known. "Okay," she said, and heard the breathless, thin sound of her own voice.

Was he smiling, or trying not to smile? She couldn't decide, and she dropped her gaze to his chest. That didn't help. The memory of his skin under her fingertips made her cheeks grow hot again. If she looked any lower she might *really* get herself in trouble.

"Whenever you have time," he continued, as if they were having a conversation instead of Mari making a complete fool of herself.

"Maybe today," she found herself saying. "I mean, you're around all the time, right?"

If she hadn't had two handfuls of clothes, she would have clapped one over her mouth to try and take back the sentence.

Her eyes flickered back up to his face. It was definite. He *was* smiling. The grim look was gone. Instead, his eyes were soft and a little darker than usual, and fixed on her face. As usual. But his look wasn't as intense as it normally was. Instead, he looked startled and amused. "Right again," he said quietly. "I'm not going anywhere. Whenever you're ready, Mari. I mean it."

"I've got to get to work," Mari blurted, her cheeks burning.

He stepped aside gracefully, as if she hadn't just said something totally idiotic. "I'll put the coffee in something a little less likely to spill," he said.

"Sure." She all but ran past him. *I'm acting like a teenager. And he didn't even try anything last night.*

*Maybe I wish he would have.*

It was more the sort of thing Elise would have said. Mari could just imagine the redhead pausing before she left the room to give one elegant come-hither look over her shoulder.

She made it to the bathroom without tripping, at least, and found herself staring at a disheveled, red-cheeked witch in the mirror—a witch with a tangled mop of blond hair and an absolutely horrified expression on her face. "Dear gods," she whispered, "what did I just do?"

*Nothing, that's what, and that's what the problem is,* Elise's voice said practically. *You're making a big deal over this, Mari. It's about time you dated someone, and he's available, and funny, and smart, and he accessorizes with nifty sharp things, not to mention the guns.*

Mari twisted on the water in the bathtub and flipped the switch above the faucet that would make the shower gurgle into life. After a few moments, steam began to fill the air. "Good gods, woman," she told herself firmly, staring into the mirror, "quit acting like a moron, okay? You think you can do that?"

*He's interested. So that's not the problem. What is the problem?*

*The problem is I like him, and he's nice and available. But what if he's like...*

She shook the thought away. He wouldn't hurt her. He'd taken one hell of a beating yesterday to protect her. And he'd never, ever raised his hand to her. She suspected the mere idea of it would horrify him. After the few bad relationships she'd had, she considered herself usually able to tell when a guy might like to belt women around a little. He definitely wasn't that type.

*But he looks at me like he wants to do something else. Like maybe kiss me.*

She stripped hurriedly and stepped into the shower. She'd be only a little late instead of glaringly late, if she was lucky. Time to stop woolgathering and get her butt into gear.

# Twelve

He handed her the stainless steel travel cup full of fresh coffee, and held her navy-blue wool peacoat up. She didn't have time to argue, so she slipped her arms into it gratefully, and he handed over her battered purse as well. "I've called a cab," he said, without preamble. "My treat since it's my fault you're late."

She visibly considered protesting, then simply nodded. Her hair was still wet, but she hadn't bothered to put it in a ponytail. The water-darkened curls fell behind her shoulders, and he restrained the urge to touch one, to see if her hair was as soft as it had been last night. "Okay," she said, ducking her head and patting her pocket for her keys. "Look, Hanson, I—"

"Mari?" It was one of her housemates. Hanson did his best to fade, but the woman had already seen him.

It was the brunette, Gretchen. She was a tall, plump, pretty girl with a faint psychic glow; not enough to be truly a Lightbringer, but more intuition that the rest of the normals. Her short dark hair was wildly spiked and disarranged, tipped with maroon dye, and her silver earrings—four hoops in each ear—clacked against each other as she moved.

"Gretchen," Mari said. "Hi. Look, I'm in a rush."

"Did he stay here last night? In your *room*?" Gretchen asked, jerking her chin at Hanson. He almost wanted to speak, deflect the woman's rancor, but Mari wouldn't like that.

Mari's eyes glittered blue, and her aura flashed once, sharply. "I am an *adult*, Gretchen," she said quietly, but with a finality to her tone Hanson had only heard once before. "I pay a double share of rent here so I can have whoever the hell I want in my room."

Gretchen's hazel eyes widened. She looked stunned. Hanson didn't blame her. It was easy to forget that Mari was incredibly powerful; she was so shy and retiring most of the time.

*She touched me.* He had to fight to keep the stupid grin from dawning over his face again. *She touched me.*

It had taken every erg of control he possessed—and a few he didn't know he had—to stay absolutely still while Mari touched his face, traced his cheekbone, touched the scar right by the corner of his mouth. The pleasure of it—her *deliberately* touching him—had almost threatened to snap his control. He was glad he'd decided to sleep fully clothed, and doubly glad she hadn't seen his definitely male reaction to the feel of her fingers on him.

Then she'd blushed and almost stammered, her eyes dark and fluttering everywhere, stealing little glances at his face. He had wanted so badly to cup her face in his hands and kiss her. He still didn't trust himself to refrain, so he dropped his eyes to the peeling linoleum of the kitchen floor and waited for events to unfold.

"Jesus, chill out," Gretchen said, raising her hands. "I was just going to—"

"Just going to what?" Mari's tone was chilly. Hanson was glad she'd never spoken to *him* like that. He would rather face a *belrakan* again than hear that icy-crisp voice directed at him. "Look, Gretchen, I love you, and I love Amy. You guys are my friends. But I've had it with either of you thinking you can control who I see, or who I have in my life. Clear?"

"He's a creep," Gretchen said finally, without so much as a glance in Hanson's direction. "We're worried about you, Mari. You haven't been yourself.—"

*You mean she's been less easy to take advantage of, don't you?* Hanson took a deep slow breath. This wasn't likely to turn physical, but they were already late. When could he intervene?

An automobile horn honked outside. He cleared his throat. "The cab's here," he offered neutrally, cutting off Gretchen's words.

"I don't make any value judgements about who you date," Mari replied tartly. "I think I can expect the same courtesy from you."

"You remember the last psycho? The one that damn near put you in the hospital? This guy's just trouble waiting to happen, Mari, and Amy and I want him out of the house." Gretchen folded her arms, leaning against the fridge.

*Hospital?* Hanson thought, and a number of things fell into place. No wonder she was so skittish and shy. He'd suspected she'd had her share of mishaps with men, this just confirmed it.

The thought of a man putting Mari in the hospital drew a red spike of rage across his vision. Hanson took a deep breath, dispelling it. He was here now.

"Save your breath." Mari turned on her heel, grabbing Hanson's coat sleeve with her free hand. "I'm moving on

Saturday. If you're going to throw Hanson out, I'll move *today*."

A chill and a flush seemed to slide down his body at the same time. She was *defending* him. And she'd implied she was dating him.

*I am the luckiest sonuvabitch on the face of this earth.* He almost didn't notice Mari was dragging him out of the kitchen, his body obeying her automatically. He shook himself free of the daze with a sharp mental slap. *Careful, Watcher. She's going outside.*

*She just implied she was dating me, didn't she? She did. Oh, gods above.*

"Mari." Gretchen trailed after them. "Mari, listen to me, please."

"Save it," Mari tossed back over her shoulder. "I'm moving ASAP, Gretchen. Thanks for showing me the light."

"Mari, wait a minute.—"

Mari unlocked and flung the front door open with two sharp movements. Then she stepped outside into the gray, thin sunlight of a cloudy morning. Rain threatened farther to the north, the sky there taking on a dark, peculiar color, but for right now it was only cloudy and cool. She still held Hanson's sleeve, and he moved automatically, following her. *If anything strikes, I'll have to disengage her very gently.* He was grinning again. *She just said she was dating me.*

Mari cursed under her breath with an inventiveness that almost surprised him.

The cab sat on the street, a yellow Checker, bright against the palette of grays and muted colors the morning revealed. "—had it up to *here*," Mari mumbled, and pulled him all the way down the walk and across the sidewalk into the street. Hanson checked for traffic automatically; there was none.

Mari flung open the cab's door and pushed at him. "Inside."

Normally he would have insisted she go first, but something warned him not to disobey her now. He meekly folded himself into the cab's back seat, smelling upholstery, curry, and cigarette smoke; the cab's heater was going full throttle. "Hello," he said to the man in the driver's seat.

Mari dropped into the seat beside him and slammed the door shut.

"The Rowangrove," Hanson supplied helpfully. "It's on the Ave, near Belmonti's."

"I get you dere," the cabby, a graying Sikh man with a cigar chomped between his lips, said. His turban was a magnificent pink. He dropped the meter flag with one practiced swipe and took off down Mari's street, a Ganesh air freshener swinging from the rearview mirror. Hanson took the precaution of spending a little Power on a small glamour, just something to muffle the sound of their voices. If Mari wanted a private conversation, Hanson would provide one. It was habitual, a courtesy to a Lightbringer.

"Bloody hell," Mari fumed, staring out the window. "Who does she think she—oh, gods. I just told her I was moving, didn't I? I'm going to have to pack. And get my deposit back from Andrews. What did I just do?"

Hanson said nothing. *You just defended me to your housemate,* he thought, his heart threatening to crack inside his rib cage. *And you said you were dating me.*

She finally looked over at him, the worried line back between her eyebrows. "I'm sorry. Gretchen's overprotective, and she... well."

*She's upset because you aren't available to fish her out of trouble,* Hanson thought sourly, *and because you won't bail her out when her boss calls from work anymore, or buy her groceries, or a hundred other little things. Good thing I'm around, Mari, they would bleed you dry.* "It's all right," he said, not because he forgave the brunette, but because Mari was examining his face, looking far more worried by the moment. "Really, Mari. I'm used to it."

"That's no excuse," she flared sharply. "She shouldn't have said that."

"I make her uncomfortable," he offered. "Thank you."

She shrugged, then sighed, delicately rubbing at her temples. "I suppose we should have that talk now," she said, with the air of a woman expecting her own execution.

*Never mind,* he thought, watching her profile as she dropped her eyes, then stared at the front seat. *I know everything I need to know.*

It was impossible, inconceivable, but he'd just been given concrete proof that she didn't dislike him. She had *touched* him.

He settled for saying, "Whenever you like." Color rose in her cheeks, a rosy stain against the pale skin. He found that absolutely charming.

*Keep your mind on your work, Watcher.* He told himself. *A moment's worth of inattention and things can go to hell in a handbasket.*

It was daylight, even if the sun was hidden behind clouds, and he was well rested. There would be nothing he couldn't handle during the day.

Except maybe one beautiful, uncertain water witch.

Mari was still blushing furiously, staring straight ahead. "So," she said. "I... um, I kind of said... well, I mean... I... you know, Hanson, I—"

"You don't have to," he said. "Really, Mari. It's enough."

"No, I think I should," she persisted, stubborn to the last. "I kind of implied to Gretchen that we were... um, you know."

"You did, kind of," he said. He couldn't seem to stop grinning.

"That wasn't very fair of me," she let out, all in one breath. "I mean, I... I kind of assumed..."

"Mari," he said, taking pity on her and schooling his face back into its plain mask, "I'm your Watcher. You're my witch. It's that simple." He watched the cabby's eyes in the rearview mirror, but the man appeared oblivious. That was good. Some people didn't like the mention of the word *witch.* "Whatever you want," he finished, almost losing his train of thought. *She touched me.* His body rose at the memory of her soft, tentative brush against his face.

Thinking about that made him think about how soft her skin was. What would it feel like to sleep with her in his arms? That didn't help him keep control.

Mari sighed. "But they could call you back," she said. "You said they rotate Watchers."

"You're my witch, Mari. Circle Lightfall doesn't have the right to order me anywhere." It was a statement of fact. He didn't belong to Circle Lightfall now, she was *his* witch, and the closer she allowed him, the happier he was. Was that why she'd been so uncertain? She thought he'd be yanked out to stand guard duty over another Lightbringer? *Sorry, no dice, Mari. I won't leave you.*

Unless, of course, she *sent* him away. That would be different. "Unless you sent me away," he said, to be absolutely honest. "You could send me away and I would have to obey. I'd watch over you, of course, but at a distance."

Mari's head turned so fast her damp curls ruffled. "Theo," she said, and trailed off uncertainly. Then she took a deep breath. "And Dante."

"Yeah," he said. "She stops his pain. You stop mine."

"This is insane," she whispered.

"We undergo intensive psychological testing," he disagreed, then could have kicked himself. *Don't disagree with her, this is the closest to her you've gotten in months, don't throw it all away, you moron!*

"I'll bet. Can't give a crazy man those guns, and knives, and God knows what else." Her eyes skittered up, touched the sword hilt poking up over his shoulder. "Hanson?"

"I'm sorry, Mari."

"No, don't be. It's okay." She waved away his apology and then settled against the back of the seat, her shoulders dropping, relaxing. "I did it myself, didn't I? I'll have to deal with the consequences."

"You didn't do anything wrong." The Rowangrove wasn't very far away from Mari's house—twelve blocks at most—and the cabby waited to take a left onto the Avenue. They only had a few more minutes in the shelter of the cab. He wished, suddenly, that the shop was a little farther away. Mari's knee pressed his; she had scooted over and was sitting right next to him. He could smell the cleanness of her freshly washed hair and the perfume of her fading anger. *She even smells pretty,* he thought with a kind of wonderment.

"I just… She's so mean to you," Mari said. "And I've had it with everyone else running my life. It's my life, right? I can do what I want."

"Well, what do you want?" he asked, before he thought about it. *No, I take it back.*

If he made her think about what she really wanted, where would that leave him?

"I think I want to move in with Theo, finish my thesis, and get a job," she said finally, looking down at her hands. "And then I'm going to buy a car. You know anything about cars?"

"A little," he admitted.

"Then you can help me keep it running."

His mouth went dry.

The cab swung through its left turn, and Hanson's habitual scanning of the street broke into his daze. Something felt different today. Different, and dangerous. The air on the Avenue was full of little prickles, and he glanced down at Mari.

"What?" She immediately craned her neck to look out the front windshield, then out her window, and then she twisted to look out the back window. "What is it? You've got that look again. What's wrong?"

"I don't know," he said. "Something seems off down here today. Just going to be careful, that's all."

Mari nodded, biting at her upper lip. I *wonder how that feels.* He had to shake himself out of the fantasy of being able to lean over, kiss her forehead, and then tilt her chin up so he could taste her.

"So," she said, the line between her eyebrows deepening slightly, "so you're not... mad?"

"About...?"

"Gretchen, and what I... said."

*Doesn't she understand?* Hanson took a deep breath, forced his fingers to relax. "Mari," he said firmly, "I don't mind at all. I..."

Words failed him. He studied her face, her blue eyes wide and worried, her fine, thick, tumbling hair beginning to dry in the onslaught of the cab's heaters, the color rising in her cheeks. What could he say? He had no right to tell her anything. He was only a Watcher.

Mari was still watching him. She made a single, nervous movement, as if prompting him to talk. He took another deep breath.

"We here!" the cabby announced, applying the brake with more vigor than was perhaps necessary. Hanson glanced up, the glamour he'd placed to keep their conversation muffled breaking with a slight subliminal snap. *Saved by a Sikh cabby.* The relief was almost matched by fresh worry. *If I didn't know any better, I'd swear I was about to tell her how goddamn much I want to...* Long practice stopped the thought. He was a Watcher. He couldn't afford to dream.

"Hanson?" Mari asked.

"I'm your Watcher," he said, finally. "I won't ever leave you, Mari."

And that was all he could say. She would laugh at him, if she knew the way his heart leapt every time he saw her, if she knew how he dreaded being away from her even long enough to kill another Dark predator. He was only a Watcher.

He didn't have any right to love her.

# Thirteen

It was a very busy morning. And Mari was glad, because she didn't have to think about Hanson, or the way he looked, or the fact that she'd just made a huge idiot of herself.

It wasn't so much that she'd defended him to Gretchen. It was high time she started speaking up, really. Gretchen and Amy didn't have any right to control her life. No, it was that she'd pretty much called him her boyfriend, and all he wanted to be was her Watcher. He had practically scrambled out of the cab to get away from her.

*Silly me,* Mari thought, *I thought he felt something for me, the way Dante likes Theo. Maybe it's a fluke. Maybe I can touch him because I'm a water witch, or a Guardian, or just a big old fool. Maybe that's it.*

But then again, Dante didn't seem to just *like* Theo. It had been pretty obvious from the first time Mari had seen Dante in the old shop, before everything had gotten so weird, that the big black-eyed man had a pretty bad case for Theo. And he'd seemed to get even more attached to her since, if that was possible. You could just tell by the way he almost held his breath whenever she looked at him. He was always so gentle, he watched her as if she was the only thing in the world that mattered.

Hanson, on the other hand, was just doing his job.

Mari sighed.

She didn't get a chance to look at the papers until the morning rush died down. Theo would have to order more of the black novena candles and the Love Me Now oil, two of the biggest sellers. Hanson was in the back room making her a cup of tea. Mari, perched on the stool behind the cash register, dug the thick sheaf of paper out of her purse and opened the sheets, glancing through them and then stopping, her forehead furrowing.

The paper was beautiful, thick, and obviously handmade. There was a thick black bold calligraphy script on one side, with notes written in a firm, somewhat spidery, leaning-forward handwriting.

Suzanne's handwriting. She would know it anywhere.

Mari's skin went cold, goose bumps rushing over her in a wave. Her entire body prickled. "Gods," she breathed.

"Suzanne."

A breath of wind stirred the air inside the shop. Mari glanced up. Nobody there, nobody outside. There was the faint clink of a mug on the counter, and Hanson's quiet watchfulness in the back room behind the blue-green curtain, but nothing else. The racks of candles and incense, the bookshelves, the racks of ritual robes and hemp clothing, the shelves of statues and metaphysical supplies all stood still and ordinary in their accustomed places.

But the painting Elise had done on the ceiling and the blue paint on the walls were glowing slightly, the colors far too rich, reacting to something. Mari shivered. Something was wrong and getting worse by the moment. She hadn't felt this type of dread since—

"Mari?" Hanson ducked out from under the curtain to the back room.

She had the sudden, intense urge to sweep the papers off the counter and behind her back, like a little girl caught with her hand in the cookie jar.

*Lemon.* The smell of lemon drifted in the air, and silk seemed to brush Mari's cheek.

"Mari." He was suddenly right next to her, taller than her, his shoulders absurdly broad, blocking out the sight of the window and the front door of the shop. "You're pale."

Mari felt something slide down her cheek, warm and wet. She dropped her eyes too late. A spot of water splashed onto the rich paper, blurring one of Suzanne's crisp little words.

"*Mari!*" He didn't yell, but his voice rattled the shop windows. His hand shot out, hovered above her shoulder, Mari almost flinched. "What is it? Mari?"

*Why does he sound so worried?*

"I'm all right," she said, in a thick, funny voice not at all like her usual bright cheerful tone. "It's just kind of a shock."

"What is?" He looked down, and Mari gave him the papers. She didn't have a choice now. Besides, her hands were shaking. And she could admit it. She wanted to hear what he would say.

He didn't look at the papers, just laid them aside carefully on the counter. Then he cupped his hands around hers, not touching them, keeping the barest distance between his skin and hers. Heat tingled up her hands, raced up her arms. His little Watcher trick, making sure she wasn't going into shock. "Mari?"

She did something that surprised herself. Mari dropped her

hands into his. He caught them reflexively, and then went so still he barely seemed to breathe.

"You hate touching me, don't you?" she whispered.

She didn't dare look up. The tension that invaded him now was different, but still dangerous. "Of course not," he said, quietly. "If you think that, I'm sorry. It's just that…" He paused, and she had the sudden lunatic idea that he was gathering courage. The thought was ludicrous. Hanson, scared of *anything*? He was *never* frightened. "I'm only a Watcher," he said, finally, his voice husky and so low she could barely hear him. "I don't have the right to… to want to touch you, Mari."

The smell of lemons and tang of power in the air was gone. Mari sighed. Had it been Suzanne? There was no way to tell. *Maybe I'm crazy.* But if she was crazy, at least she had company. Theo and Elise were also crazy.

And he was, too.

She looked up at him.

He was watching her face, and he looked worried. She'd never really seen him look worried before. Grim, amused, enraged—but never worried. She swallowed dryly. Her heart thundered.

"I didn't tell you," she said. "That man, Rossini—he gave me these papers. They have Suzanne's writing on them. He said something about a library. And…" But then she bit her lip. *Beware the Watchers, Guardian. They mean you no good.*

Hanson's hands tensed slightly. "Did he harm you?" he asked. "Touch you?"

She shook her head. "I was dizzy, and I felt so sick, like I had the flu." It was a relief to tell him. He leaned slightly forward, his entire attention on her. Nobody had ever listened to her that way, as if she was the only person in the world, as if what she said was important. "And whatever you did to keep me in the doorway, I broke it. But it was clingy, like it didn't want to let go."

"The *belrakan*," he said softly. "It would make you ill, that's why I had to put you under a keepsafe and get it away from you. It's pure contagion." Then his eyes changed. "Sorry," he said, apologizing for interrupting her.

Mari took a deep breath. "Don't tell Theo," she said. "Or Elise. Or Dante," she added hurriedly. "Please. They'll just fuss at me. I want to find out where these papers came from. I think they're about that spell, the Guardian spell. And if they are…

well, I want to know. We never got a chance to find out where Suzanne got the spell from."

He studied her face for a long moment, his hands wrapped around hers. The feel of his skin against hers, warm and hard, made a flush rise to her cheeks. Was he still doing his little heat-trick thing, or was she blushing?

"What do you know about the papers?" he asked quietly. "And where do you want to start looking?"

Mari blinked. Then her heart made a funny leaping motion inside her chest, and she had to swallow again. *He didn't even ask me why I don't want to tell the girls. He's just taking it for granted that it's what I want, so that's what he'll do. Just like always.* "I—" she began.

She didn't get a chance to finish. The temperature in the shop suddenly dropped sharply, as if a cloud had drifted over the sun. The pearly, rainy daylight seemed to dim, and Mari flinched, something scraping against her senses like a dull knife blade sawing through skin.

"*Damn* it," Hanson growled, his blue eyes turning incandescent. "Stay here, Mari. *Stay under cover.* Please?"

She nodded, shivering, the heat draining away as quickly as it had flamed through her. The shields set on the shop resonated softly, as if stroked, and the Watcher shields laid over the outside trembled, just on the verge of locking down to protect the shop—and her.

Hanson let go of her hands reluctantly, turning on his heel just as the wind rose outside. Mari could hear the lipless howl as the wind screamed down the street. Something Dark, outside, and it was probably hunting her. Or one of her friends. "Be careful," she managed around the sudden wild pounding of her heart. "Hanson? Be careful."

He turned back, his long black coat flaring sharply out and then settling. The red-black of his aura beginning to spike out, hard and hurtful, ready for battle. His eyes burned.

Mari inhaled sharply, but she didn't flinch. He caught her face, his hands cupping gently, as if she was precious. "Stay here," he repeated, as if she hadn't agreed. "Please."

Then he bent down, and before Mari had a chance to think about it, his mouth was on hers.

It was an intense kiss, but a strangely gentle one. His mouth burned, heat pooling in Mari's belly, their tongues meeting. She'd wondered almost every time she saw his mouth what it

would feel like, and she found that he tasted like city night and
male, heady spice and something dangerous, deadly. Lightning
shot through her. It had *never* been like this before.

He tore himself away, but gently, his thumb brushing her
cheekbone before he released her. "Stay," he said, his voice
still strangely husky. "Please." And then he turned again, his
coat following him like a pair of wings, and was out the door
before she could react. The bell jingled merrily as a tendril of
Watcher power pulled the door shut and the lock chucked home.

Mari slumped against the counter, trembling. Of all the
things in the world she had expected, *that* was the very last. He
had always been so careful not to touch her without her
permission, never pushing, always watching from the shadows.

"Gods," she said out loud, then looked down at the papers
lying on the counter. He hadn't even looked at them. He'd been
too busy looking at *her*. She jammed the papers back in her
purse and then stood, irresolute, behind the counter.

*I suppose maybe I might have been just a little bit wrong.*

She shivered, crossing her arms over her chest, cupping
her elbows in her hands. The street outside was dark and empty,
strangely empty for the middle of a weekday with all the shops
open. There should have been plenty of people, even with the
gloomy skies and rain threatening. *Where is everyone?* She
dropped her purse under the counter. She'd look at the papers a
little later, when he came back.

*If he comes back. He almost died last night, Dante called
that thing "Watcher's Bane." If it's so bad even the Watchers
have a name like that for it...* The thought paused as she
approached the window, the floor creaking under her boots.

Her cheeks burned. She was *blushing,* just like a stupid,
silly high school girl with a crush.

It didn't help that he was tall, sharply handsome, and had
those amazing eyes. It also didn't help that he was so careful
and gentle with her all the time. And there was a sneaking sense
of comfort in having him around. There hadn't been anything
yet that he couldn't handle.

*I can't believe I'm just waiting around in here while he
goes out and gets himself killed.* She shivered again. It wasn't
like her to be so... well, wishy-washy.

*I hate being wishy-washy.* She turned towards the step down
from the counter. *But he asked me to stay inside. He didn't
order me, like Dante sometimes does. He* asked *me to stay*

*inside.*

Thunder rumbled, making the window glass rattle. Or something like thunder.

Mari stumbled, her eyes widening, and glanced up, as if she could see the sky instead of the roof. Her lips still burned from his kiss, and another wave of heat went through her. *I must be having really early menopause,* she thought, searching for levity, *the hot flashes are something else.*

*That wasn't thunder,* a deep instinctive voice warned her. *The floor creaked. The floor doesn't creak when—*

Something tapped at the window.

Mari looked up.

There, standing outside in the eerie, dim light, was the pale, dark-haired man with the stony eyes, wearing the same hip-length coat.

Rossini.

Mari's heart slammed against her rib cage, repeated the trick, and then started pounding so hard she thought she might be having a heart attack.

He pointed at the door, and then he held something up. Another clutch of papers, this time rolled into a thick cylinder and trapped in a rubber band.

Caution warred with curiosity. He wasn't dangerous, was he? He hadn't attacked her last night, when she'd been weak and sick. And he'd called her *Guardian.*

Mari chewed at her top lip, considering. Rossini tilted his head, his slate-colored eyes fixed on her. He held the papers up, without any sign of annoyance or impatience.

Deciding, Mari walked cautiously to the door and unlocked it. Then she backed up, the shop's warding trembling with Power. He'd be foolish to start anything in here.

He slid up to the door, moving slowly along the layers of shimmering energy. Then he opened the door and stepped inside, still moving slowly.

Now that she wasn't sick and blinded, she examined his aura. It wasn't like a Watcher's. Theirs were swirls of red-black, powerful, impossible to hide and obviously deadly. Rossini's aura was sheer and blank, like a granite cliff face. "Good morning, Guardian," he said, with that same slight, respectful nod.

"Morning," she said. She had to try twice; her throat was as dry as sand. "You're rationing out Suzanne's papers."

"How else could I make an excuse to see your lovely face?" His voice was low and blind. It made her think of pebbles rubbing together inside wet dirt. She shook her head to free herself from the vision. He'd seemed normal last night. Hadn't he? "But no, I'm not *rationing* them. I can only take so much from the library at a time to avoid detection. The Librarian knows I'm up to something, but she's willing to let me do as I please. We have an agreement, the Librarian and I."

"The librarian? What library?"

"If I could tell you, I would," he said, and laid the papers on the glassed-in counter. "I saw your Watcher. He looked distracted." Rossini's lips quirked up at one corner, as if he knew far more than he was telling.

"He's *never* distracted," Mari said sharply, her temper rising. Was even this stranger going to jump on Hanson's case today? "What is it you want?"

Rossini shrugged. "I doubt you would understand even if I had the time to explain, Guardian," he said, taking a careful step back towards the door.

Mari opened her mouth to say something sharp, but there was a rumbling sound like a freight train going downhill. A confused flurry of motion, the bell over the door giving one violent sound, and then Hanson was in front of her, pushing her back so quickly she almost stumbled, his arm held straight and level, the gun cocked and pointed at Rossini.

"Get. Out," he said, each word clipped and hurtful, polished to a cutting edge.

"Hanson!" Mari tried to step around him, but he moved, swiftly and gracefully, using his body to herd her back. "Hanson, wait a minute, he—"

Rossini held his hands up, palms out. "I'm just a delivery boy, black-knife. Don't take it out on me."

Hanson pulled the hammer of the gun back. The small click seemed to slit the air inside the shop. "Now."

"Hanson, will you just—" Mari tried to go around him again, but he moved again, briefly and efficiently, keeping her sheltered behind his taller body. "Look, he just wanted to—"

Rossini backed toward the door. The bookshelves began to groan uneasily. The bell over the door tinkled, a sweet chiming sound underlying all the tension in the air. Breathless tension filled the shop, and thunder muttered again. Mari swayed, grabbing Hanson's coat. *What's wrong with the floor? Why do*

*I feel like it's moving?*

"Hanson." Mari tried again. "Look, will you please put the gun down and listen to me?"

"Later, Guardian," Rossini said.

Hanson's aura spiked with fierce, hurtful darkness.

Just then, it happened. The ground started to shake.

The windows rattled and wobbled, and the floor groaned. Mari grabbed Hanson's shoulders. *I'm not doing that. Is he doing that? No.*

Another confusing motion. Hanson's arm around her waist, and then she found herself shoving aside the blue-green curtain hanging in the door to the back room. Hanson stopped in the doorway, and it took her a second to realize what was happening. Not thunder, warnings. Warnings of an…

*Earthquake.*

They happened sometimes—not often, but the city was on a fault line. It was the only bad thing about living here.

Mari closed her eyes and hung on for dear life, wondering if this was going to be the big one. She might never get the chance to read Suzanne's writing.

# Fourteen

By the time the ground stopped shaking, Hanson was almost sure he wasn't going to die of frustration.

Mari leaned against him, her face buried against his shoulder, trembling. He could feel it through his coat, all the way down to his bones. She was soft and slender, and she fitted into his body as if she'd been made for it. All that softness, pressed against him. He wanted to wrap his body around her, feel her against him, for the rest of his life. It was the only thing that could possibly have calmed him.

An aftershock hit, and she made a low, hurt sound. Hanson braced his back against the doorjamb and stroked her hair, his fingers slipping through the blond curls. Something crashed and tinkled, breaking. He hoped a bookshelf hadn't fallen, that would be a right mess. "It's all right," he said, quietly, meaning to soothe her. "You're with me. It's all right."

He slid his fingers under the weight of her hair, cupped her nape. She was warm, almost feverish. Pleasure swirled through his nervous system, sparking violently. If he moved even slightly she would feel the affect she had on him. He could never remember a woman giving him a hard-on with just a kiss and such a short, chaste kiss as that. Hell, he could never remember a woman giving him a hard-on just by being *near* him.

A few thickly-silent minutes passed. "Gods," she said, finally, into his chest. Hanson found he was tucking his chin to look down at the top of her head. *Don't move,* he thought through the haze. *Don't move, sweetheart. Please.*

"It's all right," he said. "Just a little one. Not even a five-pointer." His voice was a soothing rumble, meant to shake the tension out of her. "I'm here, Mari. It's all right." *Don't move. Just stay here for a minute or two. Or the rest of my life.*

The bell jangled again. "*Mari!*"

It was Elise.

Hanson didn't let go of her. He couldn't. He was frozen in place, hoping she wouldn't move away. Hoping she would stay right there in his arms, where she belonged.

"Mari! Holy hell, are you all right? Mari?"

Mari raised her head. She was deathly pale, and her pupils were dilated. The trembling went through her in waves, peaking and then dying down. She had one hand wrapped in his coat and didn't let go. She had clung to him, shaking, burying her face against his chest.

*Did she have another vision?* he wondered. "Mari?" he asked, gently.

"Dear gods," she said, shakily. "Hanson."

"Now we know what an earthquake coming feels like. Damn." It wasn't the moment for levity, but they both needed it.

"*There* you are!" Elise ripped the curtain aside. "Are you all right? *Are* you?"

"I'm fine," Mari said, her chin lifting. She didn't let go of Hanson. "What are you doing here?"

"Hello to you, too. I was going to drop by for lunch. Then the earth moved, ha ha." Her cheeks were powder-pale, spots of red high up on her cheekbones. Crackling static outlined her, humming Power. Hanson's bones flared with pain, and Mari's nearness turned it into pleasure. His fingers rested against her nape, tingling rushing down his arm and spreading through his body. If she moved even slightly she would feel his arousal. "Are you okay? It was only a little one. You should have seen the stoplights bobbing back and forth."

"I think I'm okay," Mari said. Then she looked up at Hanson, her eyebrows raised.

She stared at him, her pupils shrinking. Her eyes were blue again. Her gaze fastened on his mouth, and Hanson had the completely reprehensible urge to take the curtain out of the flame witch's hands and pull it down, and then kiss Mari again. And again. And again.

"I didn't See this," she said, and her lip quivered slightly. Hanson's entire body tensed even further.

"Of course not," Elise said. "You can't. Neither can I, or Theo. Suzanne could have, but... Jeez, Mari, you can't See *everything.* You've *never* Seen a quake before, why should you start now? Come on. Are you okay?"

"I'm fine," Mari said, and seemed to mean it this time. "I *hate* these, even the small ones. Hanson... I didn't... gods. He carried me over here."

"It's a damn good thing, too." Elise looked up at him. "Thanks, Blue-Eyes. Last time a quake hit, I found her under a coffee table. Look, Mari, I'm going to turn the radio on and see what's up. The phone lines are probably a mess, but I'm going to try and call Theo."

"Okay," Mari said. "Do you mind if I faint?"

"Go ahead." Elise's lips quirked. The crackling charge of Power over her dispersed, shimmering, settling down. The shields on the shop, Watcher shields and witch-wards, went back to a low, residual hum. "Check the pipes back there, see if anything's broken, will you?" And she dropped the curtain, stamping away, her boots grinding into broken glass. Something had probably fallen off the shelves and broken.

Mari tipped her head back and looked up at him. He moved automatically so his hand cupped the back of her head, his fingers sliding through her hair. "Hanson," she said, as if reminding herself who he was.

"Mari," he replied, his eyes fixed on her face, helpless. It would be so easy to pull her forward, to—

Her hand moved against his chest. Paper crackled. "He gave me these," she whispered, and Hanson leaned forward. He stopped himself just in time. *She's alive, alive. Alive.*

"Mari," he said again. Was there anything sweeter than her name? She tasted like salt and cinnamon and liquid sweetness. He was *sweating*, almost shaking with need. He wanted to taste her mouth again.

She blinked, then freed her hand from his coat. He expected her to step away, put some distance between them, but instead she slid her fingers up his lapel. Her hand curved around the back of his neck and he shuddered, spiked honey flame spreading through him from her touch.

She pulled his head down, and he was lost, his mouth meeting hers. She actually stumbled slightly as he moved, one hand cupping the back of her head, the other flattening at the small of her back and pulling her forward. Her body seemed to melt into his. Paper crackled and shifted, crushed between them. He didn't care. Her mouth opened to his like a flower, and he drowned in the taste of her, the sliding softness of her. Her Power, blue-green now, deep and shimmering as a lagoon, folded around him, stealing through his veins, and igniting in his head like kerosene.

The kiss seemed to go on forever; paradoxically, she pulled away too soon, inhaling sharply. He opened his eyes to see her studying his face. She was flushed, her lips slightly parted, her hair tangled and mussed. He rested his forehead against hers and stared into her eyes. *A man could drown in those eyes.* He surfaced slowly from the welter of sensation. *Have some pity on me, Mariamne, please.* "Mari," he whispered hoarsely, his lips shaping the word. Then he kissed the corner of her mouth. He couldn't help himself.

"Thank you," she whispered.

*I didn't do anything.* He pressed his lips against her cheek. She moved against him, just a little, and her eyes widened.

"Anytime," he whispered back, meaning it. "Mari."

"Elise," she said. "Elise is here."

*Oh, damn.* He took a deep breath, trying to store the memory of her pressed against him. Who knew when she would let him touch her again? "You're *my* witch, Mari," he said. "Don't send me away."

She blinked again, and then the corners of her lips tilted up. Her lips looked just a little bruised, ripe for kissing again. She moved against him, this time definitely testing him. "No," she said softly, looking up into his eyes. "We have some things to talk about."

"Good gods, woman. You're going to kill me." He felt his mouth quirk up slightly.

"Really?" She moved again, and he had to forcibly restrain himself from crushing her against him. "I don't think so."

"Neither do I." He didn't want to let go of her.

Her face fell. "Don't tell them," she whispered, pleading. "Please. About the papers. I want to find out more before I tell them."

He nodded. "You don't even need to ask," he replied. "Where do you want to start looking?"

"*If* you two are ready to stop making out," Elise called sharply from the front of the store, "I really need a little *help* here."

"I don't know," Mari whispered. Then, turning her head towards the store, she called, "All right, Elise. Just a minute."

He couldn't help himself. He kissed her cheek, her temple under her silken hair, her forehead, and finally, when she turned back to him, her mouth again. He knew it was against the rules. He had no right to touch her. He had no right to even think about touching her.

She made a small, soft sound, maybe surprise, maybe pleasure, her fingers threading through his hair. When she finally broke away from him he was wishing frantically that he could pull her in and wrap around her, carry her with him everywhere. *Protect* her. He'd been distracted, not recognizing the earthquake, lured out so the *g'raian* could talk his way into the store.

And that was another thing. He couldn't leave her alone for five minutes without some sort of trouble. She seemed to attract it like a magnet attracts iron filings. "Beautiful," he whispered, his fingers moving slightly against her scalp, massaging, feeling the silk of her hair slide against his skin.

She froze. "Hanson."

"Are you two *done* yet?" Elise almost yelled. "For God's sweet sake!"

Mari jumped, nervously. "Coming," she called, and then gave him a look he couldn't decipher. "Thank you," she whispered. "For not telling them."

"You're my witch," he repeated. "You say it; I do it. All right?"

She nodded and then tried to slip away from him. Hanson found, somewhat to his surprise, that he couldn't let go. Finally, he made his arms unloosen, and she stepped away, sweeping the curtain aside. She looked back over her shoulder at him. Her hair was tangled, and her lips looked a little bruised, obviously kissed. She was, in a word, lovely, and his body leapt at the thought of walking her home. Alone. Maybe even sleeping next to her. In the dark...

"Do you know what he is?" she asked, obviously meaning the *g'raian.*

"*G'raian,*" he said automatically.

"What's that?" Then she shook her head. "No, tell me later. Can you see if anything's broken back here, or any pipes?"

He nodded once, swallowing. *Duty. Honor. Obedience.* "Anything you like, Mari," he said, harshly. "Anything."

She bit her upper lip, flushing again, and turned, dropping the curtain. "I'm coming," he heard her say.

"About damn time," Elise snapped, and Hanson had to take a deep breath. *Don't talk that way to my witch.* But the fire witch was a Lightbringer too. He couldn't attack her, he couldn't even *think* about attacking her.

It took three or four tries before he could make his fists unclench. It took another deep breath before he could remember what she'd asked him to do. If there was another aftershock, he would have to be close to her to protect her. Or if something Dark decided to take advantage of this confusion to attack.

He wasn't going to leave her alone again. Not even for a moment. Not if he could help it.

*She kissed me.* He couldn't stop the grin spreading over his face.

# Fifteen

It was a small quake, the battery-operated radio said—only a three-point-two. A single glass candlestick had jittered off a shelf and some books had fallen, but other than that the shop was unharmed. The phone lines were jammed, but Dante did get through to tell them Theo was all right and at the Red Cross shelter helping out, of course. She wanted them to check on their own houses. Mari flinched at the thought of going back home.

Elise swept up the candlestick, scolding Mari all the while. She snapped at Hanson when he reported that the pipes were fine, and she muttered thunderously under her breath as she stamped down the stairs into the stock room to check everything while Mari picked up the books and reshelved them. It was Elise's version of nervous worry, and Mari was actually secretly glad. It was, at least, one familiar thing.

Sirens echoed in the distance, and the fear-dyed mood of the city washed against the shop's shields. Hanson spent a long time making sure there was absolutely no crack or seam in the domes of energy, testing the waters outside. He was silent and grim, as if he hadn't just kissed her. Mari was glad of the shields. Before she'd met Suzanne, she would have been at the mercy of the waves of fright and confusion echoing down the street. Mari had been caught in a riot once, and it had taken her a year to recover. Something like this could have set her back for months.

It wasn't until they had locked up the store and Elise had stamped off down the street—there were new cracks in the pavement and all the traffic lights on the Ave were out, not even blinking—that Mari realized she'd forgotten to tell Elise that she needed to move. *Pronto.*

For a moment she stared after the redhead, biting gently into her upper lip and contemplating calling her back. But then she looked up at Hanson and her breath stuttered out of her lungs.

He watched her, leaning against the door to the shop, focused on her—and on everything else on the street, it seemed. His eyes were bright blue, almost glowing. *How does he look like he's paying attention to everything at once, and paying attention to me at the same time?*

Desultory rain spattered down, stopped. There would be a storm later in the afternoon to add to all the fun. Here, under the overhang, it was dry. Her stomach flipped. She was alone with him, or as alone as it was possible to be on a city street. Nothing moved under the cloudy skies. It was odd, but then again, it wasn't just a normal day.

They stood there for at least a minute, Watcher and witch, staring at each other.

"Mari?" he finally said.

She shook her head, her hair falling in her face. She stripped it back with impatient fingers. "We should go check the house."

He nodded. "Circle Lightfall could get you a house," he said, cautiously. "Or an apartment."

Mari's lungs began to burn. She'd been watching his eyes and forgot to breathe. "No," she said, and pulled in a breath. "Look, I don't want charity. Not from Circle Lightfall, not from *anyone*. Okay?"

He nodded. "What about a gift, then?" he said. "I don't have much to give you, Mari, but—"

Oddly enough, that made her laugh. He stopped, staring at her, and then glancing over her shoulder to check the street behind her. "That's okay," Mari said when she could speak again. "I don't have anything to give either, so we're even. Look, do you think you can stand to spend one more night there? Tomorrow I'm sure we'll get this all sorted out."

"As long as I don't have to sleep on that couch," he said, and then shut his mouth, looking ashamed.

That made Mari's chest hurt. "Of course you don't," she said. "Not unless you want to."

"I don't want to, but I will if you tell me to." He peeled himself away from leaning on the door and cautiously offered her his hand. "I'll walk you home."

"It's not home," she said. "But you can walk me there." She reached out, took his hand and laced her fingers through his. His eyelids dropped slightly, and the look he gave her wasn't just intense. It was *scorching.*

*I wonder what he's feeling,* Mari thought, and was powerfully tempted to find out.

Instead, she settled for pulling experimentally on his hand. "Come on," she said. "Let's go."

He obeyed, moving automatically to follow her. "I didn't dream last night," she said, "and I haven't had a vision all day today."

"That's good," he replied. "Right?"

"I think it's because of you," she said. "I slept all through last night. I haven't done that in ages."

"I hope it's me," he replied.

"You saw him," she said. "Rossini."

"I saw him." His fingers tightened slightly.

"He isn't human?" Mari persisted. She hated sounding so tentative.

"Not really. Human-looking, that's all. The world's a lot more crowded than anyone thinks."

She wanted to know what the stone-eyed man really was, but this was fascinating. "How do you find out about all this stuff?"

"Well, there's classes every Watcher takes. Anatomy of nonhuman species, classification of Dark. It's about half-and-half the first five years, field experience and class time. Then it's sink or swim with a more experienced Watcher, and after that... we get to take our turn at guard duty."

"Guard duty." Mari looked up at his profile. His jaw was set, and he scanned the street, then glanced down to make sure the pavement was clear.

"For a witch. And the gods help you if you screw up." A muscle flicked in his cheek.

"Dante said you'd... lost one," she said. "He said you hadn't been the same since."

Glass crunched underfoot. A restaurant window had shattered, and boards were nailed over it. Mari caught a flicker of uneasiness. The whole city was restless, brushing against her shields, begging, demanding to be soothed. If Mari let her shields down and let that screaming bedlam in...

"Astrid," Hanson said. "I made contact and frightened her, withdrew. Then I was fighting off the Crusade one night and a *s'lin* broke into her house. It wasn't pretty." His tone was flat, impassive, but his face was deadly white, eyes flaring blue. "She was an air witch," he said, finally.

Mari squeezed his fingers. "It wasn't your fault."

"If I hadn't frightened her, I would have been there to help her," he said harshly. "I swore to myself I'd never lose a Lightbringer. It's the worst thing a Watcher can do."

"But it wasn't your fault," Mari persisted. "You were doing the best you could."

"It wasn't good enough." He walked beside her obediently, but his fingers had turned into iron and his aura was moving uneasily. "I won't fail you, Mari. I won't let anything happen to you. "

"I know," she said, wishing she could think of something to say that would make him smile, or at least look less grim. "But it wasn't your fault."

"Mari…" He seemed at a loss for words, took a deep breath, tried again. "I should have been there, and I wasn't. I was clumsy, and a Lightbringer died because of it. You don't know, Mari. You just don't have any idea."

"Then tell me," she said. "Wait, no. Tell me what Rossini is."

"*G'raian*," he said. "Stonecatcher. You'd call him a gargoyle."

"Gargoyle? Is he…" She was trying to figure out how to ask if he was Dark.

"He's not a predator. *G'raian* don't eat Lightbringers. They prefer other prey. Suicides and depressed normals, mostly. They're mischief-makers, they love to cause trouble. I wouldn't trust anything he tells you, Mari. They love to create chaos; they feed on it." His thumb moved over the inside of her wrist, a soft touch. He was relaxing.

The touch made her breath catch. She would never have thought he could be so gentle. But he'd kissed her as if he was drowning in her, making a soft sound far back in his throat, his fingers gentle but inexorable. Her skin burned with the memory.

She stopped at the corner. No traffic on the streets. People would be stuck on the freeways, the buses weren't running, and most of the businesspeople had already gone home to check on their own houses. The gas station was cordoned off with yellow police tape. Mari hoped the underground tanks weren't leaking. Still, it was strange for everything to be so deserted. But with the way the streets felt, she didn't blame everyone for going home. The city felt as if it was just waiting for the ground to start bucking again. "Why didn't I See this?" she asked, looking up at him.

"Neither of your friends did either," he said.

"But we're Guardians. Aren't we supposed to—"

"An earthquake isn't Dark," he pointed out, then dropped his eyes.

"I hadn't thought of that." Mari sighed, pushing her hair

back from her face with her free hand. "But still…"

"It's been uneasy lately," he said. "I don't trust this. And the papers… Are you sure your Teacher wrote them?"

"Not wrote them, but wrote *on* them," she corrected absently. "And I haven't had a chance to figure out what else is on them. He said something about a Library and a Librarian."

"We can ask a few questions," he said quietly. "I've got a couple places we can start, but… you know, they're not nice places. You may not want to go to them."

"I'll go with you. I want to check the house. My altar, and maybe do some packing."

"Well," he said. "It would be better after dark. But after dark, it's more dangerous for you."

"I've got you." She couldn't believe something like that had come out of her mouth. But it was true. "You won't let anything happen to me."

*Did I just say that?*

His icy eyes lifted and moved over her face like his fingertips. "No," he said softly, but his voice was low and husky. "I won't let anything happen to you. But if you come with me, you'll have to stay close."

She nodded, biting her lip. "I've been in bad places before."

"Not like this you haven't," he said. "If you want to we'll go and start asking questions about this Library. Someone's bound to know something. It might be unpleasant, though."

"That's okay. How could things get any worse?"

"Don't say that." He glanced up, checking the street. "It's too quiet."

"Everyone's home, checking their houses and making sure their pets are all right. The last time we had a quake… well, there was a lot of damage. We're lucky this time." She realized they had just been standing there, and she stepped down off the curb. He checked for nonexistent traffic and followed, obedient.

*I'm leading around a guy in a big old black coat with guns strapped to him,* she thought, *and he's coming along just like a puppy on a leash.* "Hanson?"

"Hm?"

"I'm glad you're here." She stopped, and he halted, looking down at her again. Now that she knew what his mouth felt like, it was hard not to reach up and touch his lips to see if she could talk him into kissing her again. "I really like you."

His mouth twitched slightly. "Yeah?"

She nodded, her hair falling into her face. "Yeah."

"Then I'm happy," he said. "I adore you, Mariamne."

"Really?" It was an idiotic thing to say, but it was all she could come up with. He looked serious. He didn't say things he didn't mean. She knew that much about him, at least.

"Of course," he said, as if it was self-evident. "You're my witch."

There didn't seem to be much to say to that, so she simply walked the familiar route home with her head down and his hand in hers.

# Sixteen

Hanson stopped and half-turned. Mari stopped too, her hand caught in his, pleasure blurring up his arm in waves. "Hanson?"

"Wait," he said, and pulled her close enough that he could slide his other arm around her. It was an excuse to hold her, but it was a good one. "Wait a moment, Mari."

They were less than a block from her house, and something was wrong. Very wrong.

His aura spread along the edges of her clear glow, and he cast out, seeking. His Watcher-trained senses encountered something hard and cold that smelled of bitter salt.

He knew that smell. "Mari," he said, "maybe it's best if we don't go into your house."

"What are you—" She twisted around in his arms, her hand still caught in his. Her eyes grew round.

"Not human," Hanson growled, his voice taking on the sharp hurtful edge of Dark. *Careful. She's right next to you. Don't frighten her.* "Something else. I can *feel* it."

She glanced up at his face, flinched, and then looked back at the small clapboard house crouched under cloudy skies. "I wonder what…"

Hanson pulled her into the shadow of a laurel hedge as the front door of her house opened.

Nothing. The wind pushed at the door, made it bang against its frame. A low moan mouthed through the air.

"Oh, my God," Mari breathed. "Hanson, the door."

"Easy, Mari." It took only a moment to hide them both. It wasn't invisibility—that would be difficult and draining. Instead, the illusion-shell would simply make an onlooker's eyes slide right over them both. He restrained the urge to stroke her hair, to touch her face. Now it was time for work, for making sure she came to no harm. "Just wait for a minute. We can watch for a little while, see what's going on."

"But Gretchen…Amy…or Brandon… What if something's happened?" She was trembling again, his arm tightened around her.

"Something's happened all right," he told her. "Let's make sure something *else* doesn't happen. If the Dark has invaded your house, you'll be a target. Please, Mari."

She bit her lip. "All right," she whispered, and he bent down to press his lips to her forehead. It was a brief contact, and he shouldn't have done it because it distracted him, but she needed comfort.

He was about to say something else, but his eyes caught a sudden movement up the street. He looked over Mari's blond head and felt his hands tighten.

The *g'raian* stood in the shelter of an overhang, watching as well. He apparently had seen them both before Hanson snapped the illusion-shell up, because he stared right at them and nodded once, deliberately. A growl thundered out of Hanson's chest, shaking the thick, cool air. It smelled like a storm coming. A storm and Dark.

Mari jumped, twisting in his arms to see what he was looking at. It was too late. The *g'raian* faded back into the shadow of the overhang. "What? What's going on? Hanson?"

*If she panics,* he thought coldly, *I'll have a hard time keeping control.* He could feel the symbiote rising, conscious of the threat to her. Her nearness turned it into honey-spiked pain riding his bones. "Stay calm, Mari. I need you calm right now. I just saw your friend, the gargoyle."

"Where?" She twisted again, trying to look, his arms tightened reflexively. Mari looked up at him, her wide blue eyes dark and pained. "Hanson, *please.*"

"Mari," he said, and his voice was far too harsh, "I *need* you calm right now."

She swallowed once, hard, and nodded. "All right." But her eyes were full of a suspicious shine.

"Someone's died in your house." *She shouldn't have to deal with this.* "I need a few moments to get a better glamour on, and then I'll walk up to the front door. Let me handle this, all right?"

She nodded. "Who... You can tell that someone..."

He suppressed the urge to kiss her again. Instead, he pulled her forward. She came willingly and rested her head against his shoulder. She was shaking again. "I can tell," he said grimly. "Any Watcher could. The shields have been ripped apart from the inside, Mari."

"Something got into the house?" she said against his shoulder.

"Let me think, okay? And let me handle this. I know how to clear a scene and talk to cops. You just stay here under a keepsafe."

She wrapped her hand in his coat. "No," she whispered, tears brimming in her eyes. "Please don't leave me here. *Don't* leave me here."

"But—"

"I'm safer with you," she pointed out. "Please, Hanson. *Don't* leave me here. Please."

"Mari—"

"Please." And her eyes welled with tears.

*She is safer with me, but what if something Dark is still in there?* "All right," he heard himself say. "But *stay close* to me. There's no telling what's in there. If I tell you to run, *run*, understand?"

She nodded, her forehead rubbing his coat. He waited a few more moments, just to savor her leaning against him. "We'd better get it over with," he said finally.

They left the illusion-shell, Hanson's arm over Mari's shoulders. She stayed in the shelter of his body, his aura extending over hers, a stain at the fringes of her clear light. "Just be cool," he said to her, before they passed the mailbox. "All right? I'm here."

"All right," she whispered. "Hanson?"

"Hmm?"

"Are you sure that…"

"I'm sure."

They reached the end of the concrete walk leading up to the house and stopped, Mari uncertainly and Hanson to recon. This close, Hanson could tell the shields had been ripped open, even the Watcher shields. Streaks of pulsing energy bled away from the broken shielding. It had been torn and burst from the *inside*, the only conceivable way something Dark could break Watcher shields so messily. Hanson's attention shifted, "catching" the threads and rifts of Power and compressing them. Memorizing the marks and turning the problem over to his subconscious, he came back to himself with a shudder. Mari's eyes were round.

*Something busted this place open with psychic TNT,* he thought, and felt a shiver trace up his spine. This was beginning to look like a message. Porch boards creaked under their feet. Hanson slid his arm free of Mari's shoulders, reached up, and drew the sword free of its sheath, his glamour stretching to cover in case someone was watching. "Stay behind me," he cautioned, and Mari gave a shaky sigh.

The entry hall was dark and silent. Something had blown out all the electricity, either the earthquake or the sudden eruption of Dark. Hanson didn't want to find out.

It was in the living room that he caught a glimpse. Amy, the blond roommate, lay twisted against the couch.

Or what was left of Amy. A few strands of her sleek platinum hair were all that was left to distinguish her.

Hanson had seen plenty of carnage in his time as a Watcher, but this was something else. He let his eyes pass over the scene, once, in a swift arc. "Holy *fuck*." He pushed Mari back into the hall. "You don't want to see this, Mari. Stay here."

"What is it?" Her voice trembled. "Hanson, that looks like—" She pushed forward, but he grabbed her arm and shoved her back, taking care to block her view of the living room.

"Mari," he said harshly, "you do *not* want to see this."

"I'm not in danger, am I?" she snapped, fever spots high on her perfect cheeks. "I *order* you to let me see."

He inhaled, his control strained and his fingers tight on the sword hilt. *Obedience, Watcher.*

He half-stepped aside, careful to keep himself slightly in front of her in case anything attacked.

Mari choked. She grabbed his coat and buried her face against his back. He shouldn't have felt grimly satisfied—but he did.

"We have to pack you a bag," he said. "We can call the cops afterward. You're not staying here."

"Hanson," she breathed. "What could have... *gods*..."

"Dark. Something Dark, from the inside. Maybe one of them let something in. I don't know. Let's get you some clothes, Mari."

"I can't... oh, gods." She sounded as if she was going to be sick. He didn't blame her. "All right. Let's go."

She held on to his coat, hiding her face against his shoulder as he sidled past the living room and into the hall, trying to make sure she didn't have room to peer around him.

"Well," he said, finally. "Mari?"

Mari's door had been hacked in. It looked as if long claws had battered the flimsy wood. The doorknob was ripped out, and the shields she had placed so carefully on her sanctum were cracked and torn. Her room had been tossed thoroughly. The bed was savaged, her sheets torn into confetti, the mattress slashed. Hanson's nostrils flared. The smell was definitely Dark, and it nagged at him. Something familiar.

He didn't have time for it now. "Your room's been trashed," he said.

"Oh, *no*," she said, and the hurt in her voice was enough to make his free hand curl into a fist.

*Dammit.* He sheathed his sword. What had been here was

most likely gone, having fed and indulged in its appetite for destruction and chaos.

Mari's altar had been smashed into matchsticks, the conch shell ground into powder. Something had fed greedily on the Power here. If Mari had been here alone...

*Don't think about that.* "I guess I'd better find a place for us to spend the night," he said, listening to Mari's breathing. If she started to go into panic or shock, he would have to take her out of here. He only felt icy rage and mounting frustration. He couldn't remember where he'd smelled this type of Dark before, but it was maddeningly familiar.

"Do you think... Gretchen..."

"I don't know. I'll check..." He let his voice trail off, his eyes moving over the room. Some of it was destruction just for the joy of it, like the ripped books and the smashed stereo. The bed, in particular, was pure vandalism.

"The police," Mari said, in a choked little voice. "We can't touch anything."

*It wouldn't matter even if we did. They're not going to find anything here. Nothing but two dead bodies and destroyed furniture, and the stink of the Dark. Only that.* The symbiote moved restlessly inside his bones, and he realized that Mari's pearl necklace was missing.

"Your necklace is gone. Dammit. Come in." He pulled her into the room and set her in a blind corner. "Stay right there and don't move. I'm going to see if any of your clothes survived."

"Hanson." Her eyes were red. Brimming with tears. Glitters of wetness tracked down her cheeks.

Rage crystallized. *She shouldn't have to see this.* "What?"

"I...I have to know. Gretchen...and Amy...and Brandon."

"It's not safe," he said, turning back to her closet. There was a duffel bag tossed on the floor. It had been under her bed, he remembered, ripping it open and turning back for the closet. Whatever had torn her room up had also gone *under* her bed. That was a kind of thoroughness he wasn't used to seeing from the Dark, unless the Dark in question was very hungry. "What else do you—"

She broke for the door. He dropped the bag and blurred across the intervening space, catching her wrist and shoving her back against the wall. "*No,*" he growled, and the window rattled in its frame. "It's *not safe*, Mari. *Let me do my job!*"

She collapsed against the wall, sobbing, her wrist caught in his fingers. He was gentle, careful not to bruise her. "Shh," he said. "Hush." *I've frightened her, clumsy, stupid, and I was doing so well, damn it to hell.* "Mariamne, shhh, hush. It's all right. I'll look as soon as we have your bag packed, all right? I promise. Let me do this. I know what to do, shhh, hush. It's all right."

The sobs eventually shuddered to a stop, and she slumped against the wall. Hanson finally dared to let go of her and stepped away "Let me do my job, sweetheart, all right? Whatever was here might still be here, and if it is it will come for you and *kill* you. Stay with me. I'm your protection, Mari. Stay with me."

Her eyes flashed, extraordinarily blue. "I have to see," she said. "What if one of them is…is alive?"

"There's nothing living left in here, Mari," he replied grimly. "Now just hang on a minute, okay?"

She didn't make any gesture of assent, but she remained slumped against the wall while he packed a few items of her clothing that hadn't been shredded. *Whoever it was did a good job,* he thought grimly. *And took some time over it.* "All right," he finally said, hitching the duffel bag up on his shoulder.

"What now?" she whispered, a dazed look on her face that tore at his heart. She of all people should not have to witness this.

"Now we check the house, if you really have to see everything. And then we'll call the police, quick."

"Hanson…" She wiped at her sodden cheeks with the back of her hand.

He crossed the room again and cupped her face in his hands. "I'm right here," he said. "I'll be here all through it. I'll deal with the cops and everything else. It's part of Watcher training. You just have to look stunned."

"That won't be hard," she whispered, and the faint attempt at humor scored his heart like nothing else could.

"You don't have to look, Mari," he pointed out.

"Of course I do," she replied colorlessly. "They died because of me. Because of what I am."

# Seventeen

Mari clutched at his coat all the way back to the kitchen and the phone. Amy lay in the living room. At least he'd told her it was Amy, but Mari couldn't tell. He said there wasn't anything left living in the house, and despite her insistence on seeing she didn't protest when he simply led her to the phone.

There was too much blood, Not only that, but the *smell* was awful. It was like the worst bathroom stink she had ever smelled. It wasn't just physical; it was a psychic stench dyed into the air, fear and hatred and death and the smell of something as foul as the thing Hanson had fought off last night.

He dragged her outside to wait for the cops. Dragged not because she protested, but because her legs wouldn't work. When the cops came, and then the paramedics, he handed her over to the EMTs and neatly directed the cops away from her.

Mari pressed the back of her hand against her mouth, shivering.

"It's okay," the EMT said. She was a stout, motherly woman, with short, dark hair and a kind, brusque manner. Her nametag said *P. Joshua*. "Just try to breathe, honey."

Garish lights painted the drizzling rain. Hanson stood off to one side, giving a statement to a rumpled, bald homicide detective. If Mari didn't look closely, she could ignore the glamour closed over him, hiding his guns and the sword. He looked like a normal, concerned boyfriend, pale and jittery because he'd just seen something horrible.

The glamour also hid her duffel bag, slung against his back. *They wouldn't like us taking evidence*, he'd said before picking up the phone, his other hand loosely shackling her wrist, keeping contact with her.

*Or making sure I wouldn't bolt.* Her brain shivered, shying away from the awful thought of what lay inside the house.

Mari had been placed in the back of an ambulance, clucked over by the EMTs, and visibly dismissed by the cops. Any other day, she would have been upset when she realized Hanson had given a subtle *push* to a cop or two, getting them to disregard her.

As it was, her stomach kept trying to empty itself and her entire body felt numb and tingling.

The EMT gave her a paper cup full of coffee from a red

thermos. "Drink up, sweetie." She reminded Mari of Theo, with her wide brown eyes and no-nonsense attitude. "Come on, can't have you going into shock."

"I can't believe it," Mari heard herself say.

"Hell of a thing to come home to," the EMT said, sighing. "And on a day like today, too. You get rattled in that quake?"

Heat rose to Mari's cheeks. The memory of Hanson holding her during the earthquake, murmuring in her ear, his arms steady and solid, shouldn't make her blush. Should it?

Her stomach flipped. "Oh, gods," Mari moaned, and her hand jittered. The coffee slopped in the cup.

Hanson broke away from the cop talking to him, his aura spiking. It was a *push*, and he cut between two uniformed officers and arrived just in time to subtract the paper cup from her fingers just before she spilled it. "Hey," he said quietly, and glanced up at the EMT. "You okay?"

"I'm not." She glared up at him, knowing it wasn't his fault. "Two of my roommates are in there in pieces, Hanson. I'm *not* okay."

"We can go," he said. "I need to call Dante."

"No." She bolted to her feet. That was a mistake, because he caught her arm, keeping her from overbalancing. "Please, Hanson."

His aura stretched again, and the EMT mumbled something. "Do you want this?" he asked, holding up the paper cup.

Mari shook her head, numbly. He set it down in the back of the ambulance and slid his hand down to her elbow. "Let's get out of here. Night's falling."

Her stomach flipped again. "They're just letting us go?"

"We didn't do anything," he pointed out, his hair beginning to stick to his forehead under the drizzling rain.

"They didn't even ask me anything," she mumbled. Her teeth chattered.

Hanson's arm closed over her shoulders. A wave of heat crashed through her body. She blinked dryly, her eyes grainy. "They think they did," he said. "You were sobbing, obviously distraught, and obviously innocent. I'm the concerned boyfriend, who will take you home and take care of you. I gave them a phone number and—"

"Don't call Dante," she interrupted, her teeth chattering. "Don't call *anyone*."

"Why not?" He snapped a glance over his shoulder and

steered her around the corner. "We'll need help, and he's the only other Watcher here."

"No," she said. "No. Whatever killed them... it smelled like my vision. The... the one where Theo..." Her teeth chattered so hard it was difficult to speak.

"You're in shock," he said. "Got to get you off the street, Mari."

"Please." Her hands shook like an old alcoholic's. The street lamps were guttering to life, buzzing and beginning to cast faint orange circles on the pavement. "Promise me you won't call Theo or Dante or Elise."

"Mari, it killed both women, and the cops couldn't find Brandon in the house. He's gone." His jaw was set, his eyes burning blue. "I found out the boy has a record, too. Drunk and disorderly, assault."

"Leave Brandon out of this," she said numbly. "Please."

"The wards were broken from inside." His arm tightened over her shoulders. "Look, Mari, if we don't tell your friends, we'll have to find somewhere for you to sleep. And you need dinner."

"I can't eat," she whispered miserably. Her numb feet clumped along the pavement. *Something tore my room apart. All my books. Smashed my shell. And A-a-a-amy...* Even her mental voice stuttered, the awful vision of the couch and what it held rising into her head like a shark sliding up from dark waters.

"*Gods.*" The way he snapped the word short made it a curse. "Just a minute, Mari. Let me think."

Mari stopped, planting her boots on the sidewalk. Hanson stopped, too, glancing around first to check the area. "Promise me," Mari said through chattering teeth. "P-p-promise me."

"I promise, Mari." The words sounded torn out of him. "Now can we get you off the street?"

"I th—" Mari started, but the sound of the scream drowned out her words.

It was a long, trailing, hair-raising, spine-tingling roar of bloodcurdling rage, all the more terrible because it wasn't audible; it was a psychic cry. Mari's knees buckled. She clutched at Hanson's shoulder and heard him swear, his fingers suddenly biting into her arm, holding her up.

*What th*—Mari started to think, and then blackness swallowed her whole.

# Eighteen

*I'm no good at healing,* Hanson thought desperately, and held the bloody rag to Mari's head.

She groaned, her eyelids fluttering. He stroked her cheek, dabbed at the gash on her forehead. "Mari? Say something. Please."

"Ouch," she muttered, dreamily. "What was *that?*"

"You fainted," he said. "I don't blame you. Something screamed, probably whatever's hunting you. Sounded awful."

"I feel funny." Her hand lifted up as if to touch her head, dropped back down.

"You're in shock. Just relax, Mari. Breathe. I'm right here."

"Where are we? Are you—"

*We. She said we. Taking it for granted, thank the gods. She doesn't sound angry.* "I got us a hotel room downtown. We're safe for now. I've shielded the walls. I'm going to have to take a breather, but other than that I'm fine. It's you I'm worried about."

"Can't… afford…"

"Don't worry. I've got emergency funding from Circle Lightfall. This is what it's for." He dabbed a little more at the bloody wound. "You went down pretty hard. Hit your head on a mailbox."

That won a small chuckle from her. "I guess the mailbox won."

"Guess so. I'm sorry, Mari. I should have caught you."

"It's all right." Her eyes opened, their blueness deep and dark enough to drown in. Hanson leaned back, the damp rag clenched in his fist. "There you are," she said, wonderingly.

"Take it slow," he cautioned, as she pushed herself up on her elbows and looked around the hotel room. Hanson glanced at the room: short-pile carpet patterned with diamonds, ecru curtains drawn tight, white coverlets and wine-red bolsters on the beds. It was the most strategically safe room in the hotel, and he'd had them send up extra towels. Outside, the city breathed, enough interference here downtown to at least provide some protection from attack. They were checked in as a married couple, emergency ID shown and accepted. Thank the gods Mari hadn't barred him from using Circle Lightfall's help. The witches had refused Circle Lightfall and banned them from the city, but

Hanson was powerfully tempted to call for reinforcements. This was rapidly getting out of hand. "Just take it slow, Mari." He checked her pupils again. She didn't have a concussion. Just shock and the memory of a sight no Lightbringer should have to see.

She pushed herself upright, staring at the room. "Gods above." She reached up to touch her forehead gingerly, her fingertips barely brushing the skin. He leaned back slightly, perched on the edge of the bed. "Ow. Theo would have a fit."

"She might," he agreed. "How do you feel?"

"Awful," she replied promptly. "What *was* that?"

"Something Dark, screaming. I don't know, Mari. I just got you out of there. I didn't have the energy to fight, especially with you unconscious and bleeding." He stripped his hair back from his face, wishing he could punch something. It would get rid of the tension.

She blinked and sighed. "I guess so. Do you think it was… whatever did that to Amy and Gretchen?"

"It's possible," he admitted. "Look, you need something to eat. There's room service."

"I can't eat," she immediately disagreed, her pretty, wistful mouth turning down at the corners.

"Well, I'm hungry, and I need food. So I think you should probably eat, too, even if you're not hungry. If you drain your physical reserves you'll go into shock again. I've spent a lot of Power, and I need to rest."

*If this doesn't work I don't know what I'll do.* He let his shoulders slump as if he was tired. He wasn't hungry and could still fight. It would take a lot more than this to make wear him out, but she didn't know that. She needed to rest.

As he'd suspected, that got to her. "I didn't…" She trailed off, her fingers exploring the soreness on her forehead. Hanson had to swallow hard against a sudden flare of nausea. The thought of her hurt, in *any* way, was enough to make him sick to his stomach. "Gods, Hanson, I'm sorry. I didn't think about how tired you must be. I'm so sorry."

He shrugged. "You want to take a shower or something? I'll get us some dinner. Then we can figure out what to do."

She nodded, biting her upper lip, and he had to push down the urge to kiss her. *Hard.* Prove to himself that she was all right.

Mari examined his face. "Sounds like a good idea." She

reached up with one hand and touched his cheek. "I didn't thank you, did I?" She sounded thoughtful.

Hanson found his breath catching. Heat spilled down his face, his throat, set his heart to pounding. "It's my job," he managed around the lump in his throat.

"Oh, I know," she said softly. "But thank you anyway." Her fingers trailed down to his jaw. Helpless, he leaned into her touch, his entire body resounding like a plucked string. "If you'd been there…when whatever it was—"

"I'd have protected you," he said low and harsh, his breath tearing out of him. *Don't you understand what this does to me?* he wanted to ask her. *Don't tempt me, Mari. Don't.*

"What about Amy? And Gretchen?"

He shrugged, his entire attention on the feel of her fingertips against his face. Narcotic heat slid down his throat and spread to his chest. "Maybe. If I could save them without endangering you."

Mari blinked. Her blue eyes filled with tears. "It's my fault," she whispered. "I'm a witch, and they died because of it."

"It's not—" he began, but she shook her head, biting her upper lip.

"It's my fault," she said, and her breath hitched in a sob.

Hanson did the only thing he could think of. He gathered her up in his arms and cradled her, her head on his shoulder and the rest of her safely in his lap. He rocked her while she cried, grief and guilt shaking her. He stroked her hair and wished he knew what to say to comfort her. It was a thorny pleasure to feel her shaking against him, to be able to tangle his fingers in her hair, kiss the top of her head, and try to ignore the fact that even while she was sobbing he wanted to pull her down on the bed and—

*Don't think about that. Can't I go five minutes without thinking something like that?* He kissed her tumbled curls again. He'd never had this sort of trouble staying focused before.

The agony of tears finally shuddered to a stop. He held her, content to sit still and let her rest.

It was a long time before she sighed and scrubbed at her cheek with the back of one hand. "I'm sorry," she whispered, her voice cracked and rough from crying.

"No need," he said. "You saw something horrible today. No wonder you need a good cry." *Don't let her move. Don't let her move, please.*

She didn't move. "Why don't you cry?"

He shrugged slightly, careful not to jostle her. "I've seen too much, maybe."

"Do you think…"

He guessed what she was going to ask. "It was quick, Mari. They didn't have time to suffer."

"Are you sure?"

*No*, he thought grimly. *It played with them, whatever it was. Played with them for a long time before it finally drained them both of blood and life.* "I'm sure." His voice was husky, mostly from his dry throat.

She shuddered again. "At least that's something."

He didn't agree or disagree. Just held her until she moved, all too soon.

She slid off his lap and over to the side, and he let his hands fall to the coverlet. If he didn't, he might be tempted to touch her. Sitting next to him, he could feel her watching his face, hoped his expression wouldn't betray him.

"Hanson?"

"Hm?"

Mari leaned over, pulling down on his shoulder. He bent down, obediently, and froze when she kissed his cheek, pressing her lips onto his stubble. She stopped, considering him again, and then kissed the corner of his mouth.

*Not. Made. Of. Steel,* he thought again, taking in a sharp breath. *Gods. Help. Me.*

"You don't like me," she said finally, and the hurt in her voice made his hands curl into fists.

"It's not that," he whispered.

She wrapped her fingers around his rough-stubbled chin and pulled his head gently around. He obeyed her, fire spilling down his skin from the touch. Her lips met his again, her tongue sliding in to tease at his, soft and warm and innocent.

Mari kissed him softly, with great attention. Her eyes were closed and less than an inch from his. He breathed in her scent—cinnamon, shifting ocean tides, the clean smell of the only witch in the world he would ever want. Hanson reached up tentatively, slowly, and wound his fingers in her hair, drowning.

She pulled his T-shirt up. He worked his arms free, pulled it over his head and tossed it, breaking free of her mouth only for a moment. When her fingers brushed across his bare skin he shuddered, barbed-wire pleasure slamming through skin and nerves all the way to the bone. He held her face in his hands, kissing her desperately, lightning crackling under his skin.

"Please," he whispered against her throat, where the fragile pulse pounded. "*Please.*"

As if he knew what he was asking for.

She sighed and kissed his temple. He pulled her backward, hardly remembering they were on the bed. A confused scramble of clothing followed. He had to be careful. She didn't want any of her clothes torn, but he couldn't care less about his own. He would have cheerfully ripped even his jeans to shreds to get to her that much more quickly. Her pale, water-clear skin flushed beneath his callused hands as he traced the curve of her ribs, the dimples at the base of her spine, the wonderful arc of her hips. Mari sighed against his mouth. "Hanson."

He forced himself to go completely still, throat working and opened his eyes halfway to see her next to him, crimson standing high in her cheeks. The blush only made her eyes seem more blue.

"I really…I mean, I haven't done this in so long." The blush rose even more. He didn't look down. If he did he would only see her skin, and his own readiness. "You don't have to…"

"Mari," he interrupted harshly, through the stone buried in his throat, "if you tell me to stop, I will."

She bit her lip and slid her hand up his arm, muscle standing out hard as tile. "I don't want you to stop," she whispered.

He closed his eyes. When he opened them, she was still there, watching his face, puzzled. "Here," he said, his hands sliding down to find her waist and shifting her above him. "Move." He could almost feel her heartbeat through his palms, excitement pounding through every artery. Her skin moved against his, exquisite softness, her knees on either side of his hips. Then he let go of her, one finger at a time, forcing himself to shallow control. "Do what you like," he said, and let his hands fall to either side.

Mari braced her hands on either side of his shoulders. Her hair fell down, a curtain of golden curls, one pale breast peeking out, its candied tip begging to be kissed. *Later.* He had to take in another short breath as the thought sent another lash of pleasure through him, the mounting feedback of her skin against his clouding his brain.

She watched him for a long moment, the flush spreading down from her cheeks, past her collarbone. He forced himself to watch her face. She looked both exhilarated and scared to death. "Hanson," she whispered, then shook her head. That made both breasts peep out at him, and his hands ached with the urge to wrap around her waist and pull her onto—

She moved. He felt her legs shift, and a silken heat touched the very tip of his penis. Then, centimeter by slow centimeter, she slid down, her eyes closing heavily, his hands finding her skin again, helpless. She stopped halfway, her lips parting, and he rocked his hips up, unable to stop himself. She slid down another degree and her eyes flew open, meeting his, blue against blue.

"Still," she whispered huskily. "Be still."

*This is going to kill me,* he thought, through the confused storm haze firing through his nerves. He made a sound, whether of pleasure or assent or pleading he couldn't have said, and she took pity on him. Or maybe not, because she moved yet again, a long slow rocking movement of her hips that closed silken fire over every inch of him.

Buried in her, he shuddered helplessly and threaded his fingers through hers, struggling to remain still and failing. He wanted more.

Another exquisite friction as Mari lifted up and then settled back down, her eyes half-lidded and vulnerable, the burning in her cheeks only making her shine more brightly. Light cascaded out from her aura, a spreading haze of sapphire. He had to wait, and watch, and try to keep as still as possible while she took her pleasure, rocking against him, sometimes rising enough that he feared losing her altogether. Lowering herself onto him, impaled, hot liquid silk closing around him, jeweled sparkles rising behind his eyes until she stiffened, back arched, her glorious golden mane tossed back. A short breathless cry wrung out of her. Then he could let himself move, and it took only two short thrusts before the fire took him, too. A long pounding moment of white fire and crystalline heat singing in his blood. Then he gasped as Mari settled across his chest, her hair curtaining his face. He breathed in. Spice and salt and the clean smell of a woman.

*Mine,* he thought, wonderingly. *Mine. All mine.*

*No. She's a Lightbringer. I belong to her, not the other way around. Lucky, lucky, lucky.*

"Mari," he whispered into her hair. Her breasts were pressed against his chest, and she lay against him as if she belonged there.

She sighed, her breath brushing his shoulder. So exquisitely fragile, the light blurring out from her aura settled into a humming glow. "Wow," she breathed. "You've done this before."

"Maybe," he said, into her hair. "Or just dreamed it."

"You dream about this?"

"About you."

That made her laugh. He cherished that small sound, and he traced his fingers in small patterns against her flawless skin. The Watcher shields on the room vibrated uneasily.

"I'm hungry," she yawned. "You want dinner?"

"Absolutely." *I don't want dinner, I want to stay right here and do things to you that haven't even been invented yet.*

"I should take a shower, too." But she didn't move, simply lay draped across him. He was happy enough to stay absolutely still, hoping she didn't want to move too soon. Blessed relief from a Watcher's agony poured through his body, made the Dark inside his flesh hum, a satisfied whine. "Hanson?"

"Hmm?"

"I'm glad you're here."

"Me too, Mari. Me too." *If you only knew how glad.*

She fell asleep soon after, so he just lay close and listened to her breathe. He'd somehow done what he'd wanted to do since the first time he'd seen her—worked his way into her life, into *her*.

But her sleeping meant that he had time to think, and that was not guaranteed to give him any peace. Because something had broken into her house and destroyed her life, something that was probably hunting her even now—and it had broken out from the *inside*, which meant Hanson had failed to keep something dangerous away from her.

And that idea was enough to make him shiver.

# Nineteen

*Darkness and rain, Theo's pale and blood-streaked face, the Darkness pressing close, full of teeth and claws. And his face, his familiar face, bloodless, eyes blazing red.*

Mari sat bolt upright, gasping, her teeth chattering. Hanson was already awake next to her, and his skin burned against her chill. He caught her shoulders and took her in his arms. The mothering dark of a hotel room closed around her.

"Th-th-the vision," she stammered. "Again. The vision—"

"I'm here," he soothed. "I'm here, Mari. Hush, I'm here."

Tears slicked her cheeks. Wonderingly, she put up a hand and felt the dampness against her skin. "Gods," she whispered. "*Gods.*"

"What was it?" Quiet, neutral, his voice overpowered the sounds of the city street outside. He'd checked them into one of the most expensive hotels downtown, and she hadn't had the nerve to protest. She didn't know how he was paying for it, and at this point, she didn't care. Dinner was room service, and she'd taken a shower in the granite-tiled bathroom, numb and dry-eyed as the hot water beat against her skin.

"The v-vision. Theo dying. The smell, the *smell* is the same thing as at my house."

He flattened his hand against her shoulder. Heat coated her skin, working inward until she was no longer shivering. "Breathe, Mari. Breathe."

Air filled her lungs, blessed deep air. "Hanson."

"I'm here. Tell me." He stroked her back, a warm comforting touch, pausing at the curve of her lumbar spine, trailing back up.

Mari opened her mouth to start describing the vision. Instead, a dry, barking sob burst out of her. He hugged her, his arm over her shoulder. She buried her face in the juncture between his throat and shoulder, shaking. Hanson stroked her hair, her back, kissed her forehead, held her while she cried. Finally, she ended up in his lap, clinging to him as if he were the only solid thing in the world. He said nothing for a long time, merely playing with her hair, lifting it, threading his fingers through it, and letting it fall.

His heartbeat thudded under her ear, reassuring, steady and slow. Mari felt empty, numb. Her body twinged in assorted places, reminding her of what she'd done.

"Hanson?" she whispered.

"I'm here."

*Of course he's here. And you just rolled around the bed with him.* "What do I do now?" She sounded plaintive even to herself.

"Well, you're finished with your exams." He slid his hand under her hair, cupping her nape. "Your thesis?"

*How can he think about my thesis at a time like this?* "I j-just need to finish the bibliography," she said. "That's not what I mean. I mean about the… about Gretchen and Amy."

"You can't let your life stop. That's like letting the Dark win."

"What about Gretchen and Amy? They died because of me. Because of what I am. And the papers."

"We don't even know what's on the papers." he pointed out. "And the *g'raian*. What does he have to do with it?"

"You think… oh, gods. Do you think he *did* have something to do with it?"

"I don't know. I intend to find out."

"When?"

"Tomorrow night."

"What time is it?"

"About midnight."

"Is it too late to start tonight?" she asked wistfully.

He was so still she was afraid he'd stopped breathing. "I'd prefer not to, Mari. You're tired."

"I've slept," she said. "I'm fine."

"Let me do my job. This is what I was trained for."

"You can't order me around in the name of Circle Lightfall," she snapped, then immediately closed her mouth. Guilt flamed in the pit of her stomach.

"That's right." He still didn't move, but he inhaled sharply, smelling her hair. "I wouldn't do that. You're my witch." Oddly enough, he sounded thoughtful, not angry.

"I want to find out," she said into the hollow of his throat. "I have to find out. I don't want Theo to die." *And I die too,* she thought, shuddering. *I am going to die. But maybe I can save Theo.*

"Theo has Dante," he said. "And you have me."

*That doesn't do me any good. Not with what I just Saw.* She shuddered. "Hanson, *please*," she said, through numb lips.

"I want to start tonight. Look, can you take a shower and—"

"Why?"

"Because anyone can tell you've been rolling around the bed with me," she replied.

"No, I mean why start tonight? And would you care to join me in the shower, Lightbringer? I think I'd enjoy that." He stroked her hair, his fingers idle and warm.

Mari was surprised into a laugh. "I don't think so," she told him, skating her fingers up his ribs. Ridged smoothness of scar tissue bumped under her touch. He inhaled sharply.

"Mari," he said gently. "If you want to start tonight, don't tempt me."

*He acts like I affect him,* she thought. She trailed her fingers over his chest and felt him go absolutely still, not even breathing. *What's really going on inside that head of his?*

She could find out. It wasn't hard. All she had to do was drop her shields and she would drown in what he was feeling. Even now, she could feel his aura pressing against hers, sliding around her like a stingray gliding in warm water.

"Please," she whispered, her voice breaking on the word. Tears welled in her eyes.

"All right. Tonight. Give me ten minutes, okay?"

She nodded, but she didn't let go of him. She pressed her cheek against his shoulder. *Give me just a few more seconds,* she thought, breathing in. He still smelled safe. Her heart pounded at her wrists and throat, pulse racing. *I just want to lay here forever.*

And that was the problem, wasn't it? She liked him. She liked his acerbic wit, liked the feel of his skin against hers, and loved the way he made soft, soothing sounds deep in his throat while he kissed her. And what woman wouldn't feel traitorously warm towards a muscle-bound hunk who treated her like a princess and defended her against nightmares?

But she couldn't deny her visions. She was given her Gift for a reason.

"Mari?" he said, gently enough.

*I love you,* she thought. *I love you, and it's not enough.*

"Go," she said, and rolled away from him, curling into the tangled sheet. "Go ahead. Clean yourself up."

"Sure you don't want to join me?" he asked diffidently, and her heart cracked.

"I'm sure," she said, and felt the bed move as he made it to his feet in one smooth motion.

"Too bad. Mari?"

"Hmm?"

"Whatever your vision is, it can't be all that bad. I promise I won't leave you."

That made her chest ache even more. Mari swallowed a dry sob.

"Okay," she managed around the lump in her throat.

*I know you won't leave me, and that's why I have to leave you.* She heard him pad into the bathroom. The light came on and the door closed. She waited until she heard the water start in the shower before she rocketed to her feet, almost taking the entire sheet with her. They had tangled the bed out of all recognition.

*Because I just saw you kill Theo in a vision,* she finished. It was time to face facts. The face of the Dark in her visions had been mercifully hidden before. But she'd seen it this time, maybe because she'd been relaxed, deeply asleep.

The red-burning eyes and snarling Darkness that killed Theo wore Hanson's face.

And that meant Mari had to get as far away from him as possible.

She found her clothes tossed on the floor, her cheeks flaming. She had never taken such an active role in sex before. She'd all but hit him over the head and dragged him into a cave. *I didn't know!* she thought, pulling her jeans up, and buttoning them swiftly. She jerked her sweater over her head, nearly pulling out a hank of her hair, and then had to hunt wildly for her socks, moving as quietly as she could.

*He's got Watcher shields on the room. He'll know if I leave. Think, Mari. Think!*

*I didn't know,* the rest of her wailed. *Gretchen...Amy...I didn't know. I'm sorry, so sorry...*

*Stop that whining,* the cool, clinical voice in her head that sounded like Elise said. *You're a witch, so be a witch. Work some magick.*

Well, then.

Mari found her boots, stuffed her feet into them, and tied the laces into sloppy bows. Then she found her purse, papers crackling inside it, and her coat. She'd have to leave the duffel bag behind. It was too bad, but it was too heavy for her to carry. Fully dressed and ready to go, she stood in the middle of the room for a moment and glanced around.

Her heart twisted again. She wanted to stay.

*Too bad. It's either him or Theo, and Theo's your best friend. You can't let him kill her, no matter what.*

*No matter what.*

She closed her eyes, swaying, seeking calm. It took a good twenty deep breaths before her heartbeat responded, slowing down.

*Water,* she thought. *Sea, ocean, tide, lake. Lagoon. Water. I'm water, clear water, I flow through this. I flow through his shields like water. Water. Water.*

The chant rose from the depths of her training, Suzanne's voice calm and quiet, paralleling hers.

"Water now is all of me, from sunless lake to quiet sea, my presence now you cannot see. Water now is all of me, from sunless lake to quiet sea, my presence now you cannot see."

The chant was only a whisper, shaped by her trembling lips. Power rose inside her, stronger than ever, her head filled with the muffled sound of faraway waves on a soft shore.

She opened her eyes. The hotel room seemed to shimmer around her. She was encased in a bubble of Power, its edges fluid, fountaining up from the floor and curling around her in a spiral. For a moment, the thought of what it must look like to ordinary people—a woman standing in the middle of a hotel room, talking to herself, her fingers flicking as if playing with liquid air—made her want to giggle. Of course an ordinary person wouldn't see the Power drifting around her, wouldn't hear the ocean's steady call, would never know the fierce joy of seeing a spell take shape.

*Ordinary people wouldn't get their friends killed by being a witch,* she thought grimly, and set her jaw. She walked slowly towards the door, her concentration firming, keeping the edges of the magick solid. *I won't let it happen to Theo. I won't.*

Her hand touched the smooth metal handle of the doorknob just as the sound of the shower cut off.

*Damn.*

Mari opened the door quietly, the edges of her new water-clear aura touching the fringes of the Watcher shielding. The shields didn't even quiver. Mari passed through them with only a faint crackling feeling on the surface of her skin.

The door shut behind her with a heavy click. Her heart pounded, and it was difficult to keep concentration with adrenaline flooding her bloodstream. *Did he hear that? I hope not. Please, don't let him have heard that.*

Mari glanced down the hallway, tastefully lit with alabaster sconces. A central well of open space showed four glassed-in elevators, and she could peer all the way down to the lobby if she wanted to. He might expect her to take the elevators, so she cast around for another option. The carpet, plush and wine red, whispered under her feet. Orchids grew in a slim, black pot set on a restrained antique ebony table, artfully spotlit. The flowers stretched towards her, tasting the magick, Power dyeing the air blue.

And right over the orchids, a green "Exit" sign.

*Oh, thank the gods.* Mari walked as quickly as she could without tearing the cloak of her spell-laid camouflage. The Power obeyed far more readily than it ever had, but it strained the edges of her control, trying to leap free of her and do... what? What would it do, if she let it free to do as it wanted?

She never wanted to find out.

Mari made it to the stairway door just as the Watcher shields on the room behind her flushed a deep, angry red.

He knew she was gone.

The stairwell door closed behind her with a quiet click, and she wished she could run. Instead, she made it down the green linoleum stairs by concentrating on only one step at a time, making sure both boots were perched on a step before taking the next. She was six floors up. The concrete walls were bare here where the guests didn't usually come. Why couldn't Hanson have put them on the first floor?

*Probably something to do with safety,* she thought, choking back a giggle. *Why do I always want to laugh at times like this?*

She heard the whole building groan, dust dancing in the air. Hanson reaching out, trying to detect her.

She gasped, the sound echoing in the stairwell. She could *feel* him, having no control left over to screen out his emotion. All her strength was focused on staying hidden. Red rage, dark-green worry, sick fear turning the pit of her stomach over. He was starkly afraid for her, her name pounding inside his head.

*What did I do, what did I do, Mari, Mariamne, where are you?*

Mari's fingers curled around the metal handrail, chipped green paint flaking away under her hand. The metal would start to sing and bend soon, responding to the weight of his agony. She fought to close him out and shut his emotions off.

*Water now is all of me, from sunless lake to quiet sea, my presence now you cannot see...* She chanted over and over again, until the words ran under her thoughts, a smooth dark river cloaking her.

The red-black blur that was Hanson's aura dropped through the well of the building too quickly to be in an elevator. Then he streaked out towards the street and was swallowed up in the chaos and white noise of the city.

Mari let out a shaky breath. She made it down the stairs, out through a heavy metal door, and into the hotel lobby. A bronze statue of women dancing swayed above a fountain, dry now, probably since the earthquake. She saw the front desk, the concierge's desk, bellhops chatting with each other outside, a doorman smoking a cigarette. Now Mari could see that fog had rolled in, a thick cottony cloud wrapping the city in soft white.

*Fog is water,* Mari thought. *I can probably vanish here, too, thank the gods.*

With a silent prayer, she drifted out the front doors, and one of the bellboys shivered and glanced around as if he felt something. He was slightly psychic; Mari could see the glow in the air, and her throat went dry. It was the same kind of glow Gretchen had given out, a sort of quiet foxfire instead of Elise's bright fiery aura or Theo's deep, calm well of light.

She made it out past them, up the street to the corner, and was about to cross the street when Rossini paused right next to her.

"Lost your watchdog, Guardian?" he asked.

# Twenty

"I don't understand," Theo said, her pretty forehead creasing. "Elise said she was—"

"Begging your pardon, ma'am," Hanson interrupted, "we don't have a lot of time. I need to find her, and quickly. *Please.*"

"But what happened?" she asked. "The last I heard, she was with you. Elise said you were taking her back to her house."

Hanson was lucky the green witch was at home. She had just arrived from a long day of working at the Red Cross shelter. Thankfully, the damage from the earthquake hadn't been that bad, but there were a lot of frightened rabbits masquerading as people out there.

Dante, leaning against the wall next to the fireplace, blew out a sharp breath between his teeth. "He can't say, Theo. I'll bet she swore him to silence, and he has to obey. I'd also bet it has something to do with that tarot card reading you did."

The green witch turned pale as milk and swayed on her feet. Dante caught her elbow, blurring across the intervening space with spooky, graceful speed. Hanson's shoulders tightened. He was going to have one hell of a headache soon. *Mari. Where are you? Mari.*

It had been the only thing he could think of, to come to Dante and Theo. He couldn't tell them about the papers; Mari had made him promise. And he didn't have time to answer all their questions about the attack on Mari's house. He only needed to find his witch—and the green witch was his best bet of doing that. After all, Mari was hiding from a Watcher, not from her friends.

*Where is she?* His brain worried at the question like a tongue worrying at a sick tooth. What had he done wrong?

He knew, of course. He'd committed the one unforgivable sin. He'd presumed too much. He had no right to love her. He deserved nothing more than a lifetime of hard work and combat before an eventual inescapable death. He'd failed her, frightened her so badly she'd run off into the city. And she would be dead before long, Dark drawn to her like vultures to a fresh corpse.

He shuddered. *That* was a particularly unwelcome mental image.

"Breathe, sweetheart," Dante said softly into Theo's hair. The sight of the Watcher murmuring to his witch made Hanson wince. He'd screwed up again, and Mari was gone. "There. It's all right. We'll find her."

Three thudding crashes resounded against the front door. Hanson whirled, his coat flaring out, and his sword almost leaping free of the scabbard before he realized who it was.

Another crash and Theo's front door flung itself open. The red-haired witch stalked in, the scent of burning insulation trailing her.

"What?" she snarled, stamping down the hall and then stopping short in the doorway to the living room. The shields on Theo's house crackled with a frantic burst of energy. "I just fudged the last end of a set at the K-Bar. What the hell's happened *now?*"

"At least your instincts aren't rusty," Theo said mildly. The dappled green silk of her skirt swirled as she half-turned, smiling up at Dante. "I'm all right. Don't worry about me," she continued, and then sighed. "Elise, I'm afraid Mari's in trouble."

"Tell me something I *don't* know," Elise's green eyes flamed. Sparks popped from her fingertips. Then her eyes swept across Hanson in a brief dismissive arc. "What's *he* doing here? Isn't he supposed to be watching out for her?"

*Oh, so now I'm good enough for you, since I'm supposed to watch out for Mari?* Hanson had to take a deep breath, invoking iron control. The trouble was it *hurt*. The Dark symbiote rustled uneasily, scraping at his bones with rusty razors. The clear light coming from the Lighbringers dipped him in sharp agony. And Mari...Mari had fled from him, fled so quickly he'd lost her scent as soon as he'd left the hotel room. Fled him without even a word of warning, although she'd been too quiet. He should have known she was planning something.

"*Please*," he said, more sharply than he'd intended. His voice made the windows rattle in their frames and the pictures move uneasily on the wall. "I need to find her. She's in terrible danger, and the longer you sit around *talking*, the greater chance she'll die. So *help* me, or I'll go out hunting. I don't care either way, but stop *wasting time!*" The last words made the floor creak under his feet. *I'm two seconds away from slapping a Lightbringer,* he thought grimly. Only Mari could bring him to such absolute frustration.

"You're the one who showed up and intruded on our lives," Elsie snapped, her fiery hair lifting slightly, red-gold drifting on a faint, hot breeze. The smell of burning candle wax drifted in the still, tense air. "Both you and Stoneface over there."

"That's *enough!*" Theo said, sharply enough that both Elise and Hanson turned to stare at her. "Mari's in trouble. *Deep* trouble. Elise, fill my scrying bowl with water, will you? It's on the fireplace altar. Dante, run upstairs and fetch my athame, and get ready to feed me all the Power you can. Hanson, sit *there*." She pointed at a comfortable-looking, battered leather couch. "And just try to stay still for a few minutes. I'll get a lock on her, and we'll go find her."

Hanson dropped obediently down on the couch, his hands clenched into fists. Elise stared at Theo for a moment, then cut a venomous glance at Hanson and stalked through the living room to the fireplace, scooping up a black pottery bowl with a covering of black silk. "Goddamn Watchers," she said, making no attempt to keep her voice low. "Bringing all this shit to us."

"That's quite enough," Theo said, steel in her normally calm voice. Dante was already gone, his boots resounding on the stairs. "Right now Mari needs us, Watchers or no Watchers. If you won't help me I'll tie you up in the cellar, Elise."

"Oh, I'll help all right," Elise snapped. "I'll take out whoever's bothering her, and I'll burn down everything I have to, and I'll—"

"Water, Elise. In the scrying bowl. Hurry up."

Elise stamped into the kitchen. A thin veil of white smoke drifted in the air behind her. Theo sighed, pushing up the sleeves of her long, black sweater. Her long, dark hair was mussed, but her eyes were clear and calm. "Hanson," she said, "what happened?"

"I think I frightened her," he mumbled, looking down at his hands. *Just find her,* he thought. *I swear I'll never touch her again as long as she's safe. Please, if there are any gods listening, please just let them find her. Don't let me be too late.*

"Don't worry," Theo said, kindly enough. "She won't do anything stupid. She's too smart."

"I know she is," Hanson found himself saying. "I'm the stupid one here, ma'am."

Theo paused, tucking a strand of dark hair behind her ear. "This is the longest Mari's ever spent with a man," she told him, her green eyes depthless. A private smile tilted up the corners of her mouth. "Most of the time, they're too quick with their fists or too good at belittling her. She hasn't had an easy time of it."

Hanson's throat closed. "I would never—" he began.

"I know you wouldn't," she said, and he shut his mouth so quickly he almost heard his teeth snap together. "Be patient with her, Hanson. She's very fond of you, and I think you're the best thing that's happened to her in a long time. I think you're the Knight of Wands in her cards. Did I ever tell you about that?"

"No, ma'am." *I don't care about your goddamn tarot, ma'am. Tell me where to find my witch. That's all I want.*

Theo shrugged, pulling a low, wooden three-legged stool out from under an end table. Dante's footsteps came back down the stairs. "For a little over two years now, the Knight of Swords has been moving through my cards. It's Dante—swords are Air, the element of quickness and a foil to my Earth magick. You're Mari's Knight of Wands—Fire to her Water, if you will. She needs a little bit of prodding every now and again. She's too indecisive for her own good. And Elise...well."

"What?" Elise snapped, sliding through the door from the kitchen. The electric light tinted her hair with fiery copper. "Are you going on about that Knight of Cups bullshit again?"

"It's not bullshit, Elise. You'll die of poison if you ever swallow that tongue of yours. Now come over here and stop bitching." For once Theo didn't sound calm or tranquil. Hanson caught a flash in her eyes—green sparks—and he went very still. He would never want this witch angry with him.

Amazingly enough, Elise only rolled her eyes and brought the bowl of water to the green witch. "Here, Your Majesty. Are you going out, or am I?"

"I'm probably calmer, sweets. You just stay here."

Dante paused at the door. His coat whispered. Hanson's impatience crested, but he didn't allow himself to fidget. "Theo?" Dante's voice was soft, questioning.

"Bring me my athame, Dante, and stay behind me. Elise will anchor me, you'll feed me Power, and Hanson will watch the perimeter. All right?"

*Don't trust me,* Hanson wanted to say. *I lost my witch. She slipped through my fingers like water. I fouled up. I went too far, and I frightened her.*

"Sounds good," Dante didn't even glance at Hanson. "Keep us safe, Blue-Eyes."

Hanson could only nod. *Don't trust me. I'm not worth it.*

It was too late. Dante handed Theo her ceremonial knife, and the green witch closed her eyes. Dante went motionless, his hand on her shoulder. Elise, cross-legged with the bowl of water in her lap, let out a sharp curse and closed her own fiery eyes, her hair lifting on the hot, private breeze that seemed to follow her around.

Power rose, dyeing the air with shifting waves of green and scarlet twined together, the smell of damp earth and ozone filling the house. Hanson checked the shields. Everything was as it should be.

Everything except Mari's absence. His chest tightened again. Rage rose, and he pushed it down. He couldn't afford to get angry now. He had to be cool and logical, he had to *think*. He'd screwed up, but maybe she was still alive. If she was, he would watch over her as well as he could from a distance. He would leave her strictly alone, paying for his sin with blood if he had to.

Tension stretched under his skin, poked his bones with sharp pain. *Mari,* the screaming in his head continued. *Mari, why? What did I do? Just tell me what I did. I won't ever do it again, I swear. What did I do, Mari? Mari, Mari...*

It seemed like a long time, but it was perhaps ten minutes before Theo sagged, the singing Power in the air breaking with a sound like an elastic cord snapping. "Cathedral," she murmured. "Corner of Fifth and Vine. I remember those stained glass windows. She's frightened, and there's someone with her."

"Is that where she is?" Hanson asked. "Fifth and Vine, the cathedral?"

"Yes," Theo sighed, her voice pale, drawn-out. It was the voice of a ghost. "She'll be there in... oh, feels like half an hour, it's hard to tell, time's so funny...warping..."

The green witch stiffened, and Dante made a low, hoarse sound of pain. Elise's eyes flew open. Power crackled in the air, the smell of ozone intensifying, a lightning strike. Elise's hands shot out, and grabbed Theo's, her red lacquered fingernails digging into Theo's soft, white flesh.

"No you *don't*," she hissed through clenched teeth. "Not while I'm here. Come *back!*"

Hanson made it to his feet. *Cathedral. Fifth and Vine. Stained glass.* He knew the church from recons he'd done, learning the geography of the city so he could follow Mari unseen.

*Half an hour,* he thought, bolting for the door, hearing Theo's anguished scream behind him. He didn't have time to check on her. Dante could take care of them. They were under cover in Theo's house, and Dante was the best Watcher around. Far better than Hanson. After all, Dante hadn't scared *his* witch into running away.

Theo's door shut with a snap behind him, but Hanson was already at the garden gate, white cotton fog closing around him. His boots pounded the pavement.

*I'll get there in time,* he thought, *as long as I don't have a fight on the w—*

He had no warning. The Dark boiled out of its hiding place across the street and met him with an impact like worlds colliding. Hanson went down, claws ripping into his belly, Mari's name on his lips.

# Twenty-One

St. Mary's was built of brick, its spire reaching up into the fog. The wheeling window of rose and blue over the narrow arched front door was dull and mute now, no kiss of light to make it glow. Mari shivered. "It's under a church?" she said, and wished she hadn't spoken.

"Of course," Rossini said. "The Catholics built their holy houses over places of Power, you know that. The entrance to the Library is one such place. Of *course* it's in a church."

"Great," Mari muttered. Her pulse had just begun to return to normal. "So why are you being so helpful?" The fog had begun to weigh her hair down, sodden curls lying against her collar and moisture beading on her face. She hadn't seen a single person in the fourteen-block walk to St. Mary's. It was beginning to seem that the city, usually so full of people pushing against Mari's shields, trying to push their way into her, was now deserted except for her.

And Rossini.

*I never thought I'd wish for other people around.* She shivered again. "It's closed," she said, stupidly.

Rossini shrugged, his coat moving oddly against his shoulders. His grey eyes were burning, almost silvery through the fog now. "How do you think *I* found the Library? This is my nest, Guardian. Come, the Librarian's waiting."

For some reason, the words sent a chill up Mari's spine. She climbed the granite steps after Rossini, the stone gritty under her boot soles. *Where's Hanson?* she wondered. *What's he doing now? He's probably looking for me. Gods.* But she stopped the thought, turned away from it. Her shields were thick, the armor that protected her from the world. Her body twinged in assorted places, reminding her of him. He had whispered her name as if it was the end of the world. He had touched her as if he meant it, as if she was the only thing between him and suffering, as if—

"Wait a moment," Rossini said, and spread his hand against the ironbound wood of the door. Something rippled over his skin, and Mari flinched. The power was harsh and hurtful, not like Theo's soft, rich, green glow. Rossini's Power was flint under the dirt, bare fields too rocky for cultivation, granite thrusting up through topsoil like something waiting to be hatched.

The door creaked and swung open. The smell of church—incense, cold floors, wooden pews polished by generations of the prayerful—flooded out, and Mari shivered one more time. People had come here to spill their private agonies to one of the gods—maybe one of the gods she prayed to, maybe a different one. The Power of so many generations whispering their rosaries in the gloom closed around her, touched the nape of her neck with cool, dreadful fingers.

*I wish Hanson was here.* He would have been just behind her shoulder, his breathing silent, maybe touching her arm before she stepped through the door. His warmth would be comforting, and he would stay between her and Rossini, who was looking less and less human the more Mari really watched him.

Once inside the church, Rossini swung the heavy door closed. The *chuck* of the lock shooting home made Mari jump. She shoved her hair back, tucking wet curls behind her ears, and wished she'd thought to bring an elastic band, or a scrunchie, or *something.*

"How did you get away from your pet bruiser?" he asked, grinning, his teeth very white in the gloom of the vestibule.

Mari shrugged, her damp coat moving against her shoulders. "I'm a witch," she said, and that seemed to sum up everything. A witch. And Gretchen and Amy had died because of it. Whatever was hunting her had killed them, and nobody could find Brandon.

*How about that, friends and neighbors? Did it kill Brandon too? He didn't deserve that.*

Rossini led her through the vestibule and into the nave, ranks of pews sitting blank and expectant, a hymnal placed at each seat, the little racks for the faithful to kneel on folded up. Mellow wood gleamed in the candlelight. This church didn't extinguish the candles after the faithful left like the modern cathedrals did. No, they left them burning, earthquake hazards be damned. A little thing like a fire hazard shouldn't deter prayers from reaching the gods.

"So the entrance is under the cathedral?" she asked, looking around. A bank of candles glowed under a Pieta, Christ lying dead in his mother's arms, his mother's face the face of the Goddess, grieving for her dead Son. Saint Sebastian, pierced with arrows, silently screamed from another niche. Mari's chin came up. She wasn't going to act ashamed of her change from the Catholicism of her youth to her adoption of paganism at this late date.

"Watch," Rossini said, and led her to the right. There was another archway, and a broad, open space. Mari blinked.

A bank of candles to Saint Jude stood on one side, and another bank of candles to Saint Catherine sat on the other. At the far end of the round room, the statue of Saint Mary hovered, Mary's patient face under lit by yet more candles.

On the floor of the round room, a Labyrinth unfolded in darker flagstones. Mari looked and had to bite back the urge to giggle. Even here, in a cathedral, the pagan traditions shone through. Set amid the lighter stones of the floor, the dark flagstones made a twisting circular path to the heart of the Labyrinth.

"Walk the Labyrinth," Rossini said, "and you'll get into the Library. That way, she'll have to let you in."

"She?"

"The Librarian. The Maleficent herself. Mind you don't get on her bad side." Rossini backed up, his silvery eyes glowing in the dimness. Candlelight actually made his gaunt face a little more attractive, smoothed out the sharp edges and painted the angles with mellow gold.

"You're leaving me here?" she asked. "Wait a minute!"

"Guardian, every predator in the city—and your blue-eyed watchdog—is going to descend upon us soon. If you don't reach the center of the Labyrinth, what am I going to do? Let a Guardian be killed in my nest? That would mean I'm too weak to defend myself. So just walk and go into the Library, and find what you can. The Librarian's getting impatient. And believe me, she's one lady you don't want to disappoint. Go on now."

Mari swallowed. *I wish Hanson was here. He'd know what to do.* "I had a vision," she began, but Rossini snarled, his lip lifting up from his top teeth. Had she ever thought him handsome? His tongue was forked, and it flickered out over his chin.

"Get *in* there," Rossini rasped, "or I'll *throw* you in, witch!"

Mari looked down. The entrance to the Labyrinth lay about four feet in front of her, the only straight edge in the twisting, curving path of dark stones. *Well, what else did I come here for? He was at my house. Did he kill Gretchen and Amy? If he did, why? And why would he leave me alive?*

She took a single step towards the beginning of the path

and felt a rumble begin beneath her feet.

"Old worm's getting a little testy." Rossini sounded strained. "Go, Guardian. Now, while you still can. I haven't had fresh meat in my nest for a decade. I'd hate to have it now."

Mari stepped forward again just as the world tilted sideways. *Aftershock. Just my luck to be in a brick building when the next earthquake hits.* Her boot landed solidly on a dark flagstone. She had to concentrate to pull the rest of her body behind it, as if she was stepping onto a tightrope. A rumbling started, like a faraway freight train gathering speed.

She had to concentrate again to lift her other foot, and place it on the dark flagstones, which now seemed to hover over the lighter parts of the floor. "I don't see why this is so," she began, and looked over her shoulder towards Rossini—or where Rossini should be.

Instead, she saw only darkness, not the walls of the cathedral or the softly glowing candlelight of the altars to different saints. Power tingled and stretched under Mari's skin, responding to the flow of energy around her. This was indeed a place of power, lines of force stretching under the earth and meeting under the stone flooring, vibrating like guitar strings.

*I suppose I have no choice now, do I?* She surprised herself by laughing—and plunging forward on the thin path of dark flagstones that stretched under her booted feet.

# Twenty-Two

Hanson came back to himself slowly, piecemeal. Concrete underneath him, burning cold. Something lay over his right eye, and his bones sang with pain. That was normal. The agony was almost forgotten now, being habitual and therefore ignored. The only time he didn't feel the pain was when—

*Mari. Where's Mari?*

"Mari," he whispered, and the blood congealed on his lips crackled. His entire body screamed with pain.

*Mari.*

She'd run from him. He'd done something wrong. And then he'd blindly rushed into the fog.

A flood of green fire raced through his veins, tearing horribly at the Dark that crouched inside him. Hanson screamed, an agonized sound that ripped the night open.

"No, Theo. You can't heal this. Get back. *Hold* her, fire-hair!" Dante's voice, with the whip crack of Dark power under it. The symbiote stretched under that lash, turned it into more Power, and bones cracked, resetting. Healing.

He was healing. He'd done something stupid and was now healing.

"Mari," he heard himself say through the fog of agony. Something was wrong—they shouldn't be outside. The Lightbringers should be inside Theo's house, under cover.

"Gods." The fire witch sounded hushed, something he'd never heard before. "He's calling her name."

"Dante." The green witch's voice, raw and strained. "Please, Dante. *Please.*"

"Stop it, Theo. You can't help him. Let Stoneface do it." But Elise sounded far less acerbic. "Hold my hands, Theo. Just hold on."

"Mari," Hanson heard himself say again.

"Brace yourself, brother," Dante muttered. "This is going to hurt."

It was small consolation that it hurt less than the Lightbringer's touch. Razor-spiked fire forced its way through him, the familiar acid bite of the Dark against his human cells, remaking, reshaping, and crackling against his nervous system. Hanson opened his eyes as Dante swung away, the tall, black-eyed Watcher taking Theo in his arms, stroking her hair in the weird directionless light coming from the fog-shrouded street lamp Hanson had fetched up against when the thing threw him.

Elise bent down and offered her sleeved arm, not her hand. "Here," she said. "My skin'll hurt you. Come on up, cowboy." But she said it kindly and there was something Hanson had never seen before on her face.

Was it respect? He was too tired to care. He took her offered arm, even though he put no weight on it as he slowly made it to his feet. Streetlight shine glowed in Elise's green eyes, and the fog damped her hair down. What had hit him?

"What—" he began, his boots grinding against the pavement. Theo's garden gate glimmered down the block. Both Lightbringers were out of the house because he'd done something stupid.

"Something Dark," Elise said, her mouth turning down at the corners. "It didn't kill you, and it didn't stop to attack any of us. What does that tell you?"

"It wanted to slow me down," Hanson said, and shook himself. "My thanks, witch."

"Get the hell out of here," she said conversationally. "You've got about half an hour, from what we can tell, before she's at the church. I'll take care of Theo and Dante. Just go and get Mari out of trouble." She paused, her eyes darker than he had ever seen. "You must really love her."

*Of course I do, you idiot. Who wouldn't?* But he just shrugged.

"Go on," she said, and gave him a light, friendly push. The light spilling out from her skin scraped against his raw wounds. Dante had helped, of course, but the unfiltered power-charge could only do so much. He was weakened now, and he'd lost time. How much time?

"Go help Mari, you idiot," Elise said. "If anything happens to her I'll rip your heart out."

Hanson had no doubt she'd try. "Thank you," he said, and turned on his boot heel. His clothes crackled with dried blood.

"Just go," she said. "You must really love her." She sounded sad now. It was a night for surprises. He had never heard the fire witch sound anything but acerbic.

"Of course I do," he said over his shoulder, unable to help himself. Then he sprinted for the end of the street. He heard Theo's voice, some kind of protest, and Elise's sharp reply, before the fog swallowed the sounds whole.

*Trying to slow me down. Something trying to slow me down. What the hell is going on here?*

It didn't matter. The only thing that mattered was finding Mari. Because if something Dark knew enough to try and slow him down, there was only one possible reason. It would hunt her down and kill her while she was undefended, and Hanson would have failed again, for the very last time.

*No.* He ignored the ripping pain in his side as he sped up, blurring through the fog with more-than-human speed. *Not on my watch.*

*Not on my witch.*

# Twenty-Three

The rushing wind and empty whistling blackness hadn't made Mari almost pass out. Neither had the way the dark flagstones seemed to shiver under her feet, as if another earthquake had hit.

No, it had been reaching the center of the Labyrinth and falling through, as if she'd stepped into a manhole, that had made her hyperventilate and almost lose consciousness. The sense of rapid descent came to a shuddering screeching halt, and her boots thumped into carpeted floor. She swayed and groaned, her head giving one amazing flare of pain as she reached out to grab anything and her hands found the edge of a granite countertop.

"About time," a woman's voice said, acidly. "Nobody except Rossini has come through *that* door for a good decade."

Mari gasped.

Instead of the candlelit gloom of the cathedral or the infinite darkness surrounding the Labyrinth, she now stood on a red Persian carpet laid over hardwood floor, and her hand clutched at a mahogany counter topped with granite. Behind the counter, one pale hand resting on a stack of books, a slim woman in a dark-blue dress examined Mari critically over the top of her horn-rimmed glasses. "Well?" she prompted, her candy-red lips shaping the word impatiently. Her strictly-plucked eyebrows arched over eyes as green as bottle glass held up to the sun. She had a long nose, large gold hoop earrings, and long dark hair scraped back into a tight, no-nonsense chignon.

*She looks like Miss Switch in the old kid's books.* Mari heard herself take in a shuddering breath. "Hello," she managed, hoping her stomach wasn't about to revolt and spew dinner all over the countertop. It was a library checkout counter just the same as every other checkout counter she'd ever seen, books stacked on it, a computer humming quietly off to one side, a library cart overflowing with leather-jacketed tomes at the woman's hip.

Mari glanced around, her jaw hanging. She closed her mouth with a snap.

Shelves of books marched away, brass plaques set on the end of each bookcase. The ceiling was gray stone, arched and carved with what looked like grape clusters in the middle of a high dome. A large stained glass lamp hung from the middle of the dome, giving out a bright even light. Four different rooms opened off the central chamber, and Mari smelled the dusty good scent of paper and binding glue and leather covers.

Oddly, that comforted her. Libraries had always been safe for her.

"Well?" the Librarian prompted again, one brisk eyebrow arching ever so slightly. Her aura was a deep velvety purple, shifting over her shoulders like a cape. Mari caught the faintest whiff of violets. "You are obviously the Guardian, and I am the Librarian. You may call me Esmerelda, or simply ma'am. Either will do. Now, I believe you have some papers that belong here. You may hand them over."

Mari found herself digging in her purse. The woman's crisp, authoritative voice never rose above the couth, almost-whisper most librarians learned to use. "I'm sorry," Mari managed, her stomach deciding to settle after all.

"It's quite all right," Esmerelda the Librarian said, her mouth turning down at the corners. "Rossini had to smuggle them out to get them to you. I couldn't think of any other way to bring you here. I have the rest of the papers, and some news you might find useful, and then I will send you on your way, Guardian." The woman gave her the title as if it was a sour fruit.

Mari looked around again. The air didn't smell close in here, even though instinct told her she was deep underground. Power stirred, trembling, in the air. "Did Suzanne come here?" she asked stupidly, her fingers closing around the crumpled sheaf of papers. *You know,* she mused, *at a certain point, things just can't get much weirder, can they?*

"My sister had right of access to the Library." Esmerelda's mouth turned even further down at the corners, her candy-apple lipstick gleaming in the dim light from the Tiffany lamp perched on the counter. "As a matter of fact, she's responsible for the computer filing system, which has saved me much time and trouble. You must be the water witch. Mariamne. A good name."

*Sister? Suzanne never talked about a sister!*

What else might Suzanne not have told them? "Th-thanks." Mari presented the bedraggled, crumpled stack of paper to the Librarian, whose nose gave one elegant wrinkle as she subtracted them from Mari's fingers. "I know they're folded up, but—"

"It's no matter. Come." The Librarian's Cuban heels clicked

against the hardwood as she skirted the counter, coming out through a small wooden gate that shut and latched behind her. "In case you're wondering, this place is very old. We have certain guidelines we must follow, or we're trampled by all sorts of undesirables."

*Is that the royal "we?"* Mari had to restrain herself from giggling madly. She followed the bobbing chignon as the woman set off at a brisk pace into the room to Mari's left.

"My sister was always one of the more…active, among us," Esmerelda continued. Her spine was absolutely straight under the blue silk of her dress, and the simple shirtwaist pattern didn't do her rail-thin figure justice. She wore no jewelry except for the gold hoop earrings, and the earrings didn't dare move out of place. "She believed teaching was her calling. And with the resources of the Library, she managed to impart a fair amount of knowledge in her time. As her student, you will no doubt wish to take her place, and the resources of the Library are, of course, yours for the asking. As for the rules, they are simple: no books or notes leave this place. It's the way things must be, of course. Please do not eat or drink any more than is absolutely necessary among the books. We had a rather dreadful experience with an entire bottle of Chianti in the Hex and Curse section."

Mari swallowed dryly. Her throat clicked. The sound was loud in the dusty, still air. "Suzanne was your sister?"

"Naturally," the Librarian sniffed. "Do pay attention, you haven't much time."

"Why not?"

"Because the Library is not a vacation home, Miss. It is a Nexus." The Librarian's skirt flared as she turned down an aisle marked *Witchcraft,* subtitled *Protection.*

"A Nexus?" Mari parroted, to show she was listening. *I don't think anything this woman could say would be any weirder than the past couple of days.* She smelled something spicy and fragrant over the smell of dust and books, maybe Esmerelda's perfume. Violets mixed with spice, a heady cocktail

"A Nexus," Esmerelda confirmed. "Please do pay attention. Now, the moon rises in approximately ten minutes, and that is your cue to leave. It is a waning moon, and most difficult for me to allow access or egress from the library during that time. You may take the notes with you, of course, and you are welcome back to study them at leisure after the new moon, when I will be better able to control the avenues of… You are *not* listening,

Miss Mariamne. Please pay attention." She came to a complete halt as they exited the long aisle of bookshelves, warm golden light spilling down from another Tiffany lamp, this one hanging from the ceiling as well.

A large pine desk sat in the middle of a space surrounded by bookshelves. Paper was scattered across the desk's surface, the familiar spiky leaning-forward of Suzanne's script clearly visible. Suzanne's smell of lemons and incense hung in the air, warring with the smell of old paper and dust. A canary-colored wool poncho Suzanne had spent a month knitting lay draped over a straight-backed chair.

"Suzanne," Mari whispered. A single hot tear spilled down her cheek, surprising her. After the events of the last few days, she'd thought nothing could surprise her anymore.

"Yes." Esmerelda sounded a little less clipped and precise. She dropped the sheaf of papers down on the desk. "This is where she researched the spell that killed her. When she told me what she wanted, I was…reluctant, to say the least. But she was always stubborn, my Zsuszanna. And when Rossini told me there were three Guardians and a fourth across the Veil… well." She shrugged. "Come back whenever you like, after the next new moon, and we can prepare a pass that will allow you into the Library at will. Until then, I'm afraid you must—"

"How do I come back?" Mari sad, around the lump in her throat.

"Why, come to the cathedral and walk the Labyrinth. Really, for a witch with the power of prescience you can be *most* inattentive. Now come along, and step lively."

Mari was about to ask how old the Librarian was, but a tremor ran through the still dusty air. "Oh, *hell*," the Librarian snarled, with amazing venom. She managed to make the word sound furious and acidic all at once. "The damn binding. Again. Come *on*."

Mari stumbled after the librarian's tapping heels, down an aisle marked *Talent*, subtitled *Psychometry.* "Binding?" she gasped, a stitch starting in her side. How did the woman *move* so fast wearing those heels?

"Well, the Guardian spell is incomplete," the librarian said matter-of-factly. "And all sorts of protections and bindings on the city are wearing thin."

"Okay," Mari almost ran into the slim woman as she stopped, holding up one pale hand. Her nails were painted a light opalescent pink, surprising for such a no-nonsense type. Mari's patchwork purse tugged sharply against her shoulder, but Esmerelda was speaking. Something about the woman simply commanded attention.

"There's a fault line under this city, and it's very restless right now. The binding keeping the city from sliding down into the ground was laid by the people who lived here *before*." Esmerelda's fingertips trailed along a row of leather-bound spines. *Tell The Future With A Touch*; *Psychometry For Fun And Profit; History In Your Palms*. Mari had never seen any of these titles before. "The incomplete Guardian spell has diverted power from that binding, and the mother of all earthquakes is building. I've done what I can, and so has Rossini, but really, it's up to you."

"How do we—"

"Finish the spell. You *must* hurry." She set off again, turning to her right, and Mari scrambled to keep up.

"But I don't know anything about a Nexus or fault lines! Suzanne never told us." She gasped. How did the woman *move* so quickly?

"Really," Esmerelda sniffed archly. "What did my sister teach you, then? How to juggle and do card tricks?" The Librarian came to another abrupt halt, and Mari almost tripped as she tried to regain her balance. "Here's the safest door I can give you right now. Go straight in, turn neither right nor left, and whatever you do, don't look back. The effects of looking back are extremely unpleasant."

"I don't know anything about a Nexus," Mari repeated, feeling decidedly faint. This wasn't what she'd expected, although she didn't quite know what she'd expected from an underground Library to which a gargoyle had led her.

"Then I suppose you'll have to learn, won't you?" Esmerelda said pitilessly. "I've given you everything you need. And I'll give you a word of advice too. Stop whining. I hate whining." She stepped gracefully aside, and Mari saw a low, arched, ironbound wooden door with no knob or keyhole.

"Wait a minute," she began. "How do I—"

The Librarian touched the door with tented fingers and pushed it open. It creaked, and liquid darkness exhaled from it that smelled like iron and wet socks. "Go. For the sake of every god that ever was, *just go!*" Her eyes blazed, sparks popping from their green haze, and her candy-apple lips peeled back from sharp, ivory teeth. Mari noticed, with a sinking, swimming sort of horror, that the woman's hands were no longer pale and perfect. Instead, they were withered claws, and one was reaching out to brush at her with ancient, yellowing nails.

She didn't stop to think, just bolted through the door and into the dark, hearing a nasty, high-pitched laugh trail behind her as the librarian swung the door shut. It had been a glamour, Mari was reasonably sure—or had it been?

*Go straight ahead. Turn neither right nor left. Don't look back. Well, how do I know what's straight ahead if I can't see, and how in hell can I look back when there's no light? Nexus and binding and earthquakes, oh my.*

The dark pressed chill against her shields, and Mari hitched in a breath. Her heart hammered against her ribs. *I wish Hanson was here. He would have known how to deal with that woman.*

The thought of Hanson's irony pitted against the Librarian's brisk efficiency made Mari laugh. The laughter echoed, forlorn, and bounced back to her ears. *Where am I?* She moved forward, her hands outstretched, her canvas purse bumping her hip. Something crackled inside, but Mari was too busy worrying about the wet, close blackness to notice.

The thought of a hole opening up beneath her feet in the darkness made her feel cautiously with each toe before she trusted her weight to her leading foot. It was hard to tell if she was going straight, the dark was like a bandage pressing on her eyes. Wheels and sparkles of phantom light played across her retinas. It was completely lightless down here—wherever here was.

A dry sob rasped free of Mari's throat.

*Stop whining. I hate whining.* The woman's voice, loaded with sarcasm, made her flinch again.

"I don't whine," she said out loud, and her voice bounced back to her. It sounded like she was in a tunnel. A stone tunnel.

Soon she noticed the stony floor sloping upward. *I sure hope that's straight ahead.* She began working her way up the slope. She kept her hands moving, waving in circles so she wouldn't bump her head or sides against anything, lurching forward in a weird stutter-stepping to make sure she didn't fall in a hole.

"Really," she finally said, because the silence and darkness pressing in on her was chill enough to make her shiver, gooseflesh filling her skin, "I *don't* whine. But if I did whine,

I'd probably whine about having a boyfriend fated to kill my best friend and my roommates murdered by something that was probably looking to eat me and my room all torn up, and I wish Hanson was here because I really do—"

A sound. Was it? Had she heard a soft, sliding footstep behind her? A wet, sort of padding sound?

Mari sobbed again, the lump in her throat suddenly beating in time to her frantic pulse.

"Hanson," she whispered. "I wish you were here. Gods, I wish you were here."

Another soft sound behind her. Or were her ears deceiving her? Mari stopped, frozen, one foot lifted, both her arms held out to the side. The gooseflesh ran in waves down her back.

*Really, for a witch with the power of prescience you can be most inattentive,* the Librarian's ghostly voice taunted her.

"Mother," Mari whispered, her lips barely shaping the words, the inside of her mouth smooth and dry as glass. "Mother, watch over me, for I am your child. Sea-Queen, wind and wave, rising white from the foam, guide me. Mother, watch over me; Goddess, listen to me."

Another soft sliding sound. It was definitely a footstep, a soft, *wet* footstep.

Mari screamed and bolted, hearing the footsteps quicken behind her, a sound like hands slapping fresh liver, pattering closer and closer. A rank, thick smell of seaweed and rotting flesh seemed to close around her. She fought for breath and ran heedlessly into the stony blackness.

# Twenty-Four

Hanson used his thumb to pull the hammer back. It locked with a click, the silvery metal of the gun barrel glinting in candlelight. The fingers of his other hand sank into the thing's throat. Flesh as stiff as concrete gave way under his hand. "For the last time," he said softly, "*where?*"

"Can't...tell...you..." the *g'raian* choked, its face turning purple. "Library...safeguard...protect..."

Mari's scent was strong in the church. She *must* have been here, but the trail went cold. Hanson had quartered the entire neighborhood during the long, endless, progressively more hopeless and foggy day from sunrise to sunset, and found no sign of her. At fog-shrouded dusk the *g'raian* had ventured out, maybe to cause more mischief, and Hanson had neatly nabbed him. A little release of the sick frustration and fear he was feeling was just what the doctor ordered.

His chest ached. As soon as Mari stopped concentrating on whatever spell she'd used to slip past his defenses, he'd felt the pull that told him where she was. He'd shared a bed with her, completing the bond between Watcher and witch, and he could track her almost anywhere now.

But as soon as it had started, the call faded, flaring up and then dying with maddening inconsistency, as if someone was moving her around or trying to cloak her whereabouts.

*She can't hide forever,* he thought, his eyes hot and grainy. The gargoyle choked, his stone-colored eyes turning bright silver.

"I know how to kill stonefolk," Hanson said, still dangerously soft. "But have you ever considered I might leave you alive? Crippled? No longer able to fly?"

The thing's eyes rolled back in its head. Its hands plucked weakly at Hanson's shredded coat. The Watcher's finger tightened on the trigger.

Then he heard it. Faint, but there.

The call roared to life inside his head. Mari, close. And terrified.

*Outside. She's outside.* "You're lucky," he said as he dropped the gargoyle, who hit the stone floor amid shattered wooden pews with a thud. The candlelit shadows shifted uneasily, full of the sound of wings.

Hanson hit the cathedral's main doors from inside, breaking the locks and flinging them wide. Wood shattered, splinters whipping through the air with killing force. He landed on both feet and whirled, streaking in the direction of the call.

*Graveyard. What's she doing in the graveyard?* He cleared the wrought iron fence in a single bound, dried blood crackling on his skin. No rest all day, no chance to clean up. Just the endless search, hoping against hope she was still alive. *If she dies I'm going to kill that gargoyle before I kill myself.* He had to slow down, listening for the sound of her voice.

A dim thudding. He turned and streaked for the far corner, where a group of dark cypress trees crowded around a white marble tomb. A coldly glimmering white marble statue of a blind angel brooded on top of the squat structure, and muffled shrieks came from inside it.

Hanson's entire body went cold.

He tore the thick, wooden, iron-barred door off its hinges by the simple expedient of sinking his fingers into the metal crosspieces and setting his feet, then yanking back with every erg of strength he possessed. Metal squealed and snapped, wood exploded, and a wild-eyed Mari scrambled out of the stinking darkness inside the crypt. Her hair curled wildly, streaming back from her face. She was still screaming, her cheeks paper-pale except for splotches of hectic color high on each cheekbone.

Hanson's hands closed around her shoulders. He half-spun, bringing up the gun, pointing at whatever Dark lurked in the crypt's chill blackness.

She struggled frantically, kicking and clawing at him, probably mad with fear. "Easy, sweetheart," he said, the undertone of Power in his voice slicing through her screams. "Easy. I'm here. It's all right. I'm here."

Whatever was inside the crypt retreated. A foul stench of rotting flesh and swamp water boiled out of the stone cube. *She was in there alone for how long? I am going to torture that gargoyle to death. I swear it on my sword, I am going to clip his wings down to nubs and pull out his claws before I slit his throat an inch at a time.* "Easy, sweetheart. Shhh, Mari, Mariamne, I'm here. It's me. Relax." *Come out so I can kill you,* he thought, the gun never wavering. *Come on.* "Be easy, sweetheart. I've found you, it's all right. What were you thinking, hmmm?"

She stiffened, staring up at him, her blue eyes ringed with

white. The perfume of her fear, Power trembling, ready to escape
her control, folded around him. His nerves tingled, bathing in
it, drinking in the smell of his witch. In that moment he
understood far more about the Dark than he ever wanted to. He
was hungry for her, hungry for her light. What would he do if
she denied him?

A thick, burping chuckle echoed from the tomb's darkness.
Mari shrieked and tried to leap away, struggling wildly. Hanson
barely moved, feet planted and ready to kill whatever came out
of the dark. "Be *still*, Mari!" he barked, knowing he shouldn't
presume to order her around. She was a Lightbringer. But oddly
enough, she quit fighting him and went limp against his arm,
her chest heaving with deep, harsh breaths. A spike of painful
pleasure went though him, harp string-taut nerves relaxing. Here.
She was here, and alive. He hadn't failed. Not completely. Not
yet.

The thing inside the crypt retreated. There was a sound like
soft, wet, running footsteps, the slamming of a heavy door.
Power snapped, chill and rank in the foggy air. The smell faded
into nothingness. Whatever it was, it was gone now.

He eased the hammer on the gun back down. "It's gone,"
he said, and shoved the gun back in its holster. "What were you
thinking, you stubborn little—" *Calm down. She's frightened.*

*If she hadn't bolted,* he reminded himself, *she wouldn't be
frightened. I could have talked her out of going on this
rampage, wherever she went, and kept her safe. Instead of
spending the entire day looking for her and fretting myself
into a rage.*

The chill voice of Watcher logic had a quick answer for
that one. *If you hadn't scared her, she wouldn't have wasted
her energy by running off covered with one hell of a spell, a
spell that could hide her even from her Watcher. It's your fault,
Watcher. Yours alone.*

"Hanson?" A mere breath of sound. She leaned against him,
blinking and deathly pale, her eyes glazed. He felt the fine
tremors going through her. If she slid further into shock, he
would have to bring her out the old way, skin to skin. However
much he wanted that, he didn't think she'd understand.

"Who put you in there, Mari? Was it the gargoyle? Who
did this to you?"

She blinked up at him. "Hanson?"

"Of *course* it's me," he replied, tightly. The iron band

squeezing his chest all day suddenly loosened. Heat pricked at his eyes, and his shoulders slumped. "Gods above and below, woman, I *told* you I will come for you. I *promised* you."

"I c-c-can't." Her teeth chattered.

"Who did this to you, Mari? Hmm? Who?" The frustration and rage suddenly snapped, turned to ice. He would make whoever it was *pay*. Pay in blood if necessary, for making her afraid.

"Nobody," she said, and laughed. It was a high, panicked giggle, echoing among the gravestones, and Hanson scanned the perimeter. Nothing but fog and the nose-stinging smell of Watcher power. He'd been a little less than discreet. He'd painted the night with ten-foot tall neon signs. *Watcher here! Come and see what the ruckus is!*

"We should get you out of here." he said

She finished laughing and burst into tears, clinging to him, sobbing so hard he could barely understand what she was trying to tell him. When he did finally understand, it all made sense. He moved her through the graveyard, almost unobtrusively, half-carrying her as she stumbled. She was in shock. Whatever had happened to her hadn't physically harmed her, however.

At least he had that to comfort him.

"You saw me kill Theo?" he asked, for the third time. "You actually *saw* it?"

"Sh-sh-she was w-w-with me and you were *Dark.* You had red eyes and you—"

"I don't have red eyes, Mari. Last I checked they were blue. Here, step up. The gate's just a few feet away."

"I h-h-have to g-g-get away from y-y-you," she stammered through the sobs. "Or you'll kill Theo."

"Why didn't you tell me?" He dragged her to the gate, curled his fingers around the wrought iron, and pulled. Metal squealed and snapped. Mari stared, her eyes wide and agonized.

"You wouldn't b-b-believe me." She stumbled, her purse banging against her hip. "And the L-L-Librarian—"

"Take a breath, sweetheart. I promise you, there's no way on this green earth I'd kill Theo. She's a Lightbringer, for God's sake." Hanson half-carried her away from the church. *I'll come back and kill that gargoyle later,* he decided, and felt the symbiote retreat into enraged watchfulness at the very bottom of his mind. "You know I'd never hurt any one of you," he continued, casting around for some method of transportation.

Carrying her back to the hotel would be too slow, but there weren't any cabs around. *I can cut over to Seventh Street, that's shorter.*

She began stammering out another tale, this one about the Library under the church. While most of him was worried about getting her to safety, scanning for potential predators and making sure she didn't trip, the rest of him listened closely to her as she tried, without much success, to make some sense out of what had happened to her.

*So there's a Nexus under that church, and someone built a library.* He scanned the perimeter again. If they reached the hotel without a fight it would be a miracle. *And a fault line under the city. A fault line that's had how long to store up the mother of all earthquakes? Great. Just what we need. If that happens it could destroy the whole damn city, and what will Dante and I be able to do? Not much. Not very bloody much at all.* "A Nexus?" he asked, crossing Fifth Street and turning down the hill. *Let there be a cab on Seventh Street, huh? What do you say, gods? How about you let me be lucky this once?* "What do you know about Nexuses?"

"Nothing," she replied, her voice breaking. "But I s-saw you!"

"Forget what you think you saw. I'd never hurt Theo. Dante would take me apart if I even tried. Just like I'll take that gods-be-damned gargoyle apart as soon as I have time. Look, Mari, you *know* me. You know I wouldn't hurt your friends."

She sniffed, wiping at her sopping cheeks with the back of one expressive hand. Even now, tangled and tear soaked, she looked delicious. And the bolt of flame her skin sent through him didn't help his concentration. "I *Saw* it." Her tone was stubborn, determined and tearful.

"I know you did," he said immediately. "I don't doubt that you did. Which is why I'm going to avoid Theo like the plague, sweetheart. You wanted to save her? Fine, I won't go near her with a ten-foot pole. *Don't ever do that again,* Mari. Ever. You could have been killed. Or worse."

Another half-sob; the sound threatened to break his heart. *I promised I'd watch over her from a distance. I promised I'd never touch her again. What can I say? I'm a liar. I can't. I can't do it.* "I knew it," she said, sounding far calmer. "I knew you'd come."

"Of course," he growled, scanning the perimeter once again.

"Don't ever do that again, Mari. You're a walking target."

"I'm just fine on my own," she disagreed mournfully. "If everyone would just leave me alone I'd be all right. Instead, I have these awful visions and smelly things chasing me and killing my friends and an earthquake coming and—"

"Mari. Breathe."

She gasped. He closed his free hand around her wrist, flushing her with heat and Power to bring her out of shock. Her pulse pounded against his touch. "I would never hurt one of your friends," he murmured, taking care to move slowly so she could keep up. Agony retreated. She was here and safe in his arms.

*Whatever attacked me outside the green witch's house might still be around.* His spine ran with ice. *Got to get her under cover.*

"I Saw it," she repeated, swallowing tears.

"I know you did. But you See things that can be stopped, Mari. You've warned me, and I'll stay away from Theo, end of story."

The night turned colder, absolutely still, fog wrapping around lampposts and muffling their footsteps. Was it the Dark or was he just edgy after spoiling for a fight all day? A day spent trying to track her, getting more and more frustrated every minute.

"What is it?" she whispered, her voice breaking.

*If I don't do the right thing here, she'll start screaming again.* "Nothing much," he told her. *Lying to my witch, again.* "Come on. Maybe I should carry you."

That managed to make her speed up. She stumbled and he lifted her off her feet and set her down again. "I'm a mess," she muttered. "I'm a mess, and a coward, and a whiner, and a... Gods above, what happened to you? You're *bleeding!*"

"Whatever killed your roommates attacked me, and I've been all over the city looking for you," he said grimly, setting his jaw. *If I could draw my sword I'd feel a lot better about this. But it'll spook her, and I can't afford that. Lovely. She's emitting all over the spectrum.* "I haven't had a chance to find a quiet corner and heal up. Mari, I need you to calm down. Please. Take a deep breath. I'm here."

"Calm down, he says," she replied bitterly. "I just got chased through...wherever that was, by...whatever that was, and you want me to calm down!" A jagged, brittle laugh shook her. "I'll calm down all right. As soon as I get *out* of the Twilight Zone I'll calm *right* down."

*To hell with this.* Hanson bent briefly, scooped her up into his arms. "Hold on," he said. *Let's see if I can outrun whatever it is.*

"What are you—" she began, then swallowed a shriek as he concentrated, Power gathering like a coiled spring. When he bolted forward, she shut her eyes, what little color remaining on her face draining away, clutching at his shoulder through torn leather crackling with dried blood.

*Isn't it obvious?* he wanted to say. *I'm running when I should be fighting. You're not the coward here, Mari. It's me.*

# Twenty-Five

Mari had never seen anyone look so exhausted.

Hanson leaned against the wall, peering out the window's mostly-drawn drapes, his long, dark coat battered and his face a mess. He was bruised and cut up and covered in dried blood that cracked when he moved. He had carried her into the hotel and up to the very same room from which she'd escaped last night. Had it been last night? He said it was.

*It could have been weeks ago.* She looked down at her shaking hands. *I feel like I haven't slept in years.* The chair made a slight sound as she shifted uneasily. Despite still wearing her coat, she shivered.

"Clear enough," Hanson said, as if to himself, and his shoulders sagged.

"What?" Her voice quivered.

*Stop whining. I hate whining.* The Librarian's disdainful voice rang in Mari's memory. It was true. She was nothing but a whiner. A weakling.

"I was thinking out loud," he replied, not looking at her. He sighed. "It's clear enough outside. Give me a half hour to clean up and a couple hours to get my bones fused together, Mari, and we'll start working on—"

"No." Her own voice surprised her, firm and clear. Mari knotted her fingers together.

He still didn't look at her. The curtains moved, just as if touched by a breath of air. "No?"

"I have to get away from you," she said, tonelessly. "For everyone's safety."

"No."

"Hanson—"

"No."

"Will you just listen?"

"*No.*"

The entire room creaked, a framed Berscardi print over the plasma-screen television chattering against the wall. Mari took a deep breath, searching for calm.

*Isn't that the funniest thing. I'm not ever going to feel calm again.*

"Hanson." At least he didn't interrupt her this time. "I know what I Saw. I know you wouldn't ever *mean* to hurt Theo, but I have to try to stop what I See. I was given my talent for a reason, and I—"

"I will *not* leave you," he replied tightly, "and if you try another trick like the last one, I'll just have to track you again. And I won't be happy if I do." His eyebrows drew together. She couldn't read his expression; his face was a mask of blood and bruising.

"Are you threatening me?" She meant to sound angry, but it simply came out flat. "Look, I just had something chase me through pitch-black tunnels and came out of a graveyard right after taking a happy little trip Through The Looking Glass."

"And I nearly got killed by the same thing that slaughtered your roommates," he said expressionlessly. "Dante had to shock me back to life. I spent the entire *fucking* day looking for my witch, dealing with predators, and imagining all sorts of lovely things happening to you. Things like murder, and torture, and—"

*"Will* you *stop?"* It was her turn to make the air in the room go chill and tense, Power leaking out from her aura. She was too tired, far too tired. "Don't think I'm happy about this. I wish I didn't have to do it. But I *Saw* it! Why can't you understand? All my life I've had to give up everything and move on when I was supposed to. I've lost everything, over and over again. Now I'm going to lose you, too, and I...I..." The words stuck in her throat. Her fingers tightened, and she could feel her bones creaking.

He shot her an extraordinary, blue glance. "I'm not a toy, Mari. You can't lock me up in a cupboard and only take me out when you feel like it, and you sure as hell can't throw me away. The *only* way I'm going is if you *order* me to go back to Circle Lightfall in disgrace. You hate me, and you want to kill me? Go ahead and do that. I'll go back and commit suicide if you *order* me to, Lightbringer. There's nothing left for me."

Mari closed her mouth with a snap. "Is that what would happen?" Her voice trembled. "You're serious."

"I'm supposed to protect you," he informed her yet again. "I can't do it if you go running off. Have you ever considered that I might not kill Theo? That I might have a *choice* in the matter?"

"Look at you," she whispered. "Look at what this does to you. I don't want this to go on. I can't take this."

"Then quit running away." He tweezed the curtain aside

slightly, still staring down into the street. "Well, what have we here?" Now, he sounded thoughtful and surprised.

"What?" Mari's heart slammed against her ribs. *Gods,* she prayed, *please. Not another thing. I don't think I can handle one more weird occurrence right now. Please, please, not another one. I'm begging you.*

"Something's out there," he said, and his shoulders came back up. He didn't look like he was hurting anymore. Instead, under the mask of blood, bruises and grime, he looked lethal. Ready.

Mari swallowed what she'd intended to say. "Not another thing," she repeated out loud. "Gods. I can't stand it."

"Relax," Hanson said. "Just a small fry. Not even worth going outside for, right now. Are you going to send me back to Circle Lightfall?"

"Hanson, please."

"Are you sending me back, or not?"

She struggled with the question for a full thirty seconds. "No," she finally whispered, defeated. "I don't…No."

"Good." He closed the drapes all the way with a decisive movement. "Why don't you try to rest? I'll be ready to go in a couple of hours. I'll wake you up."

"I don't think I could rest." Instead, she leaned gingerly back, testing the chair. It was soft. She still couldn't unclench her hands.

"Try. You know, I'm almost starting to believe you're alive. You scared me." He paced across the room and checked the locks on the door again. The Watcher shields in the room's walls quivered slightly. He was testing them.

"I'm sorry," she offered inadequately.

"I thought I had done something wrong," he continued, his back to her. The leather coat was terribly battered. Whatever had attacked him had done a good job of it. Mari shuddered, shut her eyes, and sank back into the chair's embrace.

"No. Nothing wrong." Heat rose to Mari's cheeks. The bed was made, of course. Housekeeping had probably been in during the day. But it was the same bed she had slept in.

With him.

Abruptly aware of this, she shifted uneasily in the chair. *How do I tell him that he didn't do anything wrong, it's just that I care about Theo and him too goddamn much to let that vision happen?*

A small, warm breeze caressed her cheek. "Mari?" His voice was close, too close. She hadn't heard him move across the room. Her eyes flew open.

He knelt in front of the chair, studying her. The bruises and swelling were going down rapidly. She could almost *smell* the fuming dark Power running through him. "I swear to you, I won't hurt Theo. Please just don't do that to me again. I can't afford to lose you."

Mari felt her heart literally crack inside her chest. "Hanson—"

"If I frighten you so much you have to run away like that, I promised I wouldn't touch you again if I found you," he continued, his face still expressionless.

"Wait. I—" *How the hell am I supposed to respond to that? You arrogant, overbearing, conceited—*

"There's something you should know," he interrupted. "Listen. I'm only going to say this once."

"You don't have to."

"Mari. Please." He gripped the chair arms, trapping her, leaning forward until he almost touched her knees. "I was a con man," he said harshly. "I cheated people. I was born with a talent like yours, but I used it to steal. I started out *having* to steal and ended up *liking* to steal. I was addicted. I went from score to score, destroying lives. I didn't kill anyone with my hands, but I might as well have." His mouth turned down bitterly at the corners. "I hit the wall," he continued, his eyes locked with hers. "I stole from a very nasty cartel and ended up with damn near every bone in my body broken, and most of my skin gone from the gasoline they poured over me and lit with a cigarette lighter."

Mari shuddered. He *remembered* it, and she was so raw and exhausted that she could *See* it. She wanted to close her eyes, block out the images of suffering, flashes of screams and torture. He was still not telling her the complete story.

No, the whole truth was too horrific, and she Saw it anyway.

"I was in the hospital," he said, softly. "I was a cripple. I had nothing. No health insurance, no family, no friends. I cheated everyone who ever loved me, and I ended up cheating myself. And then, Circle Lightfall found me. They gave me a chance to walk again, Mari. They said it was a chance to stop hustling. It sounded like a bunch of fucking fairy tales until I saw it with my own eyes. I only joined up with Circle Lightfall because they told me I would be able to walk again. And then I got infected by that damn sense of honor." Another bitter little laugh. "I'm only telling you because you should know this about me, sweetheart. I promised I'd never touch you again if I could just bring you in alive, but sometimes, I *lie*."

"Hanson—"

"I can't figure out if I'm going to stick to that promise, or if I'm going to do what I've always done and take the easy way out." He pushed himself up to his feet, his pale eyes fixed on her face. "A man's promise is only as good as the man giving it."

"You can't," she began.

"I'm going to go outside and check the perimeter. If you leave this room, I *will* catch you before you get to the lobby. That little trick you did won't work again. So just get some rest, or whatever, and I'll be back up as soon as it's safe and I've had a chance to heal."

"Hanson."

It was too late. He swung away from her and was at the door before she could finish speaking his name, moving with that spooky, graceful speed. His coat flared in tatters, and she wondered what could have attacked him, to rip the tough leather that badly. Her stomach flipped at the thought.

"Hanson!" She tried to push herself up from the chair, but her legs wouldn't straighten. They simply spilled her back down onto the cushion. "Don't—"

The door clicked shut and locked.

"—go," she finished, and looked down at her hands, now clutching the chair arms where his hands had just been. "Don't go," she whispered. *Oh, gods. I've screwed that up royally. Just like everything else in my miserable life.* "Don't go," she repeated, since he was no longer able to hear her. "Oh, gods."

There was no answer. He was gone.

# Twenty-Six

Hanson only waited until she fell asleep, and then he let himself back into the room. She lay uncomfortably curled on the bed, fully dressed, clutching her purse to her chest. She'd obviously been crying. Tears still slicked the pale cheek he could see from across the room.

He crossed to the window again and looked out. His coat was repaired and his broken bones seamlessly mended. In another hour or two the bruises and torn muscles would be gone. He would be back to the familiar low hum of miserable discomfort. He could clean up then, get the blood off, and be a little more presentable.

Whatever it was, it was still out there. Like an incipient toothache, a slight throbbing at the edge of his sensing range, something Dark.

Something he'd felt before.

It even *smelled* maddeningly familiar, when he could catch a breath of it. Something was stalking Mari with all the craftiness and precision that Hanson himself might use to stalk a mark or another piece of Dark.

*Hunting Mari. And smart enough to realize that I'm the biggest threat to it. Or something that has a grudge against Watchers, maybe.*

Worrying about whatever was hunting them wasn't distracting him enough. Not nearly enough at all.

Oddly, the thing that cut him right down to the bone was that she didn't trust him. He knew she didn't, but intellectually knowing was not the same as having your witch flee you for something you hadn't even done yet. Even though he deserved it—deserved a lot worse, really—it still made the inside of his chest feel uncomfortably like it was being clawed by a particularly vicious small animal.

He had been so careful, so endlessly careful and patient.

*Well, that's your job, isn't it?* he told himself, staring out the window, down six stories to the dark street. Streamers of fog threaded between the street lamps, and the manholes and sewer grates steamed. The prickling, tingling, breathless feeling of another earthquake approaching ran down his back with chill, icy fingers. *You're not doing Club Med. You're a Watcher. Pain is something you just deal with, that's all. You're supposed to be patient. And careful.*

He could live with being nearly gutted by the Dark. He could live with the symbiote's rusty-nail tearing at him. He could even live with the constant crushing burden of guilt.

It was the fact that she still feared him that he couldn't live with. And not only was she still terrified of him, but she didn't even trust him not to murder a Lightbringer.

"That's what I get for staying on the straight and narrow," he muttered, his breath touching the glass with vapor. "Nice guys finish last."

*Except you've never been a nice guy.*

Could it be he was only sensing another earthquake?

No, because he'd scented the *g'raian* right before the last one. He was perfectly capable of distinguishing between incipient natural disaster and a predator on the loose. And he'd chosen one of the hotels that was fully up on its seismic bracing.

Hanson's fist touched the cold glass, more vapor spreading from the contact of his skin with the chill surface. *She doesn't even trust me not to kill the green witch.* He felt the claws go through his chest again. *She thinks I'd kill a Lightbringer. And if she thinks I'd kill Theo, what does she think I'll do to her?*

He'd sworn he wasn't going to touch her again, and she thought he was a murderous liar. She was probably right. He'd spent so long fighting he didn't even remember what peace felt like. And if he would promise in all sincerity that he would leave her alone and then want to break that promise without a single qualm, what kind of a Watcher did that make him?

What kind of *man* did that make him?

*A cheat,* he told himself bleakly. *A cheat and a liar. A swindler. A fake. A hustler.*

And Mari would never in a million years love someone like that.

The window was almost completely fogged now. He swiped his palm across the glass. A flicker of motion caught his eye. His awareness returned to the street outside, and the thick acrid perfume of Dark.

*Dammit! Slow and sloppy, Hanson. Slow and sloppy.* The condensation vanished from the glass, but between the darkness and the fog he only caught a split second's worth of movement before whatever it was vanished. Big, bigger than Mari, hulking shoulders, humanoid, moving with an uncoordinated fluidity, like a high-quality puppet yanked around by a less-than-talented amateur.

There was something oddly, disturbingly, familiar about both the shape of the thing and the way it moved. Memory teased at the edge of Hanson's brain and then fled. He swore softly and then went absolutely still, waiting.

It didn't show again. He stayed motionless at the window, most of his attention on the street, and the rest of him wondering why the sound of Mari's soft breathing comforted him so much. And wondering, as well, what he had done to make her think he would kill a Lightbringer.

# Twenty-Seven

The fog still pressed against the city, a balm of cotton wool. Mari shivered and cupped her elbows in her hands. "You're going in there?" she asked, and her voice shook a little more than she liked. Hanson loomed next to her, his pale hair slicked back and dark with the moisture in the air.

The International District was a wilderness at night. Some parts were pleasant—the parts closer to downtown, where the police still patrolled. Here, closer to the southern edge of Santiago City, a cop car was a rarity, and graffiti was scrawled across most surfaces. Even the smallest shops had bars on the doors.

"I am," he said, still in that grim, chill voice. He hadn't spoken much since waking her up, every word seemingly yanked out of him by force. "And you're coming with me." His eyes narrowed, and his mouth was a single straight line. He'd waited patiently and silently for her to take a shower and change her clothes. It was as if they had never slept next to each other, as if she hadn't kissed him.

*Stop thinking about that,* she told herself. *Just keep quiet and wait for a chance to...what? What can I do?* Her back prickled with gooseflesh, intuition warning her of danger. The entire city was breathless, hushed under a blanket of fog and anticipating the next earthquake. Now that she knew what it felt like, it was hard to ignore the growing tension. *I wish I could go down to the docks or Alkai Beach. If I was near some water I might be able to think this through and figure something out.*

Mari eyed the bar again. It looked like a rough place, from the junked-out motorcycles cowering in front to the hulking black-leather-mountain bouncer at the door. The sound of a jukebox pulsed faintly through the fog. Neon blinked in the windows. Camden Street was full of places like this, some of them rougher than others. This place had clean windows and no graffiti marking the pavement or walls outside.

That meant it was tough even by International District standards.

"Don't worry," Hanson continued. "They know me in here. Nobody's likely to start any trouble."

That shouldn't have been comforting, but it was. "How do

they know you here?" she asked. "I mean, when would you
have time to come here for a beer?"

"Watchers don't drink. I come here for information." He
moved slightly, settling inside his coat. "Just stay close to me,
Mari."

*Oh, no worries about that,* she thought, looking at the bar
as Hanson stepped out of the alley's shadow. She followed him,
wishing she hadn't worn the patched blue sweater and frayed
blue jeans. Her boots almost slid in a puddle, and she leapt over
the rest of it, landing hard and jarring her entire body. *I would
never come here by myself. This looks like a place where a
girl could get in trouble.*

Hanson didn't look back, his shoulders straight as a ruler
under the heavy black leather. Mari gulped down chill wet air.
"Hanson?"

"Hmm?" He didn't stop, didn't look over his shoulder. As a
matter of fact, he hadn't looked directly at her since she'd
awakened.

"What if there's trouble?" She stepped down into the
deserted street after him.

"I'll kill whoever starts the trouble. Don't worry, Mari.
You're safe. I'm through playing around."

*I'm not worried about me. I'm worried about you. And
Theo. And everyone else.* Mari sighed. She was carrying death
around like some sort of Typhoid Mary; and she had no idea
what Esmerelda had been talking about, Nexus and earthquake
and—

"Don't *worry*, Mari." Hanson's step slowed slightly. "This
is where some of the sentient Dark and other things hang out.
You may not be comfortable, but at least you're safe."

"Why won't I be comfortable?" *It's hard to imagine I could
get any* more *uncomfortable,* she thought with grim humor.

"Because I won't be able to hide what I am in here," he
said, slowing a little more until Mari could catch up to him.
They reached the other side of the street. Mari's shields stiffened
reflexively, the atmosphere here was thick and dangerous. Left
to her own devices, she would *never* be in this part of town at
night.

*Probably not even during the day,* she admitted to herself.
*I'm glad he's here.*

And wasn't that the strangest thing? Even though she knew
he was going to kill Theo, maybe by accident or maybe on

purpose, she was still comforted by his presence.

*He's right,* she tried to tell herself. *I sometimes See things that can be changed. They're warnings, and he says he'll stay away from Theo.*

Her conscience replied with a steely glare and pursed lips. *So what? You could just be telling yourself that because you're infatuated with him, Mariamne.*

*Not infatuated. I'm in love. Two different things.*

*Love, shmove. He's just available.*

*And my heart hurts,* she thought. *My heart aches for him. And even though I know he's dangerous to Theo, I still want to put my arms around him. Not to mention some other things I'd really like to do to him.*

They reached the sidewalk directly in front of the bar. The leather-clad bouncer didn't move, but Mari felt eyes flick down her body and return to her face.

Hanson barely paused. He stalked past the bouncer, hitting the door with the flat of his hand. Mari almost had to scramble to keep up. The bouncer's sunglasses swiveled to follow her. He was a massive, broad-shouldered hulk, wearing scarred engineer boots and a broad, black scarred belt.

Foul stagnant air loaded with Power and cigarette smoke closed around her. Jukebox noise smashed into her ears. Mari coughed, her eyes watering, and Hanson's hand closed around her elbow. Her heart leapt into her throat.

"Steady, Lightbringer," he said, his voice pitched a little louder than necessary.

Mari blinked. Her eyes watered. The jukebox came to a thumping halt, and silence broke into the air.

She received a confused impression of crowding, drinks lifted to lips, fuming cigarettes. Then there was a confused flurry of motion that ended with Mari blinking and a man on the floor. Hanson made a short, sharp movement, and there was a crackling sound. The Watcher's aura flared with dark, hurtful Power, and the gun in his hand was pressed to the man's temple. "Now," Hanson said softly, "she's with me. Clear?"

The man on the floor was rail-thin, his clothes torn and grimy. Mari had to bite back a gasp. He had gray skin, long pointed ears, and a glaring yellow eye fixed on her from underneath a battered cowboy hat. A slight rattling sound slid from his thin lips.

Hanson apparently took this as an affirmative, because he

slowly drew the gun back, his thumb easing the hammer down. "Anyone got a problem?"

Every eye in the place was fixed on Mari. And she stood there, clutching her purse like a fool. Something crackled inside her purse. *What the hell is that?*

The eyes staring at her were yellow, green, black—every shade conceivable. She saw gray skin, feathers, and every thing in here had sharp teeth. *They aren't human,* she thought, *and they're not wearing glamours. And it's after dark. I'm a zebra standing in the middle of a bunch of hungry lions.*

"No problem," the bartender barked. He was a massive sheet of muscle with spiked, wet-gleaming black hair. He looked identical to the shaved gorilla outside, except without sunglasses.

His eyes were glowing crimson.

"No problem," he repeated. "Just get what you want and get out of my bar, Black-knife."

"I want Milton, to start with. And half a bottle of Scotch wouldn't go amiss."

This caused a murmur to race around the bar. Mari found that her hands were shaking, so she sank her fingers into her purse. The crackling sound was even louder.

*It sounds like paper. But the Librarian took the papers, didn't she?*

"Me? Whaddido?" There was a general scuffle, but a man, dressed in a battered denim jacket, with a red bandanna around his high domed forehead, was shoved forward. Mari blinked. Hanson rose like a wave from kneeling next to the gray-skinned man, not even glancing at her.

"Come on, Mari," he said patiently, and she found that her body numbly obeyed, stepping forward.

*What the hell is in my purse?* She almost forgot to breathe. The man on the floor was still staring at her, making a small mewling noise.

Hanson kicked him. "Get up and get away, Gray. This isn't for you." And he laughed another bitter little laugh.

"Greedy," someone else said, in a voice that sounded thick and disused, squeaking like an unoiled hinge. "Keeping the meat all to yourself." This was from a man with red skin and a long black Fu Manchu mustache, sitting tilted back in a chair with his boots on a rickety table full of dusty bottles.

"I never did play well with others," Hanson replied. "You got something to say, Sikeda?"

"Nothin' at all," the red-skinned man replied. To prove it, he picked up a small black bowl from the table and swallowed whatever was in it, tossing it far back as if it burned.

Mari followed Hanson to the bar. His aura stretched, touching hers, wrapping around her; it was an intimate touch. Intimate enough that it reminded her of his mouth opening to hers, his hands on her hips, the small desperate sound he'd made when she slid against him.

She tore away from the thought with an almost physical effort.

The bartender eyed her greedily, then slammed a bottle down on the bar. The noise made Mari jump, and another ripple went through the room. Hanson didn't react, just picked up the bottle and half-turned. "The table," he said. "There."

Mari walked behind him and settled in the chair he held for her. *This is lunacy, I shouldn't be in here. How come nobody knows about a bunch of people that look like Star Trek aliens, right in the middle of the city?*

She knew why. Normal people wouldn't be able to see past whatever glamours these things wore. Most of the Dark things sitting in here probably didn't go out by day, and here they would have no need to wear a glamour. The persistent smell of danger and the hulk of a bouncer would keep normal people away at night, without anyone being the wiser.

Sitting in the middle of a smoky bar with their hungry eyes peeling at her skin and her aura flashing nervously, she began to understand. She saw claws tightening on bottles, wineglasses and cigarettes. Someone kicked the jukebox, and an unfamiliar, pounding wailing began to fill the air. In the back corner, drawing back into a pool of shadow, something smoky and dim with glowing red eyes watched her. She had never been the subject of such concentrated attention before.

*Everything in here feeds on something.* She shivered. *And I'm a big, tasty treat to them.*

Milton settled nervously in the leftover chair, trying not to look at Mari. He had a thin, deathly pale face, and yellow cat-slit eyes glowered over a long narrow nose. It was his teeth that fascinated Mari the most: sharp and white, looking capable of crunching bone. *How does he talk with teeth like that?*

"I din't do nothin," Milton said, shifting in his seat.

Hanson pushed the bottle across the table. "Here. Just give me whatever you've got."

Milton shivered, his thin shoulders hunching. "You ain't gonna believe me."

"That's my problem." Hanson still didn't look at Mari, but that high-powered Watcher radar was still pinging in all directions. She would have bet her last nickel that he was absolutely aware of everything and everyone in the room, including her. "Pay attention to me when I'm talking to you, Milt."

Milton shivered again. A thin thread of saliva bubbled up at the corner of his skinny mouth and leaked down his chin. "Sorry," he said. "She smells like fresh meat."

Hanson grinned. It was a chillingly good-natured smile. "I didn't ask for your comment on my witch, Milt."

"Fine, okay, whatteva." Milton shifted in his chair, the wood squeaking underneath him. Mari tore her eyes away from his teeth and looked at Hanson. Oddly enough, she felt safe. He wouldn't let anything happen to her. He'd promised.

*If I can believe that, then I can believe that he won't hurt Theo.* Her conscience didn't even twinge.

"Of course, if you're not interested…" Hanson let the sentence dangle like a cigarette.

"There's something on the streets." Milt leaned over the table, his voice dropping. "It's going through the population here like a hot knife through butter. It ain't Watcher, either. We'd know if any more of your Black Knife Brigade came through. It's *somethin' else*, and it's wearing a castoff skin."

"A castoff skin?" Hanson's eyebrows drew together. "That's odd."

"It's fucking scary. The only thing I know that can wear a skin is a *kalak*, but this is something else. It don't fly, don't take a territory, don't talk to anyone. It just sneaks around and eats. Smells like acid and ink, I've been told. Word on the street is it's taking humans *and* Others."

"That's one hell of a menu," Hanson said. His fingers rested on the Scotch bottle, and his eyes flicked over Milton, scanned the inside of the bar, and then came back to rest on the thin man. "What else you got? Anyone asking about my witch here?"

"Not a whisper. We know she's yours, Black-knife. We ain't about to go after a Lightfall doll. Only the jobbers too stupid to know otherwise do that. None of *us* are hungry enough. Besides, there's plenty of other prey, especially with the way things are now."

Hanson shrugged. "What about the earthquakes?"

"Something's drained the power from that damn native binding," the thin man spat. "Lotsa disaster coming." His teeth gleamed in a broad, razor smile. "Lotsa good eatin'."

Hanson took his hand away from the neck of the bottle. Power sparked, flared, and Mari leaned back, unable to help herself. "There you go, Milt. Take it."

The thin man grabbed at the bottle, making a saw-edged whining sound. He lifted it to his lips and then looked pleadingly over the glass rim at Hanson.

The Watcher snapped his fingers and flame blossomed. Mari let out a sharp breath. The Scotch in the bottle ignited, but the thin man wrapped his lips around the neck of the bottle and sucked in. The flame vanished, his pale face blooming with a red, healthy flush for a moment. "Gar, tha's good," he whispered, then belched resoundingly.

"Now get away," Hanson said calmly. "I'll be back later."

"Don't," Milton said. "I hate meetin' you like this. Point of fact, I hate meetin you at *all*."

"That's your misfortune, isn't it." Hanson's voice was cold enough to freeze the air. "Put the word out. Anyone caught stalking my witch won't even get a warning. Clear?"

"We already know that, Black-knife." Milton gained his feet in one lurching movement, the chair legs scraping against the dirty floor. Mari winced. "Hope I never see ya again."

"Don't bet on it." Hanson remained stock-still while the thin man backed up. Mari noticed that his knees under their tight jeans pointed in opposite directions, off to either side. It looked painful, and she shivered again as Milton backed away.

Hanson glanced at her. "Easy, Lightbringer," he said. "I'm here."

"Don't call me that," she said, just loud enough to be heard over the screeching thumps coming from the jukebox. "What do we do now?"

"We wait a little bit. What do you want me to call you?"

"How about my name? Hanson, you're acting like—"

"This isn't the time or place for this discussion," he said, tight-lipped. His eyes flamed blue.

"Hanson."

Something cold and sharp touched Mari's cheek. She didn't even see Hanson move. The flurry of motion ended with him on his feet, the gun steady and pointed at someone standing right behind her. Mari froze, her eyes fixed on Hanson's face. He looked absolutely calm, his mouth a thin straight line, eyes level, his cheeks shadowed with dark blond stubble.

"Don't make me kill you." He sounded bored.

"Just playing," a thin, reedy voice said from behind Mari's ear. "She's a cute one. Why's she hanging out with a bastard like you?"

"She's got excellent taste," Hanson returned. "*Now*."

The cold, sharp thing retreated and slid around, dropping into the chair Milton had just vacated. Mari had to swallow hard. It had red eyes and a lipless mouth full of razor teeth, and the hands were twisted, wicked claws. But worst of all was the way one eye remained fixed on her while the other scanned the smoky room. "You're no fun," it said, sniffing through its nose holes. "See what a spoilsport he is, sweetie? Now me, I'm a lot of fun."

Mari found her voice. "I don't date outside my species," she said, her words cutting through smoke and jukebox noise. *How strange, I sound like Elise.*

The thing made a hissing, snarling noise. Mari realized it was laughing, and chills raced up her spine. *Gods,* she thought, and glanced at Hanson. He had settled back into his chair, apparently relaxed. That made her feel better. "So the little doll has a voice, huh? Talk to me some more, sweets."

"Now, why would she want to waste words on you?" Hanson sounded dismissive. His eyes locked with Mari's. "What have you got?"

"Something's walking the streets, but Millie the Squeaker told you all about that. I hear there's a gargoyle trailing Blondie, and I also hear she slipped the leash and went out walking. Pity you found her. She smells tender."

"When did gargoyles get interested in witches?"

"Oh, they don't like witches. Allergic to *that* meat. But he works for the Maleficent."

"The Maleficent?"

"Librarian. Nasty piece of work. Guards the Nexus with the gargoyle. Won't even let anyone in the front door." The thing's smile stretched across its face almost ear-to-ear. *If it smiles any wider its head will open up like the top of a can.* A wave of nausea slammed into her stomach. It wasn't just nausea. It was a vision, rising like a shark through dark water, racing for her.

*No, oh no. Please, not here. Please, goddess, not here.*
"Anyone else in town?"

"Just the usual. The Brotherhood's got a presence, and the Thains are sneaking around. Just normal. Bunch of freeloaders moved in once the Crusade..." The thing trailed off, eyeing Mari again. "Wait a minute," it said, conversationally. "I'll bet the rumors are true. This is one of those meddling Guardians, isn't it?"

"Oh, maybe," Hanson said calmly. "But she's mine, *kaavi.* Go ahead, try it. I might welcome erasing another of your kind from the world."

Another snarling chuckle. "Plenty of prey anyway. Especially with the Great One coming."

The vision retreated slightly. A drop of sweat trickled down the shallow channel of Mari's spine. *Please,* she prayed. *Not here. Don't let me have a vision here.*

"The great one?"

"Big quake. The shamans bound a helluva fault under the city a long time ago. Something's torn up the binding, diverted a lot of Power from it. When that hits, there will be a feast here."

"Nice." It was as if Hanson had thrown her a line, a cord of something taut and humming. A wave of strength flooded her. The vision retreated another half step, but it still hovered, waiting. "Anyone else in town?"

"'Course not, Black-knife. You know that, or you should."

"It never hurts to ask." Hanson shrugged. "Fine. I'd thank you, but you don't deserve it."

"Harsh." The thing chortled. "Sure you don't want to come with me, sweetie?"

"Fuck off," Hanson growled, and the table moved slightly, like an obedient dog. It was a trick witches had used at séances for hundreds of years, but she'd done it accidentally. The entire bar seemed to go still.

Mari's hands knotted together in her lap. *I shouldn't have done that.*

The thing stood up, slowly. "Word of advice, Black-knife. Get that rabbit out of here before the wolves decide to form up a pack."

The vision stalked closer. Mari tried to breathe softly, but there seemed to be no air in the room. Her shields went thin and as brittle as glass, and a restless murmur slid through the bar.

"Thanks for the advice," Hanson said dryly. "Now get the

hell away from her."

Mari shut her eyes. In the mothering dark, the swirl of Hanson's red-black aura closed around the fringes of her own glow—and the twisted shapes of the other things in the room moved, as if seen through a sheet of watery glass.

The walls of the bar were shielded in a way she'd never seen before, but it was simple to look out past them. They weren't made to keep anything *in*; they were made to keep humans *out*. She wondered briefly what would have happened if she'd ever been caught here alone.

The vision moved closer, slowly, a wave of syrupy terror. Mari tried to relax, tried to breathe deeply. If she could keep some kind of control.

"Forget it," Hanson said to someone. Had he been talking? Where was she? Her head hurt, a roaring filled her ears. She'd never fought a vision so hard.

*There,* she thought.

Something stalked in the alley across the street. Mari strained her mental vision, trying desperately to see. A familiar acidic odor filled her nose.

For one blinding, breathtaking second, Mari drowned in a caustic bath of something Dark and hungry, something that sank burning tentacles into her aura. She heard screaming, the staccato report of gunfire, and a hand clamped on her nape. "Gods above." Hanson sounded strained. "Always at the worst possible time." Night air touched Mari's cheek. Hanson was running. Mari stumbled, and he pulled her along, her feet barely touching the ground.

Were they outside? Where was she?

*It crouched, hulking, something pale wrapped around one clawed fist. The Darkness closed over its face, making the features run like clay in warm water, it lifted its head with a sound like squealing metal hinges and sniffed the air for her.*

One of those awful, chilling cries rose in the darkness behind them. Hanson said nothing, but the air turned hot and prickling with a sudden charge of Power. He skidded to a stop, pushed her against a wall, and printed a bruising kiss on her forehead. "Just hold on, Mari. I'm here. Just hold on."

Mari was about to scream, but the vision swallowed her whole.

*"You must find the Library and complete the spell, Mari,"* Suzanne said, urgently. Her form rippled, shivered with an

*unearthly silvery light. Mari remembered that light from the spell that had made them Guardians. Had it come for her, too? She threw up her arms, shielding her face, as the thunder-crack of light spread out.*

*"Find...Library, Mari. Ask...your Watcher...He'll help..."*

Mari fell, but the pavement didn't catch her. Instead, darkness closed over her, darkness and an awful smell. She recognized that smell.

"Get *down!*" Hanson yelled, and then there was a crashing sound. The sense of his presence was torn away, and a hot coppery reek filled the air.

Mari blinked. A fiery curtain seemed to lift, and her body, realizing it was in danger, and shook off some of the vision. Her head pounded, bright spikes of pain digging into her temples.

Then the claws wrapped around her upper arm. Mari screamed. The touch of the thing was like acid, especially against her tissue-thin, weary shields. It burned through her brain, tearing Power free from its moorings, feeding greedily. The mental rape hurt far worse than anything she'd ever experienced, agony nailing through her entire body.

"Give it to me," the lipless voice said, as if speaking through mud. "*Give* it to me!"

Mari struggled, screaming, desperation granting her hysterical strength. She tore her arm free of the iron grasp of darkness and ran, hearing the howling, cheated scream behind her, and another sound—the sound of metal against something hard, chiming. A long twisting street lying under a blanket of fog. The wet oily glow from street lamps at even intervals. The stitch in her side gripping. Something warm and wet dripping into her eyes.

Head down, fists pumping, Mari ran blindly into the night.

# Twenty-Eight

"What are *you* doing here?"

"Theo insisted," Dante replied dryly. He looked lazy, his eyes half-closed. The smoke and steel scent of Watcher fumed away from him. "Do you know what that was?"

"I don't know," Hanson levered himself up. He hadn't lost much blood. His ribs crackled, settling into their usual positions. "It smells fucking familiar, but I can't quite—"

"We have news," Dante interrupted.

Theo peered around the black-eyed Watcher's bulk. "Why didn't you tell us Mari's house had been attacked?" she asked, and the gentle rebuke in her voice was enough to make Hanson drop his head like a little kid.

"Couldn't," he said, and looked around. *Where is she?*

Mari was gone, and so was the thing that had attacked them. He swore viciously. "Which way did she go?" Even as he asked, he already knew. He could feel the tugging inside his chest telling him her direction. She was moving rapidly, but her pace was flagging. She was already winded, probably, drained from the vision and wounded by the thing.

"Listen," Dante said, his hand closing around Hanson's arm. "It's important."

"That thing is chasing her down," Hanson said icily. "Let go of me. Don't make me kill you."

"I think I know what it is."

Hanson took a deep, tearing gulp of chill air. He'd managed to get Mari out of the bar and across the street when the vision swamped her. And then the thing that had been stalking her had dropped out of the shadows and negligently batted Hanson aside. "Let. Go." The killing rage grated against his control, and the presence of the other Lightbringer forced salt into his wounds.

"We dropped by Mari's house to see if she'd gone home," Theo said urgently. "We found where the thing came from. It holed up in the third bedroom, the one with all the posters of naked women on the walls. It seems Brandon's been playing around with some things. He stole one of Mari's books on ceremonial magick."

"And something answered," Hanson filled in grimly. It made sense. The boy had been on a cocktail of substances, easy prey. And the perfume of whatever Power he'd clumsily managed to raise would have drawn a stray predator to him. "Let go. I've got to get to Mari."

"It's a shapestealer, Hanson," Dante said grimly. His black coat melded into the shadows as he moved slightly. Theo had tried to slide around him. "One of the Greater Abyssals. The earthquake probably attracted it, and the damn kid snared its attention."

Hanson stepped back, twisting his arm free.

Dante let him go as he continued, "Use your knives. Don't hesitate, no matter what face it wears. Be careful. It has Mari's scent, and it started feeding from her before you—"

Hanson bolted for the mouth of the alley before Dante could finish his sentence. *Mari!* It was a long, despairing scream inside his head. A shapestealer. Why hadn't he thought of a shapestealer? And Brandon. He'd known something was wrong with the boy, *known* it. Why hadn't he guessed?

It might already be too late.

*If I survive this, I promise, I swear by everything holy, I'll keep my promises. I won't touch her again. I won't even look at her. Just keep her safe until I can get there, gods. Please.*

The gods knew he was a liar, but he wasn't lying this time. *Just let me get to her. Just let me get to her in time.*

# Twenty-Nine

The only thing Mari could think of was to get away from whatever was loping after her through the fog-shrouded streets. Her head burned, a reaction-headache blinding her, and great ragged holes were torn in her shielding. She bolted down a close, stinking alley, the stitch in her side feeling as if someone was turning a knife against her ribs. Hot tears dripped down her face. *Hanson,* she thought, desperately. *Where is he? He's probably somewhere around here.*

"There's a fire escape," Suzanne's voice said in her ear. *"Move, Mari!"*

Mari let out a hoarse, barking sob and obeyed. *Suzanne? Why am I hearing Suzanne?*

"Because I'm here, you idiot," her teacher's voice came back smartly. "To your right—no, your other right. Climb."

At the very end of the alley, tucked behind a Dumpster, was a fire escape ladder, mercifully pulled down for some reason. Mari sobbed again, her abraded palms closing around the metal rungs. She'd erased the skin on both palms by falling when the thing grabbed her. She began to climb, her purse bumping against her side.

"I'm going to have to take you through the spell," Suzanne said. "No time. The Great One is very close, and the binding *must* be renewed, or the entire city will be torn to pieces."

*I can't!* Mari thought frantically. Her arms and legs seemed made of lead, as if she was trapped in a nightmare, running in slow motion as some snarling monster chased her.

"Stop your ninnying and get up to the roof," her teacher's disembodied voice snapped. She sounded just like Esmerelda. "You're just lucky I could come through. This qualifies as an emergency circumstance. *Mari! No!*"

Mari's hand slipped on the rung above her. For a moment she teetered on the edge of falling, and then she jerked herself back onto the ladder. Finally, she reached the first landing and started scrambling up the stairs. How long until the roof? Tears slicked her face. Where was Hanson?

*I will always come for you,* he'd said. And he always had. But now—

"Now you'll have to complete the spell," Suzanne said. "I know the original, so I'll take you through it. Get up to the roof,

Mari. We haven't much time."

Mari cried out, the thing's harsh dark presence suddenly looming in the alley below. Its mental touch against the psychic wounds it had already created was sheer torture, fire licking at raw spaces in Mari's mind.

"Hurry!" her teacher's voice whispered urgently. "Come on, Mari. You're stronger than this. Try."

"I passed my finals," Mari gasped aloud. "If I did that, I can do anything." *Hanson, where are you? I'm frightened, and I'm a coward.*

"No coward could have done the things you've done, Mari." Now Suzanne's tone was kind. The air was loose and breathless, hushed over the dark city. Mari's boots rang on steel just as the thing below her leapt for the ladder.

Rusted metal gave with a squealing snap. Mari, glancing back over her shoulder, heard the thing thud back onto the ground. Another chilling howl rose from it, scraping Mari's nerve endings with broken glass. She fell hard, her head striking the edge of a metal step.

"Get up," Suzanne said kindly but pitilessly. "That won't hold it for long. Get *up*, Mari!"

"Hanson," Mari said. "I need you." She managed to climb to her feet. A thin, glassy growling came from underneath her, then deathly silence.

Wet salt warmth dripped down from her temple. Her head throbbed. She climbed another three flights and finally fell headlong onto the roof's rough pebbled surface. Raising her head, her hair coming free and tumbling down, she felt horrible recognition slam through her.

It was the same roof.

"Find a place to sit," Suzanne said. "You'll have to trust me, Mari. Please. The entire city will be destroyed if the binding breaks. All those innocent people."

"Gretchen," Mari whispered. "Amy."

"Sit down," her teacher replied.

The strength ran out of Mari's arms and legs. She collapsed headlong on the roof.

"Good enough," Suzanne whispered. "Now, follow me."

"Mari?" A harsh, choked whisper.

Fresh pain grated in Mari's head. Thunder rumbled, and a few stinging drops of rain pattered against the roof. *What the…?*

It wasn't natural. Something had thrown the weather

systems off, some imbalance of Power. Mari felt it like altitude pressure inside her ears. More blood trickled down her cheek.

"Mari," the voice crooned again. She recognized it just as blackness rose to swallow her.

*What's Brandon doing here?*

Mari lost consciousness.

***

She came back to herself with a jolt a half-minute later, lying full-length on the roof. Thunder crackled again. As if that had broken some sort of stasis, the rain started in earnest, dime-sized drops splattering on the already fog-damp roof.

"Mari," a thick, chuckling voice said again.

*Brandon?* Mari shook her head, pushing herself up on hands and knees. *What's he doing here?*

"There you are." The voice chuckled, and Mari raised her head, water running into her eyes. "This will only take a minute."

Her dark-adapted eyes made out a low, hulking figure, and Mari had to gulp back another scream. It looked like Brandon, or what Brandon would look like with three-inch claws and glowing sulphurous eyes. But something was wrong. He was hunched over, his shoulders massively corded with muscle, as if the steroids had twisted him into something bestial. And the voice was similar to Brandon's, but it sounded as if something thick and inhuman was working his tongue.

As she watched, stunned, the outlines of Brandon's body began to blur like hot wax. "Brandon?" Mari whispered.

Then she felt it again. The tearing, ripping, gnawing, trying to worm its way into her brain. There was a pale glitter wrapped around one clawed hand. Mari blinked water out of her eyes.

It was…pearls.

Her pearls.

*That's how it tracked me,* she realized, her throat gone dry with terror. *Whatever that thing is, it's not Brandon anymore. It may try to glamour itself like him, and maybe it would work, if it hadn't tried to eat me. I'm kind of seeing what it really looks like.*

"Run!" Suzanne's voice cracked in Mari's ear, underscored with a roll of thunder. Mari found herself scrambling to her feet, her shocked and abused body screaming an orchestra arrangement of pain. It leapt for her just as her legs gave out again.

It was that accidental fall that saved her life. She fell, just missing the swipe of claws, but the thing smashed into her anyway. Mari flew, feeling oddly weightless for a moment, and there was a huge, almost painless impact along the right side of her body. A small cry jerked out of her lips.

"Mari, no!" Suzanne sounded horrified.

An air-conditioning vent had broken her fall.

*Broken my fall, or broken me?* The rain smashed long, silver needles into the rooftop. A distant rumbling started.

"The binding," Suzanne's voice said. "Mari, please. You must try."

Mari coughed. A sharp pain lanced into her side. *If I'm going to die,* she thought through the haze of agony, *I'm going to do it right. I wish I would have found out if I passed my exams.* She closed her eyes.

"Repeat after me," Suzanne said patiently. "*Aeturnus boundis terrae, pactus Grimaen.*" Mari began to stutter along. Each word tore a fresh hole in her ribs. *I think I broke something.* She pushed herself up slowly. It took an eternity, but she finally ended up sitting against the air-conditioning vent. Rain jetted down; an amazing diamond spike of lightning split the night. Thunder smashed the sky.

"*Terabus lux boundis Janus terrae.*" She heard Suzanne's voice reciting, and her own thin, choked whisper following. The language was unlike anything she'd ever heard before, ancient words humming with Power. Something stalked in the rain, something that was going to come back and kill her. Had it killed Brandon, too? And Amy? Was it just wearing Brandon's shape? Mari coughed again. A bubble of something warm burst on her lips.

"Almost done," Suzanne said. "Repeat, *Aeternum Imperatrim terrae cogniri saldrine.*"

Mari's vision began to blur, but not before she saw a low, hunched shape in the rain.

The final sentence of the spell dropped from her numb lips, and the thunder seemed to pause midway through the sky. Power rose, a spinning oval of it. Silver light poured starkly over the rooftop and underlined each object with a knife-edged shadow. Brandon's shape wavered and blurred, and she suddenly *saw* him clearly as the angle he was moving at suddenly clicked into memory inside her skull. She had Seen this before. As the Power rose around her, Mari let out a horrified sob. *At least Theo isn't here.*

"Focus!" Suzanne said. "Don't lose it now. You *must* control it, Mari. There's no other way."

"But it hurts," Mari heard herself moan. "Hanson..."

Thunder rippled, tore at her ears. He was coming. There was no way she could escape. He was chasing her. Mari cowered behind the inadequate shelter of the air-conditioning vent.

"Make it stop!" Suzanne's voice over the sound of the storm.

"I can't!" Mari yelled back miserably. The effort of yelling made another bubble of warm salt wet burst on her lips.

Suzanne's voice turned stern. "Make it stop, Mari! You can. I know you can."

A deep, grinding roar. The ground shifted under her, the rooftop tilting as the whole building swayed, earth moving. *Earthquake.* Mari screamed miserably, and then, wonder of wonders, there was Theo.

Theo materialized from thickly gathered shadows, her heavy blue skirt weighed down with water from the lashing rain. She ran for Mari, her arms outstretched, and Mari gave a sob of relief and fresh pain mixed. She knew what was about to happen and was helpless, helpless...

And then the vision *changed.*

Theo's face was too white, her lips drawn back in a rictus, and Mari suddenly understood. It wasn't Theo. It was that *thing* wearing Theo's face and trying to find a glamour that would allow it through the shell of Power released by Suzanne's spell.

Then there was an awful crunching sound. Theo looked down, a bubble of blood bursting on her lips. Water streamed down her chalk-white face. There was a smear of blood on one pale cheek, and dark hair streamed back. She fell, her blue dress fluttering, the silk making a small ripping sound as her fingers twisted, tearing the material.

Hanson jerked the knife free of the thing's body, his face a mask of rage. His eyes burned icy blue, and his hair was slicked to his head from the force of the downpour. The roof tilted crazily. Mari fell heavily onto her abused side. The pain rose viciously and made the whole world waver as the spell tore through the holes in her aura, Power bleeding free. She was too tired to control it. The spell rode her, forcing its way through her head like some monstrous thing trying to shatter free of her skull.

"Mari!" A long, despairing scream. Rain lashed, stung her eyes. "Mari! No!" Hanson's voice.

The vision had changed. Or been scrambled, the thing's red eyes somehow blurring through Hanson's face. The flux of time trembled under Mari's skin, and then let her go.

Mari's throat swelled with the enormity of the scream. It tore out of her, rivaling the thunder, and the Power rose too, striking like a snake. Silver light closed around Mari, Suzanne's arms outstretched, the smell of lemons and clean Power suddenly drowning out the reek of Darkness.

*You did it,* Suzanne whispered inside her head. *I knew you could. They're safe now, Guardian. You did it.*

"Hanson," Mari whispered, and passed out.

# Thirty

"It almost killed her," Hanson said dully, his hands hanging by his sides. Outside, the rain lashed down. The spell played havoc with the weather system, just like the first Guardian spell, but it was already fading, a normal, early-summer storm coming in from the sea.

"But it didn't." Amazingly, this came from Elise, who stood by the kitchen window, staring out into the garden. "Brandon. That little jerk. Who did he think he was, playing around with magick? Jocks don't do magick." Her fiery hair crackled, lifting on a slight breeze. There were dark circles under her eyes.

"It's a good thing you didn't find what the spell was supposed to do," Dante observed dryly. "He was obsessed with Mari and apparently went snooping through her books. It was supposed to make her fall in love with him."

Elise let out a choked sound that would have been a laugh if it hadn't been so horrified. "Gods above," she managed. "A *forced* love spell? Was he *insane?*"

"No," Dante replied, "just stupid. It's over, at least. Now we can clear up the mess."

"A forced love spell," Elise breathed. "Gods. Didn't he know how dangerous that is? You couldn't pay *me* to cast one of those."

"Well, you're a witch," Dante pointed out, "and you're properly trained. But sometimes normals get themselves into trouble. He might have used sacrifice or sex to raise the energy for that spell. But the only thing he did was attract the shapestealer, and since he'd been fooling around without proper direction, he was vulnerable."

Hanson shut his eyes, leaning back against the kitchen wall. The smell of fresh bread and the painful tang of Lightbringer power mixed to make him sigh. He was exhausted.

His ears caught the sound of footsteps, and he opened his eyes just as Theo entered the room, the tray balanced in her hands. "You can go up," she said to him. "She's asking for you."

"Gods," Elise snorted. "She almost gets killed, and it's *him* she asks for. I'm beginning to feel more like a third wheel all the time."

"Hush," Theo said gravely. "It's our fault for not figuring out we needed to finish the Guardian spell. 'Half done's worse than not done at all,' Suzanne used to say. Hanson, did you hear me? She's asking for you. Go on up."

It was a direct order, but he still had to force himself to peel away from the wall. "Yes, ma'am," he said in a monotone, and clumped out of the room, leaving them behind. The living room folded around him—the clutter of a witch's house, knickknacks and curious scattered everywhere; Theo's altar on the fireplace hearth decorated with a rosemary wreath; cinnamon incense smoking, filling the air with sweetness.

Behind him, he heard Elise again. "Suzanne should have told us how to finish that damn spell. Hey, what's wrong with *him?*"

"He almost saw Mari die in front of him," Theo said. "Elise, would you look over these papers with me? Mari said Suzanne's sister gave them to her. Dante, would you make us some tea?"

"Your wish, witch," Hanson heard Dante say. The tone of the other Watcher's voice—amused, serious, and tender all at once—made jealousy tear at his breastbone until he took firm control of himself and walked slowly through the living room to the hall. The stairs creaked underfoot as he climbed them slowly.

*I'm putting off the inevitable,* he realized. *This is the last time I'm going to be able to be near her.*

Theo's spare room. The door loomed in front of him. He knocked briefly and pushed it open with tented fingers. He had to try twice before his voice would work. "Mari?"

"Hanson?" she whispered.

She lay on the bed, the dark green velvet comforter pulled up to her chin. Pale, pearly, rainy-day light poured in through the window, making her eyes glow even more impossibly blue. Her aura, patched and reshielded, was still thin and ragged in places, but it no longer bled blue light and the smell of ocean. The bruise running up the side of her face was yellow-green, looking weeks instead of hours old, but the slice on her scalp was healing nicely. *Good to have a healer around,* he thought, then winced. She'd been wounded because of his clumsiness. He shouldn't have allowed anything Dark to touch her. He shouldn't have taken her along, but if he'd left her behind, the shapestealer could have broken in to the hotel. He'd have been at fault either way.

"I knew you'd come." Her voice was a thin thread under the sluice of the rain. "You always come for me."

"Mari," he began helplessly. Her hair lay tangled across the pillow, and he had to close his hands into fists to keep from reaching out. He wanted to touch her so much it hurt, an ache in his very bones.

"I want you to promise me something," she managed. Her eyes drifted closed, then back open. She was having trouble staying awake.

"Go to sleep," he said, his conscience pricking him. "You need rest, Mari."

"Don't tell me what to do," she returned, but there was no heat to it. "Look, Hanson. Promise me you won't go anywhere. I want you to stay here."

The injustice swelled in his throat, robbing him of words. He'd been clumsy from the very beginning. He was a liar, a former thief, not even fit to watch over her. She had almost killed herself working that spell as the shapestealer stalked her, staving off a huge earthquake almost by herself. Theo and Elise had felt the spell, putting all their energies into it without question, but Mari had finished the Guardian spell and paid the terrible price. Even now his hands went cold and damp as he remembered her limp weight in his arms when he'd sped to bring her to Theo, praying she would live. The touch of her skin had given him no comfort because she'd had no Power left to ease his pain.

"You don't want me," she stated flatly, and that managed to hurt him even more. She *still* doubted him.

"You stubborn little *witch*," he grated out through clenched teeth. "I adore you. You know that. I don't deserve to be anywhere near you, I don't deserve to be your Watcher. I don't even deserve to know you *exist*, Mari. I'm a stupid, brainless, clumsy idiot."

She *smiled* at him, her eyes glowing. Hanson lost his breath.

"Promise me you're not going anywhere," she said, stubbornly. "That's an order from your witch, Watcher. Come over here and hold my hand. I think I'm going to cry."

He didn't remember crossing the intervening space. He was suddenly on his knees by the side of the bed, her delicate hand clasped in both of his. The familiar, buzzing narcotic pleasure of her skin slammed into him, and he could have wept with relief. "Gods," he said, "I promised that if I got to you in time…"

"To hell with whatever you promised," she said, and yawned. "Promise *me*. Promise me you'll stay with me, Hanson.

I'm tired, and I want to go to sleep."

"Mari," he began.

"I love you," she told him. "Don't leave me."

Hanson choked on his own breath. The touch of her skin was doing something funny to his head. He felt almost dizzy, swamped with delicious heat. "You *wha...* ah, um... Mari..."

"And if you decide you don't feel the same way, you can go."

"Shut up," he heard himself say. "I promise. I *promise,* Mari. I'm staying. I never want to leave."

"Good," she said. "Don't be ridiculous, all right?"

He shook his head, mute with the magnitude of his relief.

"You were right," she said, her eyes drifting closed again. "The things I See...can be changed. I was just so frightened."

"I'm sorry," he said.

"Don't be," she said. "Just...stay."

"I will," he said, and watched her fall asleep, lifting her hand every now and again to press his lips to her knuckles, and wondering why tears were sliding down his cheeks.

# Thirty-One

*Eight weeks later*

Mari carried the letter into the garage. Hanson was leaning against the stationary tool bench, looking under the raised hood of a battered '68 Mustang. His pale eyebrows were drawn together, and his leather coat lay by the side of the car, a pool of crumpled darkness. "Hey," she said, hopping down the single step. Chill concrete met her feet.

"Hm," he said, wiping his hands with an oily rag, still staring at the engine. "I think I've been going about this the wrong way."

"It's time for lunch. Elise and Theo are coming over for dinner tonight. I just got off the phone with Theo," she replied. "Quit fiddling with that thing. It'll wait."

His eyes met hers, and Mari almost lost her breath. He watched her as if she was a puzzle he was trying to fit together, seemingly perpetually astonished by something about her. Mari almost forgot what she wanted to say. Her heart had a funny habit of banging against her ribs whenever she saw him. *It isn't legal for a man to look that good,* she thought, noticing the smudge on his forehead where he'd pushed his hair back from his face with gunk-blackened fingers. He smelled like leather, metal, and motor oil now, a particularly male smell.

"What's that?" he asked. "It's The Letter, isn't it?"

Mari nodded, her throat gone dry. She pulled her blue sweater down with one hand—the weather had turned cold, and the trees were losing their leaves. "Six weeks. You'd think a *library* would be more prompt."

"What does it say?"

She turned it over in her hand. "I haven't been brave enough to open it. Come on inside. This floor is killing my feet."

He scooped up his coat with a clean, economic motion and draped it over one arm. "You're right. The car will wait. You want me to open it?" He stopped right beside her, so close she could feel the heat radiating from him.

She handed it over. "If it's bad news, I don't want to know," she said, her stomach flipping. He paused, examining her, tilting her chin up with two fingers and searching her face.

"It won't be bad news," he said firmly. "Trust me. You're *summa cum laude.* How could it be bad news?"

Mari bit her lip. "Open it up," she said breathlessly. "Please."

He tore the envelope open with no finesse, his fingers leaving black marks on the paper. Yanking the letter free, he opened it up and scanned it once. His coat slithered to the floor, forgotten. Something inside it clanked as it shifted on the floor. Then he looked at her for a long moment.

Mari shifted from foot to foot. "Well?" she finally demanded.

A lopsided grin lit his severe face. "I'm looking at the new assistant head of research at the Coleridge Library," he said. "Don't rush me. I want to savor this."

"I got the job?" Mari whispered, feeling the blood drain out of her cheeks. Hanson scooped her into his arms, whirled her in a neat circle, and did it again. Then he set her back on her feet and hugged her so hard her ribs hurt.

"You got the job," he confirmed, grinning. "Congratulations."

"Gods above," she whispered, and blinked at him. "I got the job!"

His mouth met hers. It was a warm kiss, and by the time Mari broke away her heart was racing for an entirely different reason. "You do realize this changes everything," she said.

Hanson went completely still, watching her face. Mari reached up, tracing his cheekbone with one finger, watching his eyes half close.

"What does it change?" he asked.

Mari felt a completely foolish grin break out over her face. "It means you won't get back to work anytime soon," she told him. "I think we need to celebrate properly."

That made one corner of his lips quirk up. Mari's heart thundered as he asked, "What did you have in mind?"

Heat rose to her cheeks. She tipped her head back toward the Mustang, sitting obediently on the concrete floor of the garage. "I've always wondered about the back seat in those things," she managed, her voice sounding high and a little frightened. "Oh, my gods. I'm assistant head of research."

"Great." His hands slid under her sweater, calluses scraping at her softer skin. "I like the sound of research."

"So do I," Mari agreed, paper crackling as she slid her hands up, lacing her fingers at his nape. "Care to help me research, Watcher?"

He would have said something in reply, but Mari pulled his head down, and he was too busy kissing her.

Printed in the United States
53445LVS00003B/136-174

9 781933 417004